THE SPITFIRE GIRL

FENELLA J MILLER was born in the Isle of Man. Her father was a Yorkshire man and her mother the daughter of a Rajah. She has worked as a nanny, cleaner, field worker, hotelier, chef, secondary and primary teacher and is now a full time writer.

She has over thirty-eight Regency romantic adventures published, plus four Jane Austen variations, three Victorian sagas and seven WW2 family sagas. She lives in a pretty, riverside village in Essex with her husband and British Shorthair cat. She has two adult children and three grandchildren.

THE SPITFIRE GIRL

Fenella J. Miller

www.ariafiction.com

First published in the United Kingdom in 2018 by Aria, an imprint of
Head of Zeus Ltd

9 7 5 3 1 2 4 6 8

A CIP catalogue record for this book is available from the British
Library.

ISBN 9781788548397

Aria, an imprint of Head of Zeus
First Floor East
5–8 Hardwick Street
London EC1R 4RG

About *The Spitfire Girl*

It's 1939 and the threat of war hangs over the country...

Flying instructor Ellie Simpson has grown up a tomboy.
She's never had an interest in the latest fashions or
finding a husband, her only passion is flying her beloved
Tiger Moth. But when war is declared, she is no longer
be able to do what she loves most – fly.

When Ellie is offered the opportunity to join the
Women's Auxiliary Air Force, she jumps at the chance
to help keep the brave boys in the RAF safe. But when
tragedy strikes close to home, Ellie realises that this war
could tearing both the country she loves – and her heart
– apart...

This book is for those brave women who joined the ATA and delivered aircraft all over the country in order to allow the men to fight.

<u>One</u>

Essex

July 1939

'Well, Miss Simpson, what do you think?' Joseph Cross asked as he pointed to the de Havilland 60 Moth that stood proudly on the worn grass outside the barn that served as a hanger.

Ellen wanted to hug him but thought he might not appreciate the gesture. 'I love it. Is it dual control?'

'No, but it has the usual two seats so can take a passenger.'

'Good – I've got more than enough pupils to teach. Since the government subsidy last year every Tom, Dick and Harry wants to learn to fly.'

'I hope you don't expect me to pay you any extra, young lady. I reckon you owe me far more than your wages would have been for all the lessons and hours you've spent flying my aircraft over the past five years.'

She put her hands on her hips. 'Giving my brothers and me lessons at your Flying Club couldn't have been as much as the rent you would have had to pay to use my father's farms and fields.' He was about to interrupt but she continued. 'Not forgetting the fact that Dad bought the first aircraft and both Neil and George acted as instructors until they joined the RAF.'

He scowled but she wasn't fooled for a minute. 'The cost of one lesson is usually two pounds – the three of you never paid a penny…'

'Joe, I don't want to stand here arguing anymore. I want to take her up before it gets too hot. Are you coming with me or can I go solo?'

'Circuits and bumps only, my girl, no flying off into the wild blue yonder. There are three new enquiries to be dealt with in the office – I want you to sort those out this morning.'

The other aircraft the flying club owned were a Swallow and a Gypsy Moth. Both were fitted with dual controls. Joe had several clients who liked to go up on their own and pootle about until the fuel ran out. This de Havilland had been bought to satisfy those clients.

Sidney, the ground engineer, and the only other full-time employee, wandered out from the hanger. 'Nice little machine, Ellie, sweet as a nut. You going to take it up for a spin?'

'If that's all right with you, I'd love to. I'll not be long – I just want to get the feel of it for myself.'

'The bloke what brought it said it flies like the Gypsy only a bit faster. You'll have no problem – you're a natural. I remember your first solo flight when you were no more than a nipper...'

Joe poked his head out of the office. 'No time for reminiscing, Sid, let her get on with it. Just had a bell and we've got a new pupil coming in an hour.'

'Sorry, guv, I'll not hold her up.'

She collected her helmet and goggles and scrambled into the cockpit. Even though the weather was warm she needed her flying jacket on over her dungarees. It got a bit nippy at a thousand feet above the land. After doing her pre-flight checks she taxied into position on the grass runway and took off.

An uneventful forty-five minutes later she landed smoothly and headed for the office to catch up with the paperwork. The new pupil, a middle-aged bank manager, decided after a couple of circuits of the field that he didn't want to learn to fly after all. As they'd only been in the air for a quarter of an hour there was no charge.

By the time her last pupil left the airfield it was almost six o'clock. Often they had to work until it was too dark to fly, but tonight they'd finished early. Ellen left Sid to lock up and jumped onto her bicycle. At least in the summer Dad didn't come in for his tea until late so she wouldn't have missed her meal.

She pedalled furiously down the track, swerving instinctively around the dips and ruts, covering the mile in record time. She skidded into the yard, sending half a dozen chickens squawking into the air in protest, and tossed her bike against the wall.

With luck she'd have time to wash before her parents sat down to eat. It had taken Mum months to get used to seeing her only daughter dressed in slacks or dungarees. She might be a farmer's wife now, but she'd come from a grand family and had very high standards.

The fact that Mum had been disowned when she'd married a farmer should have softened her but instead, according to Dad, it had made her even more determined to bring her children up as though they were landed gentry and not the children of a farmer.

After a quick sluice in the scullery Ellie headed to the kitchen – she was about to open the door when she realised the voices she'd heard were coming from the seldom used front parlour. Mum insisted on calling it the drawing room, but no one else did.

This must mean they had guests. She looked down at her scruffy oil-stained dungarees and wondered if she had time to nip upstairs and put on something more respectable. Unfortunately, her mother must have heard her come in.

'Ellen, you are very late this evening. Had you forgotten Neil has a twenty-four hour pass?'

She was pretty sure this was the first she'd heard of it but having her oldest brother home was a wonderful surprise. She didn't stop to think why this meant they were in the parlour, and burst in.

'Hello, little sister, I've brought a chum along. Let me introduce you to Gregory Dunlop.'

Only then did she become aware of the second RAF uniformed young man staring at her with open admiration. He was a bit shorter than Neil, but broader in the shoulders, with corn coloured hair and startlingly blue eyes.

'I'm pleased to meet you, Flying Officer Dunlop.' She wasn't sure if she should offer her hand as despite her best efforts it was far from clean.

He stepped closer and held out his and she had no option but to take it. 'I've heard so much about you, Miss Simpson, and have been pestering your brother for an invitation in order to meet you for myself.'

His grip was firm, his hand smoother than hers – but what caught her attention was his upper crust accent. 'I'm sorry to appear in my work clothes. If you don't mind waiting a few more minutes I'll pop upstairs and change into something more suitable for the occasion.'

'Please, don't worry on my account. I think you look perfectly splendid just as you are.'

He seemed reluctant to release her hand but she pulled it away firmly. He was a very attractive man and was

13

obviously interested in her, but she wasn't looking for a boyfriend.

'Run along, Ellen, you've got plenty of time to put on a frock as your father has only just come in himself. We are having a cold collation so nothing will be spoiled by waiting for another quarter of an hour.'

She smiled at her brother in resignation and he winked. They both knew there was no point in arguing once their mother had made up her mind.

She met her father in the passageway. 'Have you got to change as well, Ellie? She told me at lunchtime I've got to put on something smart.'

'It must be because of Neil's friend. He certainly sounds very posh.' She pushed open her bedroom door and was about to go in when he replied.

'Seems a lot of fuss for nothing but easier to give in than put up with a week of black looks and sour faces.' He shook his head sadly and went into the room he no longer shared with her mother. Ellie wished her parents had a happier relationship.

If there was one thing she'd learned, by watching the disintegration of what must once have been a happy union, it was this: Don't marry for love as it doesn't last. If she ever took the plunge it would be with a man she respected, liked and who shared her outlook on life.

Her mother had told her to put on a frock but she rebelled. She didn't wish to impress their visitor so would come down in what she usually wore – slacks and blouse. The only time she put on a frock was when she was forced to attend church. Most Sundays she had the excuse that she had to work at the airfield.

She checked her face was oil free and ran a brush through her hair. Satisfied she was presentable she hurried downstairs eager to catch up on Neil's news. George, her other brother, hadn't been home since January and she was desperate to hear how he was doing.

Her mother pursed her lips when Ellie came in. 'Is your father coming, Ellen?'

'I don't know, Mum, but I don't think he'll be long.' She joined her brother by the open window, leaving his friend to entertain her mother.

'I wish you wouldn't deliberately provoke her, Ellie. Why won't you call her Mother? You know how much she dislikes being called Mum, especially in front of strangers.'

She shrugged. 'Whatever she was in the past, now she's just a farmer's wife. Have you finished your training?'

He grinned and pointed to the wings on his uniform. 'I have, didn't you see these? George is still in Scotland – seems he pranged a Moth and needs longer up there.'

'He obviously didn't hurt himself or you wouldn't be so jolly. Do you know where you're going to be stationed?'

Their conversation was interrupted by the arrival of her father looking uncomfortable in a collar and tie. After he was introduced to the guest her mother clapped her hands as if wishing to attract the attention of a crowd of children.

'We shall go in to dine now that we are all here.'

Ellie hid her smile at her mother's pretentiousness behind her hand. Ham and salad hardly deserved such an introduction.

When her father mentioned the likelihood of there being a war her mother insisted that this was not a suitable topic of conversation at the dinner table. No one was particularly interested in discussing the weather and an uneasy silence fell.

'We've got another aircraft, Dad. I took her up and...'

Her mother glared at her. 'I'm sure that Flying Officer Dunlop doesn't want to hear about your highly unsuitable employment. A young lady should be interested in more feminine things, don't you agree, Mr Dunlop?'

The young man nodded solemnly. 'I'm sure that most girls would prefer to talk about fashion or flowers but your daughter is different. I've never met a female pilot before and am most impressed. How many hours solo do you have now, Miss Simpson?'

'Please call me Ellie, everyone else does.'

'And you must call me Greg.'

'Well, Greg, to answer your question, I've been flying since I was twelve – six years now – and got my A licence when I was fourteen and my instructor's certificate when I was sixteen. I've logged more than twelve hundred hours now.'

'Good God! That's a damn sight more than I have.' He couldn't fail to hear her mother's horrified gasp. Instead of being embarrassed he smiled at her. 'I apologise for my appalling language, Mrs Simpson, I do hope you will forgive me.'

'Apology accepted. I'll say no more on the matter.'

He turned to Ellie. 'I want to hear how you manage in poor weather conditions and hope you will talk to me before we leave tomorrow morning.'

Before she could answer she was instructed to clear the table and fetch the dessert. Obediently she pushed her chair back and began to collect the plates. When Greg made a move to stand up she shook her head.

Clearing the table was a woman's job, as well all the other domestic duties that she did her best to avoid. Pudding was a sherry trifle accompanied by a jug of thick, fresh cream from their dairy herd. She placed the large glass bowl on the tray and put the cream beside it. The ham salad, again all home-grown, had been excellent but this would be even better.

Murmurs of appreciation ran around the table when they saw what treat was to come. Her mother might be a snob but she was a dab hand in the kitchen, so couldn't have spent all her time swanning about the place with her nose stuck in the air, attending grand parties and going foxhunting.

She was about to take her place when the telephone rang. 'Excuse me, it's usually for me.'

'Glebe Farm, Ellie Simpson speaking.'

'Thank God – you need to get down here pronto. A silly bugger has gone up in the new kite and he's still up there,' Sid told her.

'I've got to change first but will get there as soon as I can. Is Joe there?'

'No, he rang to tell me to let this blighter take the new Moth – seems he's a friend of his or something. I'll have the Swallow ready for you.'

'Let's pray he has enough fuel for another hour.' Ellie dropped the telephone back on the hook and raced upstairs.

Her clothes were thrown in a heap on the floor and she scrambled into her grubby dungarees. Her brother was waiting at the bottom of the stairs.

'What's the flap? Can we help?'

'You could drive me to the airfield – I'll tell you why on the way.'

As she ran outside a smart MG sports car pulled up. Greg was at the wheel. 'Hop in, both of you. Ellie, you sit beside me and tell me where to go.'

This left the tiny backseat for her brother to somehow fold his considerable length into – however, he didn't argue.

The car covered the distance in a few minutes, barely time enough for her to explain what had happened.

Sid had done the pre-flight checks so all she had to do was scramble into the cockpit. The aircraft had no radio so she would have to rely on her excellent eyesight.

'I'll come with you,' Greg said. He didn't wait for her agreement but settled himself into the front seat, the one used by a pilot under instruction, and strapped himself in.

She would have preferred her brother to accompany her, but it was too late to complain. Every minute counted – the man flying the new Moth must be found and led back to the airfield. If she'd been there she would have checked the pilot's navigational skills and knowledge of the area before allowing him to fly on his own. Apparently, the man said he was going to follow the railway line that led to Clacton-on-Sea and then come back the same way.

How the hell he had managed to get lost she'd no idea. But being lost was better than having crashed. The take-off was smooth and once she'd ascended to a thousand feet she was able to see the countryside laid out below her like a patchwork quilt.

Her passenger – co-pilot really – was scanning the landscape the same way that she was. She began to fly over the rail track whilst looking from side to side. She had a bad feeling about this. She opened the throttle and headed towards the east coast. The only place the wretched man could get himself lost was if he'd gone out to sea.

They made excellent time and completed the forty-mile journey in a little over a quarter of an hour. As long as she could still see the shore she would be able to find her way back. After two fruitless searches which took her as far as Foulness to the north, and Felixstowe in the other direction, she was about to give up when Greg pointed to a speck on the horizon that could have been a bird.

If she flew close enough to be able to distinguish what it was she would be out of sight of land. He twisted in his seat and cupped his mouth so she could hear what he shouted above the engine and the rush of air.

'Let me fly – I've instrument training – we'll not get lost.'

She nodded and relinquished her hold on the controls. She leaned out as far as her harness would allow and wished she'd had the forethought to bring binoculars. As they sped towards the circling object the shape became clearer and her spirits soared.

It was the missing aircraft. As they thundered towards it the pilot saw them and climbed away from the sea. She waved frantically and received a thumbs up from the other aircraft. Greg circled the plane and headed towards safety.

She prayed he was as proficient at navigation as he'd said as there was nothing but sea in all directions. The setting sun was obscured by low cloud which would have made it even more difficult to find one's position.

Ten minutes later they were in sight of the coast and she began to relax. All they needed now was an airfield to land in – she doubted the other aircraft had enough fuel to remain in the air much longer. She knew this area pretty well. She tapped Greg on the shoulder and he understood immediately.

She resumed control of the Swallow and turned towards a small private aero club on the outskirts of Colchester where she'd landed a couple of times before. Fortunately, the grass strip was clear and she did a circuit and waggled the wings to indicate that the other plane should go down.

He landed safely and taxied to one side so she could follow. Whoever this man was, by the time she'd finished with him he was going to regret his decision to fly out to sea.

Two

Jack Reynolds remained in the aircraft until the Swallow had taxied to a standstill. He was in for a right bollocking after his stupid error – he'd flown out to sea believing he'd seen a boat in distress but when he'd arrived it had proved to be a false alarm. Someone had fallen overboard from a small fishing boat but the man had managed to scramble up the nets and back into the boat.

His intention had been to circle the craft until a lifeboat came out to rescue them. The skipper had waved him away and continued out to sea. Only then did Jack understand his predicament. The sun was hidden by clouds and the compass appeared to be on the blink. He had two choices – remain where he was in the hope that someone from the flying club would come in search of him or take a gamble and fly in the direction he thought the coast was.

He watched as two figures jumped out of the other aircraft. The pilot, a huge guy in RAF uniform, was accompanied by a bird in scruffy dungarees, flying boots, goggles and helmet.

To his astonishment it was the girl who yelled at him. 'There's no point in hiding, whoever you are, get out of my kite right now.'

He scrambled out of the cockpit and dropped to the ground. He raised his hands hoping to placate her but she continued to shout at him, much to the amusement of her companion and a couple of others who'd come out to see what all the fuss was about.

'Only a total idiot would fly out to sea like you did. Have you any idea how much that aircraft cost? We only got it this morning and you did your best to drown yourself and ditch it in the sea.' She showed no sign of stopping so he decided to end it himself.

He closed the distance between them and from a yard away made his point. 'I get your drift, miss, and so does everyone else within five miles of here. I might be stupid but I'm not deaf.'

She stared up at him. Instead of being subdued by his size she closed the gap and poked him hard in the chest. 'At least we agree on one thing. Flying Officer Dunlop will return the Moth and you can find your own way back. You'll not set foot in any of my aircraft again. I don't know who you are and I don't want to.' She raised her hand to prod him again.

This time he grabbed her wrist. 'No – if you do that again you'll regret it. Keep your hands to yourself. You're not leaving me stranded.'

He released her, expecting his message to have been received loud and clear. The next thing he knew he was flying backwards, then lost his balance and fell flat on his back. The bloody girl had shoved him over.

He was on his feet immediately but the RAF guy stepped in between them. 'Forget it, chum. A gentleman doesn't retaliate.'

'No problem as I'm no gentleman and she's certainly not a lady.'

They were of equal size and Jack reckoned he'd flatten his opponent. He was about to swing when the girl appeared.

'Please, don't fight over me. I'm so sorry, I shouldn't have pushed you.'

'I'm Ellen Simpson, this is Greg.'

'Jack Reynolds. I can't say it's a pleasure miss, but this time I'll accept your apology.'

She laughed and he wasn't sure why. Then she turned her back and walked across to the watchers and he heard her arranging for both aircraft to be refuelled. He was buggered if he was going to be left to hitch his way back to Romford.

Whilst they were both occupied he returned to the Moth. He was tempted to take the pilot's seat in the rear but decided he'd be pushing his luck if he did so. He was just snapping his harness shut when the girl turned.

She took off at a sprint towards him. If she thought either of them could manhandle him out they were in for a shock. Whether she liked it or not he was flying back.

This must have occurred to her as she stopped her mad dash and stalked back to join her companion. The plane was refuelled and he waited for the RAF chap to climb in behind him. He kept his eyes firmly to the front and ignored the thumping and rocking as Dunlop settled in.

He glanced sideways as the smaller Swallow revved up and taxied away. Bloody hell! The girl had chosen to pilot the de Havilland. He wasn't sure he was ready to be flown by a bird.

*

Ellie buckled in and did her pre-flight checks before preparing to take off. A hefty ground engineer spun the propeller and she was ready. Reynolds was going to be very sorry indeed that he'd got into her aircraft. Her fury had been replaced by a grim determination to demonstrate just what she thought of him.

She wondered if he'd ever flown upside down – if he hadn't, she hoped he would be suitably uncomfortable. Once they were airborne she flew until she could see the railway track which she intended to follow as it would lead her safely back to the airfield.

The clouds were low and if she was being sensible she would have remained below them, but today caution and common sense were going to be ignored. The man sitting rigidly in front of her had known he couldn't be chucked out of the plane. However, she was going to make his journey as unpleasant as possible.

She opened the throttle and sent the aircraft speeding into the thick cloud. She continued to climb until she was in bright sunshine. The compass was between her knees and difficult to see if you weren't experienced. She would be perfectly safe flying above the cumulous if she kept heading south south west. She peered down and a cold chill ran down her spine. The compass wasn't working.

For a moment she froze – unable to register the catastrophe. This must have been why Reynolds hadn't been able to return and she'd not allowed him to explain. Then she relaxed and allowed her flying experience to take over. They were on a course away from the sea so there was no chance of doing the same thing he had.

She would climb another five hundred feet and then dive as if she'd lost control. She hoped he didn't try to interfere. As they plunged at maximum speed through the clouds she forgot her anger as the sheer joy of flying took over.

Her passenger had turned in his seat and she was delighted to see his face was white and he was yelling something at her. She laughed and allowed the aircraft to continue its apparently deadly descent until they shot out of the greyness and she throttled back, lifted the nose and sped along beneath the clouds in full control.

She recognised the countryside beneath her and adjusted her course so she was heading in the right direction again. When they arrived at the airfield she circled a couple of times allowing Greg to taxi out of the way so she could go in safely.

Sid was waiting alongside her brother and they greeted her with a wave. As soon as they were stationary she clicked her harness and jumped out – but not quickly enough. When she was unbalanced, with one foot raised, Reynolds leaned out and shoved her in the small of the back. She went sailing through the air to land painfully on hands and knees on the grass.

She scrambled up and this time had no intention of interfering if either her brother or Greg intended to thump Reynolds. She was hoisted to her feet by Neil.

'Up you come, little sister. What did you do to yank his chain?'

Before she could answer, the nasty blighter who'd pushed her arrived at their side. 'This bloody stupid girl did her best to kill us both.'

She ignored him and spoke to her brother. 'I told him he'd have to find his own way home but he got into the plane anyway. I just showed him the error of his ways.' She nodded at Sid. 'Make sure that man pays for the extra fuel and hours before he leaves.'

Greg was waiting in the car and this time she travelled in the back and allowed her brother to take the passenger seat in the front. She was in no mood for conversation, even if she could have been heard over the noise of the engine and the sound of the air rushing by.

The car skidded to a halt outside the farmhouse and she was out before either of the others. She had no wish to discuss what had happened. No one had ever treated her so badly. She hoped Joe had the sense not to let him fly with them again.

Once she was safely in the sanctuary of her bedroom she flung herself on the slippery, satin covered eiderdown. She hadn't removed her boots, which was a major sin in this house. She didn't have time for such niceties – and not for the first time she wished she'd been born a boy and wasn't hemmed in by petty restrictions.

She closed her eyes and reviewed the events of the past couple of hours. What had she learned from this experience? That not all pilots were gentlemen and some were also stupid. Greg was from the top drawer, was charming, handsome and a friend of her favourite brother – he had stood up for her. Her lips curved – had she found herself a boyfriend?

Jack Reynolds had red hair – not a favourite of hers – and was certainly not a gentleman. He had also pushed her out of the plane. Mum would be horrified if she knew what her dear daughter was thinking at this very moment.

My God! The compass hadn't worked in the new aircraft. If she'd allowed him to get a word in edgeways he would have told her himself. This was why he'd been unable to return to land. It didn't explain why he'd been out there in the first place but she had a horrible sinking feeling that she'd misjudged him.

She jumped off the bed and rushed downstairs to the telephone. A murmur of voices was coming from the sitting room so she would be safe to use it without being overheard.

When the operator answered she gave Joe's number and waited to be connected. She hoped it wouldn't be his wife who picked up the receiver. When her boss answered she dispensed with the formalities and launched immediately into her reason for ringing so late.

'Joe, I think I might have made a dreadful mistake. Do you have a number for Mr Reynolds? I must speak to him immediately.'

She heard what she thought was a chuckle but couldn't be sure. 'I'll get him – he's staying with us – he's my nephew.'

There was a clatter as the receiver was put down and then a lengthy pause – so long that she thought Reynolds wasn't coming to the phone. Then there were footsteps and he was there.

'Well, Miss Simpson, what do you want? It had better be urgent – I don't take kindly to being disturbed at this time of the night.'

'What were you doing over the sea?'

He gave her a brief explanation.

'I thought it must be something like that. I want to apologise for jumping to conclusions – well to apologise for everything really. I'm afraid I have a quick temper...'

'I apologise for assuming that because you're a girl you couldn't be a decent pilot.'

He didn't say he was sorry for sending her face first into the dirt. A surge of annoyance made her forget she had rung up to put things right.

'You should have noticed on your pre-flight check that the compass wasn't working. I take it that was lack of experience and not stupidity.' Hardly a conciliatory thing to say in the circumstances.

*

Jack bit back what he'd been about to say. His uncle thought a lot of this girl and he didn't want to sour their relationship by f-ing and blinding at her.

'I learned to fly ten years ago and have been working as a stunt pilot in America for the past three years.'

There was no response from the other end and for a moment he thought she'd hung up. Then she responded and sounded quite different.

'Really? I'd love to do that but women aren't considered good enough.'

'A biplane like the Moth isn't fast enough for all the stunts I did, but I could teach you a few if you'd like me to?'

Why the hell had he offered to spend time with this girl? She wasn't his type; he went for a curvaceous blonde dame while she was tall, skinny and dark. He had enquired about joining the RAF and was told he wouldn't hear anything for a couple of weeks so he had time to kill. He might as well spend it teaching her to loop the loop. In fact, he might actually enjoy it.

'That would be wonderful but I'm not sure Joe would approve. Anyway, Mr Reynolds, we're too busy to use one of the aircraft for something so frivolous. Sid, our ground engineer, only just keeps up with the running repairs as it is.'

This wasn't the answer he'd been expecting. Calling his profession frivolous made him decide to pursue it. He wasn't used to being turned down and this just made him more determined to get his own way.

'Okay, your loss. Good night, Miss Simpson.' He hung up before she had time to respond and hoped his rudeness had annoyed her.

When he rejoined his uncle and aunt in the front room he'd already come up with a scheme that would further his plans. 'Uncle Joe, your Miss Simpson says you're run off your feet. How about I give you a hand until I leave? I've got my instructor's certificate and am also a qualified ground engineer.'

31

'I didn't like to ask, lad, but your help would be appreciated. Mind you, the way things are going in Europe I reckon there'll be a war before long and then everything will change.'

'That's why I came back – I didn't want to be stranded on the other side of the Atlantic and not able to do my bit. I'm going to volunteer as they'll be taking as many suitable young men as they can find when it starts. You wouldn't believe the rigmarole I went through. They checked my logbook from cover to cover and if they weren't desperate for qualified pilots I don't reckon they'd take me. I'm not officer material.'

'Whatever do you mean, Jack? Why wouldn't they want you in the RAF?' His aunt seemed really upset that he might have been slighted by the toffee-nosed blokes who'd interviewed him.

'I don't have the proper education. Remember I left school without qualifications and Uncle Joe was my instructor, not some posh geezer. If you hadn't given me the chance I'd be working in a factory and never had the opportunity to do what I did in the States.'

'I promised my sister I'd take care of you, lad, and was glad to do so. Joan and I weren't blessed with kiddies of our own and we think of you as a son. Nothing's too good for you, Jack.'

They were right – they were the only family he had. 'Thank you, both of you. I'll not let you down. Now, tell me about this Ellen Simpson. I've never met a female pilot before – it's not the sort of thing you think a girl would be interested in.'

His uncle explained how the girl had become part of his business, and the more he heard about the family the more intrigued he was. 'From what you've said, Uncle Joe, Glebe Farm is one of the biggest in the area and her old man isn't short of a bob or two. He isn't top drawer but must be wealthy or he couldn't have afforded to send his children to those schools you mentioned.'

'Fred Simpson has plenty of cash tucked away. He could buy a grand house if he wanted and mix with the rich folk, which would please his missus. However, he's not like that and that's been a bone of contention between them ever since they were married.'

'I'd like to talk to the two RAF blokes before they go back – any idea how much leave they've got?'

'Neil Simpson said they have to be back at base tomorrow evening so you should have plenty of time for a natter before they leave. Don't know much about the other chap, but if he is a friend of Neil's, he's all right by me.'

Three

Ellie stared at the silent phone and then put it back on the hooks. What a very rude man he was – but as he was Joe's nephew she would have to be civil to him if she saw him again. He'd probably come back to England to enlist in the RAF, so even if he did hang about the airfield, it wouldn't be for long. All men aged between twenty and twenty-one were liable to be called up but she thought he was quite a bit older than that.

She would keep out of his way as much as possible. They were desperately short of instructors so if he was qualified to teach then he'd be a godsend – despite the fact that he wasn't very polite. No doubt he would be on his best behaviour with their pupils.

The sitting room door swung open and Greg came out. 'I thought you'd turned in, Ellie. I'm going outside for a smoke – do you care to join me?'

She was about to refuse but changed her mind. 'I don't smoke – but I'll come outside for a chat if you like.'

They had only reached the back door when her brother joined them. 'We've not had time to talk, little sister, and God knows when we'll get another twenty-four hour pass.'

They headed to the back garden where Mum grew the lush borders of perennial flowers and even had a rose garden. There was a stone bench halfway down the lawn which would be ideal as it seated three easily.

The moon was full and made it easy to find their way in the darkness. Her night vision was excellent and she supposed that both men were the same – you couldn't be a good pilot if you couldn't see in the dark.

Greg, the only one smoking, stood a short distance away and she was touched by his consideration. Once she and her brother were settled the three of them discussed the earlier events.

'It's supposed to be redheads who have a quick temper, Ellie, but considering the provocation Reynolds was remarkably restrained,' her brother said with a smile.

'Don't remind me, I'll make more of an effort if I see him tomorrow. I don't want to talk about him anymore; I'm far more interested in what you two are going to be doing now you've finished your training and have your wings.'

'It's possible we're going to be stationed at Hornchurch – I hope so as I could come home if I get a few hours free. They've already got several Spitfire squadrons stationed there. We've got a few more weeks intensive training so we can fly one of them and then we should be told exactly where we're going to be.'

'What made you both choose to be fighter pilots rather than bomber or coastal command?'

Greg answered from the darkness – she could see the glowing end of his cigarette but nothing else. 'I don't remember being given a choice – we were just told by the high-up bods. I think if either of us had been any taller we would have to have been in a bomber as we wouldn't have fitted in the cockpit of a fighter.'

'Do you think we'll be ready when war's declared? People are already hoarding tinned stuff and sugar and mum told me we've had our gas masks since last year.'

'Certainly, there's a lot going on in the RAF – I'm sure we'll have enough aircraft to defend the country when the time comes.'

'We've had a waiting list for flying lessons since last year. I think the government's making sure there are hundreds of civilian pilots who can be trained more easily than someone with no experience at all,' Ellie said.

'Have any of the chaps objected to being taught by a female and especially one as young as you?'

'A few – if they kick up too much with us then Joe takes them on. In the past two years I think at least a hundred have gone solo. I can't tell you how thrilled I am when one of my pupils gets his first licence.'

Neil spoke from beside her. 'This airfield is so close to Hornchurch you might well get some RAF bods to train.

Going solo isn't enough – they have to have instrument training and be able to fly at night. Bloody horrible it was when I did it. I can't see how we're going to fly at night as we can hardly chase enemy planes if we can't see them.'

'I wish I could join the RAF. I'm sure I could fly a Spitfire or a Hurricane.'

'Probably could – but fighting a war is a man's job. I'm sure there'll be plenty of things you can do that won't involve shooting down aircraft or dropping bombs on civilians.'

His words instantly squashed her enthusiasm. 'You're right. I wouldn't be able to do it.'

Greg appeared at her side and sat down. He smelt of cigarettes and engine oil. 'It's not something any of us want to do but the alternative is far worse. If we don't want those Nazi bastards in their jackboots marching up our streets we have no option but to fight to protect our country.'

Her pleasure in the evening had gone. Although everyone knew that war with Germany was inevitable, the Prime Minister had told them he'd signed a peace treaty with Hitler. People were putting on a brave face and pretending that if there was a war, it would be over in a few months – that it could never last as long as the last one.

'Let's not talk about it. We all know what's coming but I intend to ignore it for as long as I can. This past year has been great fun and I've been able to do the one thing I really love – which is fly.'

He shifted so his thigh was touching hers and she couldn't move away because her brother was sitting right next to her. Her only option was to stand up, which she did.

'I'm going in. If you feel like coming down to the airfield and giving us a hand, you would be very welcome. Good night, Greg, good night, big brother.' Before she could stop him, their guest was on his feet. Such gallantry was misplaced – she much preferred to be treated like one of the boys.

*

When Ellie came downstairs she discovered her mother wasn't down. Dad would have had to get his own breakfast – if she'd known she would have got up early and done it for him. Mum must have a migraine. She couldn't think of anything else that would keep her from her sacred duty.

The Aga never went out which made the kitchen unpleasantly hot in the summer. Fortunately, at seven in the morning the room was still bearable. Her brother and Greg would be down soon expecting a hot breakfast. The farm produced its own bacon, eggs and milk so there was always plenty to eat. The vegetable garden produced more than enough to feed the family and the three workers they employed.

There'd be no fresh bread this morning so they would have to make do with yesterday's and toast it. The kettle was singing, the bacon crisp and the eggs ready to go in when Neil and Greg wandered in.

'Good morning, little sister, where's Mum?'

'She's probably got one of her headaches. Everything's ready so why don't you sit down?'

'Anything I can do?' Greg asked.

'No, all under control, thank you.'

She deftly flipped the eggs then began to dish up. Soon they were all sitting down to a perfectly cooked breakfast. They munched in companionable silence for a while.

'Are you going up to see if Mum wants anything?' Neil said.

'She doesn't like to be disturbed when she's got a migraine. But I do have to sort something out for lunch.'

Whilst they continued to devour everything in sight she threw together four plates of ham salad and put them under a damp cloth in the pantry. Next to this was the remainder of the sherry trifle. It was a bit grand for a working man's lunch, but couldn't be helped.

Normally Dad and the men would get a hot meal – working on a farm was hard work. They wouldn't be impressed with her cold offering. By the time she'd finished her domestic duties her brother and Greg had finished and were busy clearing the table.

'We'll wash this up for you. Better we don't smell of chickens when we go back later.'

Neil knew this was her next task as Mum was in charge of the fowl. 'Thanks, I won't be long. Are you coming down to the airfield or pottering about here?'

'I'm going to show Greg round the farm and then take him into Romford. We'll grab a bite to eat there and join you after that.'

'I've got two pupils going solo this afternoon so won't be up myself.'

The chickens were clucking and fussing in the barn. They were used to being let out at dawn and their displeasure was audible. 'All right, stop that racket, I'm here now.' She grabbed three scoops of grain and tipped them into a bucket before opening the door.

Three dozen grumpy hens and half a dozen cockerels rushed out. She scattered the feed and left them happily munching. She quickly checked their water feeder was full and then went to collect any overnight eggs.

There were three broody hens sitting on clutches and she left them a handful of grain each. Mum did well out of the eggs. Ellie wondered if things would change when the war began. There would be rationing but she couldn't see how the government could prevent farmers from eating more than their ration when they produced all their own food. No doubt some officious bloke would come and tell them what to do when it all kicked off.

Her first pupil was due at nine o'clock which meant she didn't have time to clean the eggs before she left for work. The two that were taking their first solo flight would have a final lesson this morning as well.

The eggs must be left in the scullery to be dealt with later. When she burst in, the washing-up was finished but there was no sign of the visitors. She hadn't heard the car leaving so they must be somewhere outside but she had no time to look for them.

The kitchen was pristine, the kettle refilled and the table laid. Her brother had done all her chores so she could leave immediately. Her bicycle was propped where she'd left it. She didn't want to yell her goodbyes as Mum's bedroom faced the yard.

Cycling to the airfield every day was a pleasure unless it was tipping down or knee deep in snow. From her vantage point on the saddle she could see over the hedges. Their prize dairy herd was grazing peacefully in one field, the porkers were snuffling around in another. Glebe Farm was mixed arable and livestock, as were most of the farms locally.

From the look of the wheat and barley it would be an early harvest and a good one. They were already lifting the early potatoes and if she pedalled along here after nine o'clock she would hear the chirpy voices of the local women, who came in en masse to potato pick.

They brought their children with them and the little ones played happily together whilst their mothers worked.

The horses had gone several years ago and everything was mechanised now. Tractors were much quicker and more efficient but she missed the two shires. Her happy reminiscences were rudely brought to a halt when a car hooted loudly behind her. She lost her balance and rode straight into the hedge.

*

Jack turned into the track that led to the airfield and saw the Simpson girl riding along oblivious to the fact she was blocking the way. The Austin Seven he was driving was new and purred like a contented kitten. Perhaps she couldn't hear his approach. He pressed the horn and to his horror she wobbled and went headfirst into the bushes.

Shit and derision! He stamped on the brake and jumped out of the car not bothering to close the door behind him. It was ominously silent. Why wasn't she yelling and swearing at him?

If she was hurt he'd never forgive himself. The rear wheel of the bike was still spinning but the front half was embedded in the hawthorn spikes. Where the hell was she?

He peered over the greenery and saw what had happened. The girl had been catapulted over the hedge and must be unconscious on the other side. 'Miss Simpson, Ellie, are you hurt?' There was no answer and he leaned into the vicious thorns in an attempt to see if she was spreadeagled close to the edge of the field where he couldn't see her.

He tried yelling again. 'Ellie, for God's sake answer me?'

'I'm perfectly fine, no thanks to you.'

She spoke from right behind him and shock made him grab two handfuls of hawthorn bush. The thorns embedded themselves in his fingers and palms. His foul language made her laugh.

He stepped away from the bushes to examine his lacerated hands. 'For Christ's sake, what is it with you? You should be called Cassandra, not Ellen.'

Her fists clenched. He braced himself, not wishing to end up in the thorns for a second time.

'Mr Reynolds, you are a blithering idiot. First you attempt to ditch our new aircraft and now you've ruined my bike. I can only imagine that Joe calls you his favourite nephew because he doesn't have any others.'

He was about to apologise but she held up her hand. 'Don't just stand there like a useless article – get my bike out of the hedge. I'm going to be late for work.'

He ignored her and returned to his car. He started the engine and revved it loudly expecting her to leap sideways in order to get out of his way. She did the opposite and positioned herself firmly in the middle of the lane. The only way he was going to move forward was by driving over her.

They glared at each other through the windscreen. This was ridiculous. He was behaving like a kid – one of them needed to act like an adult. He would get the bloody bike out of the bloody hedge for her but if she didn't watch out she would end up the same way as her bike.

She stood by in silence as he struggled to remove the damn thing. He gave it another heave and this time was successful. He staggered back with the bike in his hands and lost his balance, ending up in the mud at her feet with it on top of him.

Again, she surprised him. Instead of enjoying his humiliation she removed the bike. 'Let me help you up, Mr Reynolds.' Then her expression changed to one of concern. 'There's blood all over your hands. You should have worn gloves...'

He sat up and examined them. 'Serves me right. Only a few scratches, nothing to worry about. Will you call me Jack?'

Her smile turned her face from ordinary to rather attractive. 'Okay. My bike's had it. Do you think it will squeeze into the back of your car? Sid will be able to fix it if we can get it to him.'

'Can you drive?' This seemed a stupid question but it was possible she could fly planes but not drive a car.

'I can – why do you ask?'

'You need to get to work and your bike is too big to fit in the back. Take the car and I'll carry the bike to the airfield.'

She nodded. 'Thanks, makes sense as you're the one who caused the damage. I'll see you later.'

He was about to explain how to start the vehicle but she was already inside and obviously knew what she was doing. She drove away without a second glance, leaving him to stagger the remaining distance carrying her broken bicycle.

It took him half an hour to complete the journey and if he'd expected to be greeted with thanks and enthusiasm he would have been disappointed. The mechanic, who was doing something complicated to a bit of an engine, gestured towards the wall.

'Stick it over there, mate, I'll get to it later. Joe wants you to fix the compass on the new kite. You'll find the tools you'll need over there.'

'I need the rest room first. Also, do you have any overalls I can borrow?'

The man grunted and jerked his head in the direction of a door at the far side of the hanger. Either the bloke was a grumpy bastard or he was taking Ellie's side. Once he'd cleaned up and pulled on a disgustingly dirty pair of overalls he was ready to fix the compass.

He supposed that Uncle Joe had told the old guy his nephew was a competent ground engineer. When you came to think about it his uncle being involved in a toffs' activity like flying was a bit strange. The money to start it up had come from wheeling and dealing in the East End. Probably best not to enquire too closely exactly how this had been obtained.

It took him a while to unstick the needle on the compass and put it back in place. While he was busy another car rolled up. The Swallow took off a short while later and was still out when he'd finished. He double-checked everything was working properly and then gathered up his tools and scrambled out of the cockpit.

His uncle banged on the window of the office and beckoned him in. He didn't look very happy.

Four

Ellie's morning improved once she'd arrived at the airfield. Both Joe and Sid were sympathetic and agreed that Jack was a nitwit. She got on with the paperwork she had to fill in before her students could do their first solo flight and forgot all about him.

Giles Humphry performed perfectly and she was certain he would have no difficulty on his solo excursion later that day. He landed smoothly and taxied the aircraft off the runway.

'That was really good, Giles. You'll be fine this afternoon.'

The young man nodded happily. 'I want to get as many hours as I can under my belt before things go pear-shaped. I'm going to join the RAF when it does.'

'I don't know why you're spending all this money on lessons when they'll teach you for nothing.'

He grinned. 'That's what the pater keeps telling me every time he sees me. I want to join with experience not start from scratch. Anyway, I've loved these past few months and it gives me a legitimate excuse to be away from the bank.'

'Fair enough. I'll see you later. Excuse me, but my boss wants me in the office.'

Joe was waving frantically. He was rarely upset about anything so this didn't bode well. She burst in to find that her nemesis was already there. She ignored him.

'What's up? Have we got a ministry inspection or something?'

'Worse than that. My Phyllis says the police have been ransacking the house. Some bleeder has squealed and I'm in for the high jump.'

She'd never inquired about how he'd come to get into flying when he wasn't the sort of person usually associated with an aero club. From what she knew of the matter these were usually set up by toffee-nosed people and were as exclusive as the local golf club.

'Will they confiscate the aircraft?' As soon as she'd spoken she realised she should have asked about his welfare.

Jack answered. 'I didn't know until today that everything here is in my name. I own the club and they can't touch it.'

'What about you, Joe? Have you done something illegal?'

He chuckled and his belly bounced up and down underneath his shirt. 'Nothing they can prove, my love. But there's a lot of nasty buggers after my blood and things could get a bit spicy for me until it settles down.'

'What do you want me to do?'

'You don't have to do anything, Ellie, just carry on as normal. My Jack is taking over. I'd better get off home before the local constabulary turn up to arrest me. Your ma wouldn't take kindly to that.' With a cheerful wave he waddled out and drove away in a puff of oily smoke.

She now had to find a way to work with her new boss. He might not be as accommodating as Joe, and she really didn't want to lose this job. She had no other qualifications because she had not stayed on at school to get her higher certificate. She had been sent to a prestigious boarding school, which she'd hated every moment of, as her mother had the vain hope her daughter would become a debutante and take after her. Ellie eventually persuaded her father to release her from this hell. If she wasn't at the airfield she would have to work on the farm as she had no intention of becoming a shop girl or a filing clerk.

She fiddled about with the papers on the desk and the silence became oppressive. She'd better say something.

'Do you want me to show you the ropes?'

'No thank you, my uncle's already done that. For God's sake sit so we can have a sensible conversation.'

Hastily she pulled out a chair and plonked herself down on it. She still didn't look at him as for some reason just the sight of his fiery red hair set her nerves on edge.

'Do you have your instructor's certificate?' This question was addressed to the table.

'Ellie, you're being childish. We've got to work together and you've got to accept that I'm your boss. Look at me – I can't have a conversation with the top of your head.'

She straightened and glared at him. 'You didn't answer me. If you can instruct as well we can take on some of those on the waiting list. As you can see, we're fully booked six days a week.'

He appeared unmoved by her stare and replied as if they were the best of friends. 'I have and we can. I have already rung half a dozen of them and the first is coming tomorrow morning for a two-hour lesson.'

'So I can just carry on as usual then? Do you want me to continue to do the books and correspondence?'

He nodded and flicked through the large leather-bound book in which all the appointments were made. 'You don't appear to have had any holiday or a complete weekend off since you started. From now on you can have Saturday as well as Sunday.'

The last thing she wanted was to spend time at home. Mum would have her in a frock and paying calls on her friends before she could say Jack Robinson – or perhaps that should be Jack Reynolds now.

'Thank you, but I have my regulars and I don't intend to let them down. The Air Ministry was most insistent that the more civilians who can fly the better and that's why the lessons are being subsidised by the government at the moment.'

He leaned back in his chair and viewed her through narrowed eyes. 'Please yourself. If you'd rather be here than at home that's your business.'

She thought he'd finished and was about to stand up when he waved her back into her chair. 'I'm going to put your wages up and give you a bonus for every person that goes solo, starting today.'

*

If Jack had announced that he was a Nazi she couldn't have looked more surprised. Uncle Joe had been ruthlessly exploiting the girl's love of flying and he was glad he was in a position to put that right.

'You don't have to do that. I'm quite happy with what I already get. I don't want to put the business in jeopardy...'

'Is that what the old bugger told you? You should be paid more than double what you're getting. You're worth it.'

'You don't understand the arrangement we had. My brothers and I got free lessons in exchange for Dad leasing him the fields and barns for nothing. Then we worked here once we were qualified in exchange for free use of the aircraft. Joe insisted that I took some wages as well when things got busy a couple of years ago.'

He frowned. 'It's worse than I thought then. Doesn't your old man own the Swallow as well? Is he getting a percentage of the profits?'

She looked puzzled. 'I've no idea. Joe arranged it, I wasn't involved. I expect it's all above board.'

He doubted that very much. 'If you don't mind I'll speak to your dad and find out exactly what the arrangement is. When would be a good time?'

'He's far too busy to see anyone at the moment – it's harvest time you know. Maybe in a couple of months he'll be able to spare you an hour or so.'

Why didn't she want him to meet him? 'Forget about it. I'll give him a bell some time. Right, let's leave it there, shall we? Your next pupil is just arriving.'

She stood up and smiled, but there was no warmth in it. 'Thanks for the rise. Actually, Joe puts most of my money in the bank for me. I don't want it at the moment and I've no idea how much I've got in there. He just gives me a few bob when I need it.'

'You could always look in your bank book.'

'Bank book? I've never seen it – I expect Joe keeps it in the safe.' The door banged and she was gone. How could someone so intelligent be so stupid?

His uncle had been pocketing her wages and cooking the books. He doubted there was a bank account for Ellie. If his suspicions were correct then he would put things right with his own money. He might not like the girl but she didn't deserve to be cheated like this.

He spent the next hour carefully examining the contents of the safe and he was unsurprised to discover he was right. In fact, things were far worse than he'd expected. If he'd known the true state of affairs he'd never have agreed to become involved. He glanced at his watch. Even farmers went home for lunch so if he nipped up there now he could speak to her dad and get matters straight.

Sid was in the hangar working on the older Moth. 'I'm off out for an hour. Can you answer the phone?'

'Sorry, I don't go in the office. Ellie will be back shortly and she's got no one else until two o'clock when her two solos are coming. I've got to get on – she needs this to be ready by then.'

Jack nodded and continued towards his car. There was no point in arguing and he didn't want to upset such a valuable member of staff. According to the wages book there were two ground mechanics, an apprentice plus two instructors and a receptionist working here. This was complete crap. Fond as he was of his uncle, the man was an out and out crook.

He was using this business to filter his illegal cash. Joe wasn't a fool – he'd have known that his dishonesty would be discovered so why the hell had he left him in charge? This was something he'd find out tonight when he went home.

On the short drive over to the farm he decided he would employ the staff who should already have been working there and make sure everything was above board. If the police came to investigate he wanted to be certain his name wasn't dragged into the dirt as well.

As he turned into the yard a tractor chugged up and three hot and sweaty men jumped down from it. He didn't need to ask which one Mr Simpson was. Ellie looked just like him.

He ducked out of the car and strode across with his hand outstretched. 'Mr Simpson, I'm sorry to disturb you. I'm Jack Reynolds, Joe's nephew. I've taken over the airfield.'

The older man didn't look at all surprised to see him. 'You'd better come in, lad, you can talk to me whilst I eat.'

The kitchen was suffocatingly hot and there was no sign of a Mrs Simpson. One of the labourers pushed a kettle onto the heat and the other snatched up two sets of cutlery and put it on a waiting tray.

'Go through. I'll just have a bit of a wash, collect my lunch, and we'll go into the study. It's the third door on the left.'

Jack did as he was asked and was relieved it was much cooler this side of the house. He wondered where the wife was but it was none of his concern. He pushed up the window at the far end of the room and a welcome breeze drifted in.

The study had a well-used look. There were a couple of ancient armchairs in front of the fireplace, a wireless on the mantelpiece and a desk with a stack of papers on it. There were a couple of attractive watercolours on one wall, the other covered by overflowing bookcases. He didn't have time to examine the titles as Mr Simpson elbowed his way through the door.

'Take a seat, young man. I've brought you a cup of tea but can't find you anything to eat. The wife has a migraine.'

'I'll get straight to the point, sir, my uncle has handed the business over to me because he's about to be arrested.'

'Guessed as much. Is my Ellie going to be involved?'

*

Neil and Greg arrived as the second solo flight was taking place – the first had been completed successfully and the delighted young man was hopping from one foot to the other as he watched his friend in the air.

Ellie glanced across and waved but then turned her full attention to the circling plane. She always warned her students to expect the aircraft to feel much lighter with only one person in it and therefore it would travel faster. They had to do three circuits and landings and as long as one of these was perfect he would be cleared to continue solo.

This didn't mean they were fully trained and free to fly wherever they wanted. The next step would be to learn to navigate using a map and the landscape. They had also to learn to do a forced landing and deal with bad weather conditions before they were issued with an A licence.

Watching a first solo flight must be how a mother bird felt when her fledglings left the nest. Ellie was always anxious until the first landing and take-off was completed successfully. The second would-be pilot was coming in now. She held her breath and her hands clenched. He was approaching too fast – no – he was going to be all right. He'd throttled back and the plane bounced safely across the strip.

She gave him the thumbs up and he taxied round and took off smoothly. Her brother and his friend arrived at her side.

'So far so good. He's doing fine, little sister. Can we take the de Havilland up for a spin?'

'I'm not sure. Things are different here now. Joe's nephew, Jack Reynolds, is now the owner. I can't give you the go-ahead without his permission. He went out a while ago but should be back soon.'

'No problem. Do you think he'll mind if we make everyone a cuppa? We got some sticky buns from the baker you like in Romford. More than enough to go around.'

'In which case I'm sure Jack won't object. You know where everything is.'

Greg raised a hand in salute and smiled but didn't add anything to the conversation. She returned her full attention to what was going on in the sky above her and was relieved when the flight was over. Her pupil had scraped through his solo and could now go onto the next step.

Jack arrived as she was signing the pilot's log book; he didn't look too happy. Hopefully he'd keep his ill-humour to himself until the paying customers had gone.

Greg had found a couple of old packing cases and put them outside the office to use as temporary tables. A tray of steaming mugs was on one and on the other were a couple of battered tin plates which held a dozen sticky buns. She hadn't had time for lunch and her stomach growled loudly.

'Are you going to have a celebratory cup of tea before you leave?' Ellie asked the successful pilot.

'Sorry, old thing, we have to dash. Some bigwig from head office is visiting the bank today and I'm expected to put in an appearance. See you same time next week – thanks for getting us this far.'

He rushed off with his friend and she waved goodbye before heading for her belated lunch. Jack called her back. 'Ellie, hang on a minute, I need to talk to you in private.'

She waited for him to catch up. They were still far enough away from the office to talk without being overheard. 'What's wrong? I noticed you were looking grumpy when you arrived.'

'I've been to see your father. He didn't buy that plane over there, Joe did, but he asked if your dad would put it in his name.'

This didn't sound good at all. 'Why would he want to do that?' She had a pretty good idea but hoped she was wrong.

Jack confirmed her worst fears. She'd been hoodwinked by her employer and for the past two years he'd been using her, and the airfield, to hide money derived from his criminal activities in London.

She swallowed a lump in her throat. 'When the aero-club opened I spent all my holidays down here. Mum disapproved but Dad took my side. I knew I'd persuade Joe and Dad to allow me to learn to fly. I can't regret him being here but am horrified Joe has been using us.

'So, let me get this straight – I don't have anything in the bank? Nothing for a rainy day? I've been slaving away here for absolutely nothing?'

'That's about the size of it. Don't worry about your wages as I intend to put that straight. When my uncle told me he'd started an aero club and was thinking of putting it in my name when I came back, I was touched by his kindness. I'm fond of him and my aunt, but what he did was unforgivable.'

'I can't believe Joe's all bad. He's been very kind to me and he taught my brothers and me to fly. How did an East Ender become a pilot? This whole thing's very peculiar.' Her stomach gurgled again quite audibly and he laughed.

'Come on, you need to eat. You're a skinny bird and can't afford to miss your meals. I intend to fatten you up whilst I'm here.'

She was about to take umbrage when she realised he was teasing her. 'Thank you very much. It's good to know you have my best interests at heart.' She put a hand on his arm. 'Please, don't say anything in front of them. Mum would be mortified if anyone outside the family heard about this. She already thinks I'm a disgrace – if she ever discovers I've been working for a criminal she'll throw me out.'

'We'll talk later. Don't worry, Ellie, I'll make sure nothing unpleasant happens to you or your family because of this.'

Five

Over the next few days Ellie got on with her job, and apart from the fact that Jack was now in charge, things were pretty much the same as always. He'd not said anything about his uncle and she didn't intend to ask. The only difference was that she now had a bank book in which there was a satisfyingly large sum of money deposited – more than enough for a week of thunderstorms let alone a rainy day.

She was so busy she scarcely had time to worry about the ever more unpleasant news about impending war. Mum had shown her a leaflet about the proposed evacuation of over three million children from all the major cities in the country. This would take place if war was declared but only a minority of the population thought this was likely. Her mother was one of the minority. Romford wasn't part of this mass exodus but equally, it wasn't considered safe enough to send city children.

Keeping out of Jack's way meant there were no more arguments between them. He had taken on a woman, Gladys Smith, to run the office and another full-time mechanic to help Sid maintain the three aircraft. With both of them taking pupils business was booming and she no longer felt guilty about being paid a proper wage.

At the end of the month George, her other brother, got a twenty-four hour pass to celebrate being given his wings. Mum decided they would have a party and was busy baking and making for the occasion.

'You must ask Mr Reynolds to come, Ellen. George would enjoy speaking to another pilot,' her mother said on the morning of the party.

'I can't ask him at such short notice, Mum, he'll think he's being invited as an afterthought.'

'Nonsense, he'll be delighted to be included. It's a great shame Flying Officer Dunlop and Neil can't get another pass.'

'Neil said that Greg is with Bomber Command, but he's going to be a fighter pilot. He's joining a squadron at Duxford – such a pity he can't be at Hornchurch.'

Dad was having a rare day off and looked up from the newspaper he was reading at the kitchen table. 'Neil told me his friend came top in all the navigation stuff and they want those sort of blokes as bomber pilots. They could have to fly hundreds of miles...'

'Please don't discuss such things. No one at church thinks there's going to be a war and I agree with them.' Mum glared at her. 'Don't just sit there, young lady, do as you're told. Go and make that phone call immediately.'

Ellie exchanged a glance with her father. Mum refused to accept that anything was going to change but they knew different. Hitler wouldn't stick to the truce and Britain would be forced to go to war if they didn't want to be invaded. After all, everybody in the country wouldn't have been issued with a gasmask last year if the government didn't expect there to be a war.

Although she had this weekend free, Jack would be working as usual. There were the usual clicks and whirs as the telephone operator connected her and then finally he answered.

'Jack, my mother has insisted that I invite you to our party this evening. It's to celebrate George getting his wings. I'm sure you've made other plans and we won't be offended if you can't come.'

There was a pause before he answered. 'Actually, I'm at a loose end tonight. I'd be delighted to come – I take it I have to wear a jacket and tie.'

She couldn't stop her giggle. 'Good grief! It's grander than that. Black tie, or at the very least a very smart suit. Mum wouldn't let you in the house in a sport's jacket.'

'Bloody hell! Are you expecting the King?'

'You'd think so, the fuss she's making. However, all the grand folks in the neighbourhood will be there dressed up to the nines. She's insisting that I wear my one and only evening dress. Dad is threatening to hide in the cowshed.'

He chuckled. 'Go on, tell me exactly what I've got to endure if I do come.'

'We've got three village ladies coming to wait, the cowman will be directing traffic and she's even booked some sort of musical entertainment. It's going to be absolutely hideous, if you've got any sense you'll stay well away.'

'I wouldn't miss it. I could do with a laugh. Will there be plenty to drink?'

'Mum's teetotal.' She heard his groan and laughed. 'Don't worry, Dad only agreed to have this party on the understanding there'd be plenty of alcohol.'

'What time does it kick off? I don't finish here until six o'clock. Although I've got digs in the village now I'll still need an hour to get my glad rags on.'

'It's not a sit-down dinner, thank goodness, just a running buffet. The invitations that were sent out said seven thirty so you've got ample time.'

'Righto. See you later. Thanks for the invite.' The line went dead.

If Jack was coming as well as George then it wouldn't be so bad after all. The three of them could circulate for a bit and then disappear to the rose garden as she had with Greg and Neil a few weeks ago.

A long, boring day stretched in front of her. She wasn't even needed to assist with the preparations due to the paid helpers. Her dress was ready, she'd washed her hair and had a bath last night, and it was too hot and stuffy in her bedroom to hide up there with a book. The only place she was free of the petty restrictions of her mother was at the airfield.

Her life had been miserable until she was twelve, when out of nowhere Dad had leased the fields and barns to Joe. It hadn't gone down well with Mum, but this time Dad had insisted. Joe was an unlikely person to start an aero-club. He was a rough diamond, but nonetheless was an excellent pilot. She smiled as she recalled the hours she'd spent hanging around the airfield. Joe had taken her up several times and when Neil and George asked Dad if they could have lessons she had added her pleas to theirs.

Mum had reluctantly agreed as flying was a skill she approved off – usually only the wealthy had anything to do with aircraft. Ellie had not been given permission but Joe taught her at the same time as her brothers. She was able to endure her hideous boarding school during term time because she had the escape of flying when she returned home. At school she was always the odd one out because she had no interest in society events, debutantes or the antics of the rich and famous.

She decided she would cycle to the airfield and see if there was anything she could do in the office as Gladys, the receptionist, didn't work at the weekend.

'Mum, Dad, Jack asked me to go down and help out. Don't worry, I'll be back in good time to get ready.'

Today she wasn't wearing her usual baggy dungarees but a floral, cotton dress that she didn't hate as much as the other garments Mum had bought her.

Cycling in a frock wasn't as easy as dungarees but fortunately her knickers remained unseen and she met no one on her journey. She pedalled up the track, her skirt blowing wildly over her knees, eager to find something useful to do for the remainder of the day.

*

Jack was in the cockpit of the new plane checking the compass was still okay when a flash of something blue caught his eye. What he'd seen had been Ellie's skirt flapping about – and that wasn't all he could see even from this distance.

Holy cow! That girl certainly had great pins and he could see all the way up to her panties. He bet she didn't know she was showing everyone her underwear. He'd never seen her out of scruffy dungarees – she was more of a tomboy than a classy bird and until now he'd not thought her worth a second glance.

He waited until she chucked her bike in its usual place against the wall of the office before letting her know where he was and what he'd seen. 'You'd be better off in slacks if you're going to peddle about the countryside, Ellie.'

She spun round and stared at him.

He began his leisurely descent from the de Havilland before continuing. 'Pink's a great colour on you.'

For a moment she looked puzzled and glanced down at her dress. Then she turned scarlet as she realised he was referring to her knickers. Immediately he regretted his teasing – she wasn't much more than a kid really – and he was old enough and ugly enough to know better.

'Sorry, shouldn't have said that. It was in poor taste. I hope you've come to man the telephone as I don't think you're dressed to do anything else safely.'

'I have. I don't want paying – I just want something to keep me occupied. The house is in pandemonium. Would you believe that Mum has had a marquee put up? It's to be "an alfresco party". That's all very well if it stays fine, but what about if it rains?'

He put his arm around her shoulders and gave her a brotherly hug. She flinched at his touch. He reckoned there wasn't much hugging done in the Simpson house. 'I'm looking forward to it. Don't often get the chance to mix with the upper echelons of society. I hope they don't think I'm your butler.'

'Not a chance. According to my mum a butler's usually grander than the people he works for. You'd only have to open your mouth and everyone would know.' She grinned up at him, more relaxed now. 'You've got a very strange accent – part East End, part posh and something else I don't recognise.'

'I've been living in the States for the past few years but grew up in the East End.'

'Yes, that's it. You sound a bit American sometimes. By the way, try and avoid using bad language tonight as it wouldn't go down very well with the snobby lot who are coming.'

He wasn't sure if he was offended or amused by her comment. 'I'll do my best, ma'am, but we common boys can't be relied on.'

The strident sound of the telephone ringing interrupted their conversation. 'I'll answer that. You get on with whatever you are going to do and I'll take care of the office for the rest of the day.'

Her bossy attitude was irritating but he supposed having been more or less in charge of the place the past year it was hardly surprising.

The day was made easier having Ellie in the office. Sid, like her, seemed to prefer to be at work than at home. She emerged from the office. The sound of a motorbike approaching meant his next pupil was here. This bloke had clocked up enough hours to be going solo but, according to the notes, steadfastly refused to do so.

'I'm going now, Mum just rang and demanded that I come home. I'll see you later.' She collected her bike but then hesitated before getting on. She was worried about showing her knickers not only to him but also to the man who'd come for his lesson.

He came to her rescue. 'Right, Mr Jenkins, shall we get on with it?' He gestured towards the cockpit and immediately his pupil began to climb in the front seat. Jack kept his back firmly towards the girl and heard her cycle away at high speed. He was tempted to look round, but he'd embarrassed her enough today already.

After an uneventful and boring lesson, he signed the log book and was about to make an appointment for the next lesson. 'You'll be going solo next time; you are more than ready for it. The government wants as many civilians with their A licences as possible in case there's a war.'

'Good heavens, young man, there won't be any hostilities. And even if I'm wrong, which I rarely am, I certainly won't be joining the RAF so I can't think it matters if I'm qualified or not. I'm not ready to go up on my own. I'm the best judge of my abilities and I expect you to respect my opinion.'

'If you say so, sir. Just let us know when you want to go solo.'

The man was the last person you'd expect to ride a motorbike, he was more a sedan sort of bloke. Sid had already gone. All Jack had to do was taxi the Swallow into the hangar and then he could go. Ellie had locked the office and left the keys on the box where he could see them.

If he was going to arrive on time he'd better get a shifty on. His landlady had agreed he could have his weekly bath this evening and he wanted the water to be hot. He found the primitive arrangement of a galvanised tin bath beside the copper in the scullery a necessary evil. He was used to indoor plumbing, central heating and being able to have a shower whenever he wanted. It had been a bit of a shock adjusting to life in backward Britain.

*

'You look lovely, Ellie love, you should dress up more often. You don't make the most of yourself,' Dad said fondly.

'You don't look so bad yourself. But we're both far too brown for evening dress. We'll look like a couple of gypsies compared to the other guests.' She attempted to pull up the front of her low-cut gown without success. She wasn't comfortable exposing so much of her bosom. An unwelcome flush engulfed her as she remembered that she'd shown Jack Reynolds her knickers earlier today.

'How many are coming, Dad? There's enough food and drink to feed a small army.'

'No idea, love, I leave that sort of thing to your mum. I reckon there'll be a hundred or so if the number of chairs and tables she borrowed from the church are anything to go by.'

They heard her mother calling from the marquee and both of them turned tail and dashed off in opposite directions. She stumbled, the unfamiliar heeled evening shoes unbalancing her. If she'd had her way she would have worn flat shoes – she was quite tall enough already. Mum had insisted she wear the footwear purchased to complement the frock so she'd had no choice if she didn't want a major row.

She'd already received a long lecture about not having long hair which could be put up into something more elegant. To stop the criticism Ellie had agreed to apply a small amount of lipstick, something she never used.

The home paddock was to be used for car parking. Lanterns had been put up on the trees so people wouldn't break their necks when they returned to their cars. It did look rather pretty and would look even better when it got dark.

She spied George lurking in the shrubbery and hurried over to join him. He was nearest to her in age, being three years her senior, but he was more like her mother in temperament so they'd never really been close. She thought he regretted the fact Mum was estranged from her posh family. He was the only one of the siblings that had enjoyed boarding school and mixing with the children of grand folks.

'Are you hiding too?'

'I certainly am. I can't imagine why our mother wanted to do something so elaborate. I hardly think that getting my wings is a cause for such a grand party.'

'She's been desperate to entertain on a lavish scale and this might well be her last chance. You know better than I do that whatever people think there's going to be a war sooner rather than later. When that starts there'll be no more outside parties.'

'There's a hell of a lot of pilots and aircraft being produced if the government doesn't anticipate a war. It's going to be down to us bods in the RAF to keep that bastard Hitler out of the country. From what I've heard the Luftwaffe is twice the size of us and their pilots are better trained too.'

This was hardly a cheerful conversation. She shivered in her thin, silk gown, even though the sun was still up. 'I don't want to think about it tonight. Let's talk about something else.' She pointed to her outfit. 'Will I pass muster? You're so lucky you can just wear your uniform and don't have to put on a dickie bow like all the other men.'

'You look remarkably pretty – in fact quite lovely. Whoever picked that gown out for you knew what they were doing. Green is your colour and matches your eyes.'

Her mouth dropped open. 'Good God! When did you become so sophisticated? I didn't even know you were aware what colour my eyes are.'

His laugh attracted the attention of their mother who had been searching for them.

71

'People will be arriving at any moment. This party is in your honour, George, so you must be there to greet them as they arrive.' Her mouth thinned and she pointed at Ellie's shoes. 'Look at that – you've already got mud over the heels. Go inside and clean them up and do try and stay tidy. I don't want you to embarrass me in front of my friends.'

Ellie's pleasure in the evening was squashed by this remark. She picked up her skirt and made her way, as quickly as she could without breaking her neck, towards the house to do as she was told. Nobody would notice if she stayed in her room – she was the least important member of the family. A constant disappointment to her mother who had wanted a daughter like herself.

From the vantage point of her bedroom window she watched the procession of smart cars arriving. From these vehicles emerged exactly the sort of people she wasn't comfortable with. They were all dressed to the nines; the women in diamonds and floor-length gowns and the men in dinner jackets and bow ties.

Soon the noise of the revellers drowned out the sound of the blackbirds. The evening was full of plummy voices and clinking glasses. There weren't many young people and only three others that she'd seen in uniform – all of them wearing the distinctive grey-blue of the RAF. She leaned out of the open window to see if George had recognised any of them.

She wouldn't go down until Jack arrived unless she was sent for. The marquee was on the huge lawn at the back, facing towards the house and she could see into it. Some of the guests she recognised from her bi-annual visits to church but a lot of them were strangers to her.

She was about withdraw from her position when someone spoke from just under the window. 'Are you coming down to join me or do I have to come up and get you? I didn't put on this suit for my own benefit, you know.'

Jack's laughing comment almost caused her to fall headfirst. 'Thank goodness you're here. I've been lurking in my bedroom as I don't know anyone else apart from my brother and he's far too busy being the centre of attention to want me anywhere near him.'

She left the window open and headed for the garden. For the first time since she met him she was actually pleased to see Jack.

<u>Six</u>

Jack waited by the front door, which was propped open for the occasion, for what he supposed could be considered his date. Ellie wouldn't be a boring companion. In fact, if they managed to spend more than an hour together without arguing he'd reckon the evening a success.

He had his back to the house but heard the tip tap of evening shoes behind him, so turned. Bloody hell! What a difference a pretty dress made – coming towards him was a lovely young woman with curves in all the right places.

'I know – I feel like Cinderella going to meet Prince Charming.'

She must have seen his look of astonishment but didn't seem bothered by it. 'You look swell, Ellie, that gown is perfect on you.'

'Do you mind if I hang on to your arm, I'm terrified I'm going to trip over my skirt or fall off my heels?'

Obediently he held out his arm and she slipped hers though it. 'Where to? I'm parched – you promised me there'd be plenty to drink so lead me to the bar.'

'I want to introduce you to George on the way. He's the one on the left with a silly moustache, in case you're wondering.'

Her brother was talking to a couple of other RAF guys who had their backs to them. He smiled. 'You've got to pick up the front of your gown or you'll put your foot through it.'

She snatched up a handful of material. 'Stupid thing – believe me I wouldn't be wearing this if I had any other option.'

'I'm glad you did. I'd no idea there was a pretty girl under all the baggy clothes.'

Instead of being pleased by his compliment she snorted in disgust. 'I'm not looking for a boyfriend, so there's no need to flirt with me. My priority is flying and I can't see that changing any time soon.'

He couldn't prevent his chuckle. 'Believe me, sweetheart, you're just not my type. Too young and too skinny – I prefer my birds with a bit more meat on them.'

Again, she surprised him. 'Well that's a relief, I should hate to hurt your feelings by turning you down.'

One of the RAF guys spun round as if poked in the butt by a sharp object. 'Ellie – as I live and breathe. What are you doing here?'

'Michael isn't it? I live here. Your invitation was from Mr and Mrs Simpson. I'd have thought you might have made the connection.'

'Actually, old bean, I'm staying with Bertie here, just came along for the ride.' He guffawed and beamed at all them.

The man was an idiot. The RAF would take anyone as long as they came from the right family. So much for one of the criteria being that the applicant must be highly educated and intelligent.

He must have been scowling as Ellie dug him sharply in the ribs. 'I taught Michael to fly. He was my first pupil to go solo.'

'Hi, pleased to meet you. Excuse us, guys, we need a drink.' He deliberately emphasised the American twang in his accent and was amused to hear them muttering about "uncivilised colonials" behind his back.

'What do you want to drink, honey?'

She giggled and pinched his arm. 'You can stop that now, I'm not impressed. I don't drink alcohol, it doesn't agree with me. I'll have lemonade, please.'

He ordered a pint of beer, picked up a glass for her, and took them back to her. He would have had to be blind not to notice the attention Ellie was getting from the men. A couple of old goats were heading her way and he hastily stepped in front of them.

'Excuse me, gents, the lady's spoken for.' They backed off muttering to each other.

'I wish I'd worn my dungarees. I don't like being stared at like a prize heifer in a sale ring. You should have let them come – I could flatten them easily even dressed in this silly outfit.'

'Here, Ellie, drink your lemonade and behave yourself. Shall we go and find ourselves a quiet spot where we can sit and laugh at the other guests?'

She pointed to a couple of chairs that hadn't been positioned around the tables ready for people to sit and eat their supper. 'Pinch those. Give me your drink and I'll carry it for you. Don't frown at me, Jack Reynolds, I'm perfectly capable of holding up my dress and transporting two drinks without falling flat on my face now that I've got used to them.'

He wasn't so sure but handed his beer over anyway. 'Right – where are we going with these?'

'Follow me, I know the perfect place.'

She led him away from the party and into the rose garden. 'We can sit under that tree, the sun's still hot and you must be suffocating in that suit.' She smiled at him. 'I should have said, you scrub up really well too. Even though it's not a dinner jacket, it's a very smart suit.'

'Thank you, ma'am, I aim to please.'

'And I, sir, am the Queen of Sheba.' Her laughter filled the garden and he joined in.

He positioned the chairs in the shade and then reclaimed his beer. Somehow, she'd managed to carry it without spilling a drop. Maybe she wasn't as clumsy as he thought.

From their position they could see what was going on in the marquee but wouldn't be seen themselves. An ideal place for two people who didn't enjoy parties. He took an appreciative swallow of his warm beer. 'British beer is an acquired taste, but I much prefer it to the American version. It's the one thing I missed when I was over there – that and the fish and chips.'

They sat in a strangely companionable silence for a while and then she spoilt the moment.

*

'What's going on with Joe? Has he been arrested and if so what for?' Ellie watched him slop his beer onto his trousers and immediately regretted having asked, even though she was entitled to know what was going on.

'He's "helping police with their enquiries" at the moment. How much do you know about how he came to be your boss?'

'Nothing at all. To tell you the truth I've always been curious as to how someone from the East End ended up with a flying club. Not the sort of thing you'd expect from someone with his background.'

'Too common do you mean?'

She was about to apologise when he laughed. 'I'm surprised you hadn't asked him yourself – not backward at coming forward, are you?' He swallowed a third of his beer with obvious relish before continuing. 'My aunt, like your mother, married beneath herself. However, unlike your grandparents, her family were all right with it. My aunt's old man had an ancient kite left over from the last lot and he taught Uncle Joe to fly in it. He was hooked and spent as much time as he could in the old plane until it became too decrepit to get off the ground.

'When things got too hot for him in the Smoke he upped sticks and moved to Romford. Then a few years ago he cashed in his assets and decided to start his own club.'

'Well that's one mystery solved.' She hesitated, not sure she wanted to know how Joe had made his ill-gotten gains. She wasn't comfortable with the fact that she'd been working for a criminal for the past few years. 'What did he do? You still haven't told me why the police are involved after so long.'

'He's not violent, if that's what you're worried about. He had a pawn shop – dealt with things that fell off the back of a lorry, if you know what I mean.'

'I see. You do realise I'd never have been working there if I'd known. My parents...'

'Your dad does know. Uncle Joe explained it all to him when the arrangement was made to lease the fields and barns.'

'Dad would never condone dishonesty of any sort. I don't understand. Why would he agree to work with a criminal? It just doesn't make sense.'

'I'm equally puzzled. My uncle refused to tell me. You'll have to ask him yourself. Why don't you do it now?'

She was about to tell him she wasn't that stupid when she realised he was teasing. Something else occurred to her. 'Has the airfield always been in your name?'

'Yes. I thought Uncle Joe was just setting up something by way of an inheritance but now I'm not so sure. I think it's only in my name to keep the police away.'

'You don't seem especially bothered that you own a business bought with stolen money. I suppose you've always known Joe was a bad lot.'

'Not when I was a nipper. I realised when he gave me the money to go to America that there was something up. We'd always been close and now he wanted to pack me off to the other side of the world. It didn't make sense, but I didn't argue as I was desperate to make flying my livelihood and there was no way of doing it over here.'

'I don't blame you really. If I got the chance to spend all my life in the air I'd be off like a shot. I know once the war starts civilian flying will have to stop. I suppose I'll stay here and help my dad run the farm as he's going to lose at least one of his workers. The other two are too ancient to be called up.'

She sipped her lemonade while she decided if she should do the right thing and hand in her notice or do what she wanted and stay.

'It's a hard one isn't it, Ellie? Before you make your decision there's something I want to tell you, but you mustn't breathe a word to anyone else. I've had an enquiry from some bigwig in the Government and it seems likely we're going to be put on the list of suitable places to train RAF pilots once the war starts. This would mean you could carry on flying and be doing your bit for the country.'

'That makes it easier, thank you for telling me. I'll stay. If my dad isn't bothered about where the money came from then I'm not going to worry either.'

The sun slid below the horizon leaving the sky bathed in a glorious red light. If she'd been a religious person she might have taken this as a sign from above. Then the dusk was filled with the lovely sound of violins. The trio had started to play.

'Isn't that beautiful. There's going to be dancing later in the marquee.'

In her elegant evening gown, sitting next to a handsome young man, surrounded by the flickering light from dozens of lanterns, she felt like a princess from a fairy tale.

'I hope you're not suggesting that I dance with you? I can do the polka and jitterbug and that's about my limit. I doubt that either of those will be on the cards tonight.'

'Jitterbug? I've never heard of that – is it some Yankee craze?'

He put his empty glass down with a thump and surged to his feet. 'If you can ignore that wailing and scraping and imagine you're listening to something lively by Glenn Miller, I'll teach you how to do it.'

'No chance. I can just about waltz, I had to learn the basics at school, but doubt I could do even that dressed as I am. You can show me when I've got my dungarees on – they often have Glenn Miller on the wireless and Sid has that on all the time when he's working.'

'In which case, I need another drink. Shall we go and upset a few of the guests? I got a few snotty looks when I came in because I wasn't dressed appropriately.'

'I don't think so. I'm going in, thank you for coming.' She remembered to pick up her skirts before she hurried away. As Jack had only come because she'd asked him she shouldn't really desert him like this, but she wasn't in the mood for his kind of fun.

She half expected him to call her back but he didn't. With the front and back doors open the house was pleasantly cool. The kitchen was out of bounds as the temporary staff were busy in there but she could really do with a sandwich and a cup of tea.

As she passed the sitting room she decided she would hide in there until the kitchen was empty. She hadn't had any lunch and breakfast was hours ago. The room was dark and she was about to switch on the light when a voice spoke from the gloom.

'Is that you, lovey?'

'Dad – you shouldn't be in here. Mum will be livid. I don't care, but you have to live with her.'

'Come and sit down, nobody will find us if we don't put the light on. Your mum's having far too good a time showing off to her grand friends to miss either of us tonight.'

It was tricky curling up in one of the comfortable armchairs in her long dress but she managed it eventually without tearing the material. Her uncomfortable shoes had been kicked off already.

'Jack says you knew that Joe was a criminal so why did you let him have the fields?' She hadn't intended to blurt it out so bluntly but somehow it was easier to say what she was thinking when they were both sitting in the darkness.

'I was expecting you to ask me that question when I heard that Joe was being investigated again.' There was a long pause before he continued. 'I'm sorry, Ellie, but I can't tell you the reason. You'll have to trust me. Joe's dishonest, but he's not a bad man. I would never have let you anywhere near him if I thought differently.'

This wasn't the answer she wanted but she would have to respect his wishes and not push for more. 'If Mum ever finds out – well – I just hope she doesn't.'

'As long as your Jack's in charge down there and Joe keeps his distance, I reckon nothing will come out.'

'He's not my Jack – he's my boss. I don't particularly like him, if I'm being honest. I must have more of Mum in me than I realised. He's too much of a rough diamond for me. I much prefer Greg, and if I went out with anybody it would be him.'

'Funny you should mention that, he rang when you were out and he's coming tonight. In fact, he should be here anytime. So good thing you haven't gone up or you would have missed him. He is exactly the sort of young man your mother and I want you to walk out with.'

'Hang on a minute, Dad, I've only met him once. Don't have us marching up the aisle already.'

He chuckled. 'Don't worry, lovey, you'll get no pressure from me. Eighteen is far too young to think of getting married. I don't want to lose you for another few years.'

'That's a relief then.' She carefully stood up and shook out her dress hoping it wasn't too creased. It took her several minutes to locate her shoes and ram her feet into them. 'I'd better go and look for him I suppose. Why hasn't Neil come?'

'Your brother hasn't got a pass tonight. I think Greg has taken a shine to you, Ellie. It's not that far from his London home to Romford in a fast car like his. He said he'd be here by nine and it's later than that already.'

'It's a good thing you told me or I'd have been in bed by now. Are you coming out again? Jack's spoiling for a fight and I dread to think what would happen if he causes a fuss this evening.'

With a loud sigh he emerged from his chair. 'I'll find him and bring him back here. To tell you the truth, he's more my cup of tea than Greg Dunlop. I've got a decent bottle of whiskey tucked away somewhere, we can share that and he can tell me about his daring deeds in America.'

*

Greg was regretting his impulsive decision to drive thirty miles on the off chance that he'd get a look in with Ellie Simpson. He'd had a couple of relationships, but both had been with debs. He'd never met anyone quite like Neil's sister and he was inexplicably drawn to her.

He saw the lanterns swinging in the wind a couple of miles from the farm and that made finding the place so much easier. A local appeared and offered to park his car. As he was already late, Greg hopped over the door and left him to it.

Where would he find the girl he'd driven so far to see? He hadn't expected to see so many guests – this party looked more like one of the grand affairs his mother held than an informal country get-together. His lips curved. He'd hardly be wearing a dinner jacket if it was informal.

Violin music mingled with the sound of the blackbirds in the trees and he could see dozens of immaculately clad couples mingling in a smart marquee, a barn now doubling as a bar.

He couldn't see Mr or Mrs Simpson or Ellie. He wasn't sure he'd actually recognise her in an evening dress but she would be the only one with cropped hair so should stand out. She was probably one of the tallest women here as well.

Then he saw a slender girl in a lavender silk, figure-hugging dress coming towards him. She looked spectacular and worth every mile of the drive.

<u>Seven</u>

'Ellie, you look quite stunning. I hope you don't mind me gate-crashing but I wanted to see you again.'

'Thank you for saying so and thank you for coming. Let me find you a drink. Most people have gone to the marquee as supper is being served.' She pointed to the bar which was now fairly quiet. 'You look very dashing too. I thought service men had to stay in their uniforms even when they went off base.'

'I've just completed my orientation and expect to be going to join 107 squadron at Wattisham soon. As I'm not officially attached at the moment I can do as I damn well please.'

'How exciting, Neil is going to be based at Gravesend – he's going to be a Spitfire pilot. What will you be flying?'

'A Blenheim 1f. Now, that's quite enough talk about me. What have you been doing for the past couple of weeks?'

He didn't go for the beer but had a glass of bubbly and she had another lemonade. He was almost as easy to talk to as Jack and they found themselves a quiet corner and chatted about everything from the latest film showing in Romford to what they had both been reading.

'We had better go and get something to eat before it's all gone.' Ellie put her arm through his and they headed to the marquee. Although it was finger food the guests had still sat down to eat. There were no places left at any of the tables.

'Never mind, I can go to the kitchen and get something for both of us. Why don't you go back to the bar and bring us a couple of drinks – at least there are some chairs in there.' She left him replenishing his glass and promised she wouldn't be long.

After almost twisting her ankle on the way she removed her shoes and chucked them onto the stairs as she went in. This meant the hem of her dress would trail in the dirt but better that than breaking her neck so she'd better nip upstairs and find herself something else to wear. After rummaging for several minutes in the bottom of a wardrobe she found some plimsolls and pushed her bare feet into them. Hardly glamorous, but they were far more comfortable.

There was no one in the kitchen but there still seemed to be plenty of food waiting to go out. She snatched a plate from the dresser and filled it with a random selection of items. If Greg was anything like her brothers he didn't care what he ate as long as there was plenty of it.

It was just as quick to return to the barn via the back door and she was less likely to be seen shoeless by the other guests. Greg must be wondering what had kept her as she'd been gone far longer than she'd anticipated.

With a handful of her skirt in one hand and the piled plate in the other she stepped out into the darkness. It took a moment for her vision to adjust and whilst she was stationary someone approached.

'I thought you'd gone to bed, Ellie, but I'm glad you didn't. Were you coming to find me with that?' Jack strolled into view.

Her tongue stuck to the roof of her mouth and she couldn't think of a sensible reply. Whatever she said, whatever she did, someone was going to be cross with her. Then the matter was taken out of her hands as Greg appeared from the direction of the bar.

'There you are, I was beginning to think you'd abandoned me,' he said. He ignored Jack, which was a mistake.

'Who the hell are you? I thought you had better taste, Ellie, and didn't go for the posh boys.' Jack was now standing beside her giving quite the wrong impression.

Greg seemed to grow several inches and changed from a charming, friendly man into someone quite formidable. 'Greg Dunlop, friend of the family. Ellie is with me.'

The two men stared at each other. They were of similar size and if Jack decided he wanted to fight it could go either way. She refused to be squabbled over like two dogs with one bone.

'I'm not *with* anyone.' She shoved the laden plate towards Greg. 'Here you are. Why don't you share it with Jack as I'm going to bed.'

He had to take it or it would have dropped to the floor. She hurried inside leaving the two of them to sort it out for themselves. She was sorry Jack had intervened as she'd been enjoying her chat with Greg. Men didn't seem to grow up as girls did – they still behaved like children in the playground. A woman wouldn't fight over a man, she'd have too much sense.

Maybe she would see Greg again as he was going to be stationed fairly close and whilst the fragile truce held he wouldn't have much to do. The fighter planes often flew over the farm practising their dogfights but bombers could hardly practice dropping bombs. She wasn't sure if the aircrew of these bigger aircraft were sent on imaginary missions – but she'd certainly never seen any in the sky over Romford.

On her way through the deserted kitchen she helped herself to a second plate. What she really wanted was a cuppa, but she didn't think it wise to dawdle in the kitchen just in case Jack or Greg came to find her. Going to work on Monday was going to be interesting.

*

Jack turned to watch Ellie disappear. 'Well that's us told. Did you notice she's got canvas shoes on?' His flash of anger had been ridiculous and unnecessary. He held out his hand with a friendly smile. 'Jack Reynolds, I own the aero club where she works. I've had too much drink and apologise for my behaviour.'

The other bloke carefully put the plate of food into his left hand so he could offer his right. 'Pleased to meet you again. Actually, I'm a friend of her brother Neil, only met Ellie once before.'

They shook hands and Jack liked the guy despite the fact that he belonged to a social class he despised. 'I remember now; I didn't recognise you out of uniform.' He gestured towards the plate. 'Seems a pity to waste all that food. I could do with another beer – shall we share this at the bar?'

They polished off the plate in double quick time but Jack was still hungry. 'That hardly touched the sides – I'm not a fan of this sort of thing. Can't see the point myself. What's wrong with a normal sandwich?'

'Nothing at all, in my opinion. Can you get me a beer this time? I'll run a sortie to the kitchen and find us something else to eat.'

The bar was a bit busier now as people finished their fancy supper and came in search of something to wet their whistle. Although he'd made an effort to mingle, and those he'd spoken to had been scrupulously polite, the fact that he was the only one in a lounge suit made him feel uncomfortable. He shouldn't have come to this sort of shindig, it wasn't his cup of tea.

The barman served him first which didn't go down well with the toffee-nosed lot waiting politely in a queue, but he ignored the dirty looks and took the two pints back to the chairs he and Greg had commandeered. These were positioned just outside the barn, up against the wall, and fortunately nobody else had pinched them.

He carefully put the second brimming glass under a chair and then sat down nursing his own beer. He shouldn't really have any more as he was already half-pissed and soon he wouldn't be safe to drive himself home. If he ate some more of the fancy food, that should soak up some of the alcohol.

He ought to have recognised Greg even though he was dressed like a penguin – but then he'd been more concerned with Ellie's behaviour than the other pilot. Anyway, one bloke in RAF uniform looked very like another to him. Maybe when he eventually joined up he'd become less noticeable but he doubted it – conker-coloured hair made him easily recognisable.

'Here we are; I think I did better than you, old chap. Got a plateful for each of us this time.' Greg handed one over and then took the other chair. He didn't ask where his drink was, just groped between his legs and emerged triumphantly with his pint.

They munched and slurped happily and there was no need for conversation, which was a good thing as he didn't have much to say. He didn't make small talk and the less he heard about the approaching war the better. There were no lanterns this side of the barn and he couldn't see the face of the guy beside him. He was jolted out of his alcoholic doze when Greg spoke.

'I have to ask, are you interested in Ellie?'

'Bloody hell! Not at all – not my type. You go ahead, mate, if you fancy her. I'll not tread on your toes.'

'Really? I thought you seemed a bit proprietorial earlier.'

'I apologised for that. She's like a kid sister to me so I'm going to keep an eye on her, aren't I? Just make sure you don't take advantage. She's had no experience with men.'

'My intentions are strictly honourable.' The chair scraped against the wall as he stood up. 'I'd better go and say hello to Mrs Simpson. You staying here or coming with me?'

'I'm going home when I finish this beer. I've got to be at the airfield first thing – got a couple of new pupils coming to see if they want to learn to fly.'

He wandered off leaving Jack to think about the brief conversation. Strictly honourable? This meant Greg was already considering marrying Ellie if she'd have him. Seemed daft to him to be making such an important decision after just two meetings.

He pushed himself to his feet and was shocked how much his head spun. He shouldn't have had that last pint, it had pushed him over the edge. His landlady would take a dim view if he turned up on the doorstep in this condition so he'd better spend the night at the airfield.

There was an old rug in the back of the car which would do to sleep on. The night was warm so he wouldn't need a blanket over him. He'd shaved just before he came out so wouldn't look too rough in the morning. With luck there would still be milk to go in his tea and hopefully the biscuit tin would be full as well.

He walked more or less straight to the field where the cars were parked. The lanterns bobbing about in the trees made it easy for him to find his car amongst all the others. He certainly wouldn't fly when he was pissed but he reckoned he was perfectly safe to drive his car down a deserted track without coming to grief.

His headlights lit up the airfield like searchlights. There was a flicker of movement in the office. Some bugger was after the petty cash tin. He put his foot down and skidded to a halt inches from the door. Whoever was in there couldn't escape without going past him, and even drunk he was a match for most men.

*

Ellie was up early and decided she'd much rather work for free at the airfield than for free at home. Dad was on the farm somewhere hiding from Mum who was on the

94

war path because he'd not lived up to her exacting standards last night. She had heard them rowing late into the night. Mum didn't do anything as common as shouting but her voice had carried through the walls. Dad had retired long before the party was over so Mum must have barged into his room to harangue him. He wouldn't have been happy about this invasion of his privacy. Their marriage had been a mistake – one she was never going to make herself.

Today she was in slacks and there was no danger of showing her underwear to anyone. The church clock in the village had struck eight o'clock a few minutes ago but Jack was already here.

Why had he parked so close to the office? The door was ajar but there was no sign of him through the window. She dumped her bicycle in its usual place and saw the three aircraft were safely in the hangar. He'd obviously taxied them in before he'd left for his digs last night. There were no lessons booked until ten so she was puzzled as to why he'd got there so early.

As she approached the steps that led to the office she heard what sounded like a groan coming from inside. The hair on the back of her neck stood up. 'Is that you in there, Jack? Is something wrong?'

There was no answer. Slowly she pushed open the door and for a moment was too horrified to move. Jack was slumped under the table and his smart suit was covered in blood.

She'd done a basic first aid course when she'd got her instructor's licence so knew what to do. She dropped to her knees beside him and felt for a pulse. Thank God! It was weak but regular. Blood was seeping from somewhere and this had to be stopped if he was to survive.

She scrambled to her feet and grabbed the first aid tin from the shelf. She doubted there was anything really useful for a gunshot wound – but that's what it was – so she'd have to make do. Should she call for an ambulance as it would probably take them half an hour to arrive? Then what about the police? They must be rung as well.

To do both would take too long so she would attend to the patient and then make the phone calls. She grabbed the office scissors, cut through his jacket and shirt and removed half of both, along with the sleeve. The bullet had gone through the fleshy part of his upper arm – not his shoulder at all.

There was a small bottle of Dettol in the tin which would be really useful. She tore off a wad of cotton wool and tipped water from the kettle onto it. She began to carefully wipe away the worst of the blood from the oozing bullet wound.

Then she did the same for the exit wound. In order to do this, she had to lean him against her knee which meant she now had blood all over her slacks. This would be hard to explain when she went home. Once she was sure the injury was clean she tipped neat Dettol over both and the shock of this work Jack up.

'Jesus H Christ, that hurt,' he said, his voice coming out more like a hiss than words.

'I've nearly finished. I've just got to put on a bandage. Can you sit still for me?'

He didn't answer and his eyes closed. He'd passed out again. She put a sterile pad on either side of his arm and held them in place with a tightly wound bandage. There was little left in the tin by the time she'd completed her ministrations.

His skin was clammy and cold. They kept a picnic rug somewhere and that would be ideal to put around his shoulders until the ambulance arrived to take him to hospital. After a quick search she found it under a pile of old newspapers and draped it around him. She was worried that he was still unconscious.

She left him propped against the wall. She'd never had to ask the operator to connect her to the ambulance or the police and her hand shook as she picked up the receiver.

'No, no police. No ambulance either.' Jack had woken up.

'You've been shot. You need to go to hospital urgently and the police have to be told.'

He grimaced and forced his eyes open. 'Please, for me, no calls.'

'You've lost so much blood...'

'Cup of hot sweet tea. No need for hospital. I'll be fine in a bit.'

She was going to refuse but he looked so desperate, and his colour was a little better, so she relented. 'I'll make you some tea and then you can tell me what happened. I'll decide after that what I'm going to do.'

She tipped the remainder of the water into a mug and held it to his mouth so he could drink. He finished it greedily. Her emergency first aid appeared to be working as there was no fresh blood seeping through the bandage.

She nipped outside to fill the kettle from the tank then lit the paraffin stove. This was fairly efficient but smelt horrible. She'd brought a large slice of fruit cake for her breakfast but his need was greater than hers. If he ate this and drank a cup of tea then she might not need to call out the ambulance.

His right arm was the one with the injury and he was left-handed which would make things easier for him. He appeared to be sleeping rather than unconscious which gave her a few moments to recover from the shock.

There were two phone calls she had to make but these were to the people coming for their first lesson later this morning. It wouldn't do the reputation of the business any good for anyone to find the owner had been shot.

She told both of them Jack had been called away on a family emergency. She rebooked their appointments for the following weekend and by that time the kettle was singing.

'Jack, wake up, I've got a cup of tea for you. I want you to drink it and eat this piece of cake.' She was crouching down beside him holding the mug and the plate.

He opened his eyes and this time he looked more himself. 'I think I can manage on my own, but one thing at a time.'

She handed over the tea and watched anxiously to see if he could hold the mug without spilling it all over himself. He swallowed it down with no difficulty; she removed it from his hand and offered him the plate. He took the cake and that went down as quickly.

'You're obviously recovering fast. But those holes in your arm need stitching...

'I've got a friend who can do that for me. I don't want anyone to know about this. Give me your word that what happened here will remain a secret.'

Eight

Ellie pushed a chair to the far side of the office and sat staring at him through narrowed eyes whilst nursing her tea. He was going to have to work hard to convince her not to call the police or drag him off to the nearest hospital.

He might as well tell her the truth as he couldn't think of any convincing lies that would make sense. He told her his reason for coming here – that was the easy part.

'I was bloody stupid. I should have realised the bastard in the office had something to do with my uncle. If I'd been sober I wouldn't have made such a daft mistake. I charged in and he shot me.' A cold sweat dripped down his back. 'I tripped over the step on my way in. If I hadn't I'd be dead now.'

'What was he looking for?' She glanced around and he followed her gaze.

'God knows – but he didn't find it otherwise the place would be turned over. I reckon I arrived a few moments after him and he hadn't started his search.'

'Didn't you see a car or motorbike on the way down the track?'

He shook his head and wished he hadn't as the pain made his head spin. It was his bloody arm that was shot so why did his shoulder hurt almost as much? He swallowed a few times and then felt okay. 'No, I don't know how he got here. All I can think of is that he came across the fields on foot. Don't look at me like that, love, I'm not going to peg it just yet.'

'There's some aspirin in the drawer; would you like some?'

'Please, and another cuppa would go down a treat too.'

He dozed whilst she did this. He wasn't feeling too clever but it could be a hangover as much as his injury. He hoped so.

She woke him by touching his arm. 'Here you are, plenty of sugar again. I'm going to search but it would help if you could give me an inkling of what it is I'm looking for. I suppose I should be shocked that Joe is involved with would-be murderers – but I'm not really. The worst sort of criminals live in the East End and he must have acquired something from one of them.'

'All the more reason to find whatever it is and give it back to them before somebody actually does get killed. They'll be back, I'm certain of it.'

Her face drained of colour and she stared wide-eyed out of the window as if expecting a man waving a gun to magically appear.

'Sorry, that was crass of me. They won't be back in the daylight. You can be bloody sure someone's watching this place and waiting to see whether the rozzers turn up.'

'Is it going to be more dangerous or less if we don't call them?'

'Less – much less. Uncle Joe is in it up to his neck and I don't want the boys in blue poking around anymore than they are already. I don't approve of his lifestyle, but he's always been good to me and I'm not going to turn him in.'

She slopped her tea as she picked up the mug and he wished she hadn't been involved in this. Mind you – if she hadn't decided to come in early he could be dead by now.

'I've been thinking. Although Joe was in the office more than he was in the air, I've been in and out of here every day for the past four years. It's not especially spacious so I'm sure I'd have seen something like a cashbox full of jewellery or something.'

'I agree. Therefore, it must be a document of some sort. Joe must have come across something valuable and decided to hang onto it in case it came in useful.'

'Could he have been blackmailing a gangster?'

He managed a feeble chuckle and she appreciated the effort. 'I doubt it – they would have come for him before this. It has to be... bloody hell! I don't know what it is but I think I can guess why they're looking for it now.

They didn't mind Joe having it, but now the police are investigating his affairs things have changed.'

She finished her tea and stood up. 'It has to be somewhere I wouldn't touch. I'm going to start searching in that pile of old newspapers. I've always wondered why he kept so many as I've never seen him read any of them. I suggested throwing them out last year and he shouted at me and told me to leave them alone.'

She carried the pile over to the table that served as a desk and began methodically looking through the pages. If there was anything of interest amongst them she was the girl to find it.

He shifted uncomfortably. He needed a pee and he didn't think he was going to be able to get to his feet without her assistance.

'Ellie, I had God knows how many pints of beer yesterday and…'

She dropped the papers as they were red hot and sprung to her feet. 'Golly! I should have thought of that myself. Hang on, I'll get you a bucket.'

She dashed off and he tried to stand up but failed miserably. The thought of the poor girl having to empty his piss into the Elsan wasn't a happy one.

*

There was no bucket so Jack would have to manage with an empty oil can. This sort of thing was easier for a man. Another one of life's disappointments.

'This will have to do. I'll move your car somewhere more sensible and leave you to it.' She was about to close the door when something occurred to her. 'Do you need help with anything?' She kept her fingers crossed that he didn't.

'Sod off, Ellie, I'll call you when I'm finished.'

There was plenty to get on with outside. Fortunately, no one else was working today, but someone had booked a three-hour jaunt in the de Havilland this afternoon. At some point this morning she would have to taxi the aircraft out onto the strip and do a quick pre-flight check. It would also need refuelling. She'd no idea where the pilot intended to take the plane as he hadn't filed his flight plan.

A plan wasn't strictly necessary, but a sensible precaution. Before any aircraft left the airfield, Joe insisted he knew exactly where they were going and that the pilot was quite clear where he could land in an emergency. Flying out to sea was strictly forbidden. She supposed the company rules didn't apply to relatives.

Petrol was delivered in large cans every week from the local garage. These were kept in a separate building far enough away from the hangar that in the event of a fire nothing else would go up in flames. The Moth had to be taken to the fuel and not the other way around.

How long would it take Jack to pee in the can? He should be finished by now and it would be safe to go back and remove it. She'd given it to him with the lid so at least she wouldn't have to view the contents or get it all over her hands when she carried it out.

Moving the car to a more sensible parking place took her ten minutes. She noticed there was a rug on the back seat so she grabbed that and took it with her. Even if he didn't want it over him he could use it to lean on and make himself more comfortable.

Despite the seriousness of the situation she couldn't help smiling. If Jack was anything like either of her brothers he'd be squirming in embarrassment. It wouldn't do any harm. In her opinion he was far too full of himself.

She paused on the top step. 'Is it safe to come in?'

'Yes.'

He was nursing the half full container between his knees. Hastily she rammed on the lid making sure she didn't make eye contact. 'I'll just get rid of this and then get on with the search.'

The contents slopped about inside; it was surprisingly heavy. She wasn't going to do any more at the moment than put it somewhere outside where no one else would inadvertently open it. He could dispose of it himself when he was better.

When she returned to the office he was looking a lot brighter but still far too pale. She added the rug to the one he was already covered in and he didn't complain. 'I know you don't want to go to the hospital but how do you propose to get to your friend? You can't even stand up and I certainly can't move you on my own.'

'Hand me the telephone and I'll make the arrangements myself. You get on with your search.'

He was far too fond of issuing orders but this time she would let it go as he was probably feeling really rotten about everything.

When he was connected Jack didn't give any details about his injury, just asking for whoever it was to come immediately to collect him. She returned the telephone to the table and continued rummaging through the newspapers.

'Will your friend be here soon? Do I need to have finished this before he gets here?'

'He's coming from London. Please try and find it. I can't leave knowing whatever it is might still be here and those bastards will be coming back for it.'

She resumed her task and was beginning to think it a wasted effort when a long brown envelope slipped out of the paper she was flicking through.

'I've found it.' She looked around expecting him to be sharing her relief but he was either asleep or unconscious and didn't react. She pushed her find into her slacks' pocket, quickly re-stacked the newspapers and replaced them on the shelf.

'Jack, Jack,' she squeezed his good arm but got no response. She checked his pulse; it was no weaker than before and still regular, but this time he wasn't just dozing but unconscious. This couldn't be a good sign. Could he have internal injuries from his fall? If his friend didn't arrive in the next ten minutes she was going to ring for an ambulance and he would just have to jolly well lump it.

Her bandages were still in place and neither wound was bleeding heavily enough to discolour them. She hoped she was worrying unnecessarily and that he was just deeply asleep. There wasn't any blood on the floor – it had all soaked into his clothes. There must be some on the wall behind him but she couldn't do anything about that now. It would have to be cleaned when he had gone.

Should she cancel the man bringing his girlfriend for a joyride? What if the man with the gun came back? She'd given her word she wouldn't talk about what had happened to anyone, otherwise she would ring Dad and ask him to come over.

Now she was being ridiculous – he would be somewhere on the farm and she could hardly tell her mother why she wanted him so urgently.

Then the welcome sound of a powerful car approaching made the decision for her. She was about to rush out to greet the driver when it occurred to her it could be someone else looking for the paper and not

Jack's friend. There wasn't much she could do about it apart from hand over the envelope and pray they would be satisfied with that.

If she stood to one side of the window she could see out without being seen. Jack remained oblivious and she wasn't sure if that was a good thing or not.

The car pulled up smoothly a few yards from the office and not one, but two men got out. One was medium height, slightly bald and wearing glasses – her pulse steadied. He looked harmless enough. The other one was tall and solidly built and had a broken nose.

Her stomach plummeted again. He could certainly be a villain. She didn't know what to do. Should she go out and meet them or hide in here? The matter was taken out of her hands. They were heading her way. Good grief! She was being quite ridiculous – the bespectacled man was holding a medical bag.

She reached the door at the same time as them. 'You must be Jack's friends. I don't know if he's sleeping or unconscious. Thank you for coming I was about to ring for the ambulance.'

She shuffled back so they could come in and there was scarcely room for all four of them in the small space. 'I'm Jimmy Hunt, medical chap. What's the silly bugger been up to this time?'

'Someone shot him last night. I found him when I got here this morning and have done the best I can but I'm sure he needs stitches.'

'Nige, give me a hand to move him outside. I need to get a proper look and it's too cramped in here.'

Ellie had expected some sort of reaction when she'd announced that the patient had been shot, but neither of them seemed at all put out by her shocking news. 'I'll spread out the rugs on the grass and you can put him on one of those.'

Hastily she tossed them down and watched as the two of them staggered out of the office with Jack. Nige – presumably Nigel – at the heavy end and the doc with Jack's feet. She stepped aside and they gently put him down.

The doc checked Jack's vital signs and she was relieved to see him nod as if satisfied with what he discovered.

'Good. From what I can see he is in no immediate danger. His pulse is strong and steady. He's asleep, his body's recuperating from the loss of blood, not unconscious.'

'I'm Nigel DeVere, and you are?' The big man with a broken nose smiled and held out his hand.

'Ellie Simpson. I work here.' She ignored his gesture.

'Good show – we chaps need a little woman to keep us in order. Any chance of a cup of tea?'

'Actually, I need to get an aircraft ready. Although the pre-flight checks are always done by the pilot, it's better if an experienced instructor does them first.'

He stared at her as if she'd grown two heads. 'Are you talking about yourself? Surely not? Women don't fly aeroplanes in my experience.'

How did someone as sensible as Jack have such a twerp for a friend? 'Then, Mr DeVere, your experience is very limited. Have you never heard of Amy Johnson? There are young men in the RAF today that I taught to fly.' She pointed to the office. 'You'll find the kettle and a paraffin stove in there. Feel free to help yourself.'

She turned her back on him and walked over to speak to Doctor Hunt. 'Does he need to go to hospital? He was adamant that he didn't want to.'

'Gunshot wounds are always reported to the authorities so probably best if he doesn't go. You've done an excellent job patching him up for now. We'll take him with us and I'll stitch him up at my surgery. Do you know why someone shot him?'

She shook her head. 'He interrupted a burglar he thinks was after the cash box. There are a lot of unpleasant people in Romford. I expect they thought our flying club was somewhere a bit smarter than this.'

The doctor didn't believe a word of it but he didn't pursue it. 'Will you be all right here on your own? There's no chance they might come back?'

'Not in daylight certainly. I've only got one client to deal with today and as soon as they've gone I'll lock-up and go home. It was just unlucky that Jack was here last night,' she explained and Doctor Hunt laughed.

'Typical Jack. In case you're wondering how we know each other, we went to the same school. He kept the bullies at bay and made my life bearable. I owe him a lot.'

'I take it that Mr DeVere isn't a friend of his.' She could hear this objectionable man banging about in the office. She was glad she had the envelope in her pocket.

'No, he was at med school with me but dropped out. Does something in the city nowadays. I'm sorry you had to put up with his nonsense. I had to bring someone strong enough to lift Jack – I couldn't do it on my own. Take no notice of Nigel.'

'I've met plenty like him and have learned to ignore them. How long will Jack be out of action?'

'Once I've stitched him up he'll just need a day or two to recuperate. I'm not sure he'll be fit to fly, that could take few days. To be on the safe side, I think he'd better wait until the stitches come out.'

'Do you have to take him to London? Couldn't you do it in my kitchen at home? You could boil your instruments and then Jack could stay with us until he's back on his feet.'

'Are you sure your parents won't object? If Jack wants to keep this quiet, it might be better if he comes with me.'

<u>Nine</u>

Jack roused himself sufficiently to speak. 'I'd prefer to go to Glebe Farm. Ellie, you'll need to ring your dad and tell him what's happened.'

'I can't go home right now as we've got someone coming. Once I've refuelled and done the checks I can leave for a while. You mustn't be lying there when he arrives.'

He thought he could manage to get to his feet with a bit of help. 'Jimmy, give me a hand up and I'll wait in the office. Are you in a rush to get away?'

'The day is yours, my friend.'

Nigel came out to grab his other arm and he and Jimmy managed to get him on his feet. He had a thumping headache and not only his other arm but his right shoulder was bloody painful – but apart from that he didn't feel too bad.

'You can let go now, thanks. I can stagger inside on my own.' He was glad to collapse in one of the chairs. The newspapers had been put back on the shelf. Had Ellie found anything before his mates turned up?

He took the mug of tea that Nigel had made and nodded his thanks. From where he sat he could see the hangar. There was no sign of Ellie so she must be in there getting the de Havilland ready. There was the throaty sound of the engine and then the nose of the aircraft appeared.

It was really a two-man job to start this plane, one inside and one turning the propeller. He should have sent Nigel out to give her a hand.

'Miss Simpson said she is a qualified instructor. A bit of an exaggeration, isn't it? No man worth his salt would agree to be instructed by a woman and especially one as young as her.' Nigel was old school and thought women should remain in the kitchen.

'She's a brilliant flyer. Best I've ever seen either male or female. She's been qualified since she was fourteen years old and already has several hundred hours in her log book.'

'If you say so, old chap. Bit smitten with her, are you? Can't expect you to give me an honest opinion.'

This man was a total shmuck and he wished Jimmy had found someone else to accompany him. He didn't trust DeVere not to blab. If he wasn't incapacitated, he would flatten him.

Not trusting himself to say anything polite, Jack fixed his attention firmly on Ellie as she expertly taxied onto the strip and then over to the fuel store.

'Jimmy, can you nip out and help Ellie refuel the Tiger Moth? She can do it on her own, but it will be much quicker if you give a hand.'

'We can both go – you need to rest. Doctor's orders.' He winked and Jack grinned. His friend wasn't daft, he'd keep an eye on Ellie for him and see she didn't lose her temper.

The phone rang making him slop his tea in his lap. He could reach it from where he was sitting so he carefully picked up the receiver.

'Glebe Aero Club – Reynolds speaking.'

'It's Mrs Smith. I was that worried when you didn't come home last night, Mr Reynolds. I'm sorry if I've bothered you but I just wanted to make sure you were all right.'

His landlady sounded upset and this wasn't like her. The fact that she'd walked all the way to the telephone box was also distinctly odd.

'Is something wrong, Mrs Smith? I'm absolutely fine – I had a bit too much to drink and thought it better not to turn up the worse for wear so spent the night here.'

'It's just that there's been a bit of trouble in the village. A stranger was asking after you and someone told him that you were lodging with me. If it wasn't for my Bobby I think he might have tried to get in the house.'

Bobby was her huge, friendly mutt who ran away from the local tomcat – a real pantywaist most of the time. If the dog had been aggressive then the man had definitely been dodgy. He gripped the receiver and a shaft of agony travelled from his arm, across his back and into his damaged shoulder.

'I'm sorry you were frightened because of me. I'll send someone to collect my things later today. I'll find somewhere else to live. I think my uncle has got himself into a bit of bother and some lowlife believes I can help them out.'

'I didn't want to ask you to go, but I think it best. I'll put everything into your case and have it waiting...'

'Thank you very much. I don't want a refund for the two weeks I've paid for. I'd be grateful if you don't mention about my uncle to anyone else. I'm going to London to sort things out and you won't be bothered again.'

The pips went and she put down the phone with a clatter. He flicked the bar and the operator responded. He prayed that Mr Simpson would be home for lunch and that his wife wouldn't pick up the phone.

'Glebe Farm,' a gruff voice said.

'Mr Simpson, Jack Reynolds here. Ellie has invited me to stay with you and I want to check that Mrs Simpson won't object. I had a bit of an accident last night and... and I've got a doctor with me and he needs to put in a few stitches.'

'The wife has gone away for a week or so. You come whenever you want. If my Ellie is happy then it's all right with me.'

*

By the time Ellie had, with the assistance of Jack's friends, refuelled and completed the pre-flight checks the young man and his girlfriend who were hiring the aircraft for the afternoon rolled up. She managed to complete the paperwork without the man needing to go into the office.

She watched the de Havilland take off safely. Jimmy – he'd insisted she call him by his first name – spoke from beside her.

'I'm impressed, Ellie. I doubt many young ladies could do what you do. Ignore Nigel, I try to.'

'I'm glad my father's happy to have Jack stay with us. I was thinking that maybe De Vere could go home in your car and we could use the Austin? You could take that as Jack won't be using it for a while.'

'Good idea. Sooner the blighter gets on his way the better.'

His unpleasant companion was more than happy to oblige and drove away immediately. Jack appeared at the office door more or less upright.

'I reckon I can get into the car if I can lean on your shoulder, Jimmy.'

He managed it but looked very unwell by the time he was slumped on the front seat. 'You drive, Jimmy, I'll cycle in front of you. I'll need my bike to get back here.'

The office was locked so there was nothing else to do. The brown envelope was burning a hole in her pocket and she was determined to give it to Jack at the earliest opportunity.

Her father was looking remarkably cheerful considering Mum had abandoned him. When Jack had told her Mum had gone away she had been more relieved than anything else.

'Thank you for agreeing to this, Dad.'

'Happy to, love, not had so much excitement since I was in the trenches.'

He'd somehow survived the last war but this was the first time he'd mentioned it. No one who had returned from France spoke about their experiences.

Between Jimmy and her dad they got Jack into the kitchen. Her stomach lurched when she saw what Dad had done. The kitchen table had been cleared and the kettle and a couple of saucepans were simmering on the range.

'I'll leave you three to get on with things.'

'Don't you want to help me stitch him up? Then next time you'll know how to do it yourself,' Jimmy said.

She was about to agree when Jack, who was leaning against the table getting his breath back, spoke up. 'Push off, sweetheart, you've done more than enough already.' He managed a lopsided grin. 'Isn't there something domestic you could be getting on with?'

117

'Cheek! Dad, did you get a room ready for him?'

'No, thought you could do it a lot quicker than me.'

'In which case I'll do that before I leave. He can go in George's room.'

It was a good thing Mum had gone as she would never have allowed Jack to stay. The house seemed calmer, friendlier somehow, without Mum there. She and Dad would manage quite happily without being constantly criticised.

*

An hour later she was pedalling furiously in the opposite direction. Jack was safely installed upstairs and Jimmy had driven off in the Austin. Dad said he was happy to clear up the kitchen but he wouldn't be able to prepare a meal. He was needed for milking as the cowman had a dicky stomach.

The envelope was now hidden in an old suitcase on top of the wardrobe in Jack's room. There had been no opportunity to tell him she'd found it as they'd not been alone together. She was sure this was something he didn't want anyone else to know about.

She had to get back so she could clean the blood from the wall and floor of the office. She could hardly sign the log book and take the client's money anywhere else.

Whilst she was at home she'd changed back into her usual uniform of dungarees and these were ideal for scrambling about on the floor with a bucket of water and scrubbing brush. She stood up and examined her work. There was still a faint stain on both the floor and wall but she doubted anyone would see it unless they were looking. With one of the chairs strategically placed over the damp patch the office was ready.

With Jack out of action for at least a week she would have to cancel a few of the bookings. Some of the new clients didn't want to be taught by a girl so postponed their lessons until Jack was likely to be back. The others she fitted in around her own schedule. This meant she would be working longer hours, including the weekend.

Someone would have to do the domestic chores and prepare the meals for the invalid, as well as the three farm labourers and her dad. It would have to be a woman who wouldn't gossip, someone who needed a bit of extra cash.

On the way home she would call in and speak to Mrs Branston, recently widowed and finding it hard to make ends meet. Mrs B lived on the edge of the village in a cottage owned by her dad. He'd suspended her rent indefinitely so there was no danger of her being turned out of her home. Mrs B would jump at the chance to help the family and would keep anything she heard or saw to herself.

Her mission was successful and she arrived home in good spirits. Fortunately, it wasn't late and she had plenty of time to prepare something for the evening meal. One of the benefits of living on a mixed farm was that there was always a fully stocked larder.

From the lowing and mooing coming from the cowshed Dad was in there doing the milking. The farm labourers went home for their tea so she only had to make food for the three of them.

As soon as she got in she dashed upstairs and knocked on Jack's door. He called out for her to come in and she pushed it open. He was sitting up in bed reading a newspaper and apart from being a bit pale looked surprisingly well.

'I'm just going to wash and change and will then be getting on with supper. Would you like a cup of tea or something to be going on with?'

'Come in and shut the door. I've more important things on my mind than a hot drink.'

*

Ellie looked a bit put out at his abrupt tone but for once didn't argue the toss. 'Did you find what you were looking for?'

She pointed to a battered suitcase on top of the wardrobe. 'I did, and I put the envelope in there. Do you want to read it?'

'No – absolutely not. I take it you didn't open it.' She shook her head. 'The less either of us know about this the better. Jimmy said I'm to stay put the rest of today but can potter about downstairs tomorrow. I'll need to use your telephone.'

'That might be a bit tricky. I've taken on Mrs Branston from the village to act as housekeeper until my mother comes home.'

'Bloody hell! Does that mean she'll be here all day?'

'I'm afraid it does. She's starting at six to make Dad's breakfast, then she'll do a hot meal for lunchtime. I suppose I could suggest that she goes home for a couple of hours after that and then comes back to make supper for us all.'

'If you don't mind, that would be great. I can't risk anyone overhearing my conversations.' She waited as if expecting him to tell her more. 'I'm going to ring my uncle and tell him I've got the envelope. It's up to him to contact whoever is looking for it and no doubt they'll let me know what to do next.'

'And what if Joe's already in custody? I'm sure your aunt won't know anything about it. What will you do then?'

'God knows! I can hardly post an advert in The Daily Sketch…'

'I don't see why not. Everybody reads a newspaper, although I'm not sure The Daily Sketch is the best one in the circumstances.'

'The newspapers on the shelf – can you remember what was in the pile?

'Mainly Evening Standards, Daily Sketches and Expresses. It would be a lot cheaper to put a personal ad in an evening paper –they were full of them. We need to think of the wording and, as we don't know the name of the man we want to contact, that's going to be difficult.'

'I'll ring Joe tomorrow. It's possible he's still at home and we can just post the envelope to him and forget about it.'

'If there's nothing else, I must go and change. Dad's been really understanding about all this and the least he deserves is a hot meal when he comes home.' She paused at the door. 'Did he say anything about my mother? I have a nasty feeling she's left him. She's been threatening to go for years and I think his behaviour at her party was the last straw.'

'What did he do, for God's sake?'

'He refused to mix with her guests for more than half an hour and then he was rude to those that he did speak to. They'll be happier apart. I know that's a shocking thing to say but why should people stay together when they're making each other miserable?'

'It's what folks do. I won't get married unless I'm sure we'll stick together. My aunt stuck with Joe and I think that's how it should be.'

She stared at him if he was something unpleasant she'd discovered stuck to the bottom of her shoe. 'Well, Mr Reynolds, I'm glad we've got that clear.'

The fact that she didn't slam the door, but closed it quietly, made him feel like a heel. What had made him spout off that rubbish? Hardly tactful in the circumstances. He closed his eyes and flopped back on the pillows wishing he'd kept his trap shut. He liked Ellie, she'd saved his life if Jimmy was to be believed, and now he'd alienated her – maybe for good.

His gaze kept returning to the suitcase. He'd said it would be better if he didn't know the contents of the envelope but maybe he was wrong about that as well. He rolled out of bed and stood up slowly. His legs felt as if they belonged to someone else but apart from that he was fine.

He staggered across the room like an old man. His right arm was in a sling. He wasn't sure if he could use his left to stretch up without worsening his injury. If he was going to discover what Joe had been hiding, he had no choice.

The suitcase was heavier than he'd expected and he lost his grip. It crashed to the floor scattering its contents onto the central rug. He staggered a few steps, lost his balance and fell onto his knees. The impact jarred his shoulder and his head spun with the pain.

The door burst open and Ellie erupted into the room. She dropped to her knees beside him all signs of her previous animosity gone. 'Let me help you up. If you hang onto the bed post with your good arm I think we can manage it.'

His stomach was churning and for a horrible moment he thought he was going to vomit. Then it passed and he was able to answer. 'Give me a minute. I'm okay – just shocked. I'll get up on my own.'

She didn't argue but waited quietly beside him whilst he gathered himself. He grasped the end of the bed and heaved. His knees almost buckled again and if she hadn't steadied him he would have gone down a second time.

'Two steps to the left and you'll be in bed again.'

He gritted his teeth and did as she said. She had to lift his legs from the floor and put them between the sheets as he didn't have the strength to do it himself. It took him several minutes to feel well enough to speak.

'It's a good thing your dad gave me some pyjamas as I usually sleep starkers.' This wasn't what he'd intended to say but it was what he'd been thinking. He opened his eyes expecting her to look a bit embarrassed by his comment.

She was laughing at him. 'I'm a farm girl, I grew up with two brothers, there's nothing you've got that I haven't seen before.'

Ten

Jack's eyes widened and he glanced at his crotch. He must think he'd exposed himself. She flushed scarlet. 'Don't worry, you remained decent throughout.'

To cover her embarrassment, she dropped to the floor and began to scramble about collecting the assorted detritus spilled from the old suitcase. There were dozens of photographs of strangers strutting about in a grand house and for a moment she was puzzled.

'These must be my mother's missing family. I'm not sure if I told you that she comes from an aristocratic lot who disowned her when she married my dad.' She was so engrossed in these she forgot the reason the suitcase was on the floor in the first place.

'Pass me the envelope, Ellie, I've decided I want to read it after all. You can look at your relations later.'

'Just a minute, I can't leave all this on the floor in case Dad comes up.' The brown envelope was lurking under some letters tied with a ribbon. She tossed it onto the bed without getting up.

She placed the interesting photographs and letters to one side and then scooped up all the rest and dumped it back in the case. She snapped it shut again and heaved it on top of the wardrobe.

'Are you sure you're all right, Jack? I must get on with making our supper.' There was no answer and for a horrible moment she thought he'd passed out again.

She spun round. He was holding a single sheet of paper in his hand. From his expression whatever was written there was far worse than he'd imagined.

'Can I see?'

He shook his head. 'Holy shit! No – you can't read this. I wish that I hadn't. There are some things you just don't want to know about your family.'

'Fair enough. Do you want me to return it to the suitcase?'

'Not much point now – like Pandora's box, the information's out and can't be put back.'

She left him to his thoughts, not sure that his analogy was correct. He was the only person who knew what was on that sheet of paper so, as far as she was concerned, not much had changed.

*

The remainder of the evening she was so busy she didn't have time to think about either the mysterious sheet of paper or the bundle of letters and photographs. Dad seemed his usual cheerful self and was pleased she'd had the initiative to employ a housekeeper.

'I like Mrs B, good sort of woman. Maybe she'd like to live in? She could have the two rooms that your grandma used to use when she couldn't get up the stairs anymore.'

'Does that mean Mum isn't coming back?'

'I'm afraid it does, love. We agreed it was for the best. I'm going to set her up with her own bank account and she can live wherever she likes and mix with the toffee-nosed lot she seems to prefer to us ordinary folk.'

'How did you meet? I've always wondered.'

He smiled sadly. 'At the races. A friend of mine had a runner in the same race as her father. We met in the owner's paddock. It was just before the last war.' He seemed lost in thought and she didn't like to interrupt. Perhaps if he remembered the reasons he'd fallen in love with her all those years ago he might make more of a push to get her back.

'Your ma got a bit tiddly and I had to step in when one of her lot tried to take advantage. You get your rebellious streak from her – because her pa was so against us courting it just made her more determined. In the end we eloped. She was overage so there was no difficulty getting married and my parents, your grandad and grandma were still alive then.'

'You must have been very much in love with each other. It's such a shame it has to end like this.'

'To tell you the truth, Ellie, I don't reckon your ma realised what would happen. She thought her family

127

would accept me because my family had plenty of money even if they didn't flash it about like they did. When they rejected her she wasn't too bothered, as she expected me to buy her a big house so she could mix with all the snooty folk in the neighbourhood.'

'Why didn't you? This house isn't big enough for two families. I certainly wouldn't want to share a kitchen with my mother-in-law.'

'I was young, didn't think about things like that at the time. When I did, it was too late, Neil was on the way. Then I volunteered and Charlotte had to stay here without me. I didn't expect to be gone for four years.'

Ellie seemed to recall that she'd been told her grandfather had died just after her dad had returned. Of course, he could hardly move away and abandon Grandma then. George had been born the following year and she had followed three years after that.

'Will Mum stay in touch with us? I do love her even though sometimes it seems as if I don't.' Something occurred to her. 'Is she so against alcohol now because of the way you met?'

'Probably – I never asked her. We jogged along all right until she moved into another room. It's been like living with a stranger ever since. I don't want to speak ill of your mum, love, but she's never been happy here. I reckon she regretted her impulsive decision within a few weeks of being married. She'll be better off, and so will we.'

'I suppose I'd better let Neil and George know what's going on. Might be a bit awkward if one of them turns up and finds Jack living here and Mum moved out.'

'I'm going to bed; will you lock up? Don't forget the chickens.' They didn't embrace; her family had never been physically affectionate with each other.

She made herself a cup of cocoa after she'd completed her evening tasks. This was a nightly ritual regardless of the weather. There was sufficient for two mugs so she made one for Jack as well. She put some biscuits on a plate with the cocoa, switched off the lights and carried the tray upstairs.

There were five bedrooms in the farmhouse – four upstairs and one, the one that Mrs B might move into, next to the kitchen. There had always been a bathroom and lavatory upstairs in her lifetime and there was another washroom and WC next door to the scullery.

Grand houses often had several bathrooms, and radiators in each room to keep them warm, but her grandfather hadn't gone as far as that with Glebe Farm. In the winter they froze in their bedrooms like everyone else in the village. Fires were only allowed upstairs if someone was ill.

She carried the tray into her room and put her cocoa down. She didn't want any biscuits; he could have all those. The letters and photographs she'd dumped on her bed could be looked at later.

There was a light coming from under Jack's door so she knew he was awake.

*

Jack heard Ellie go past and was going to call out but didn't want to disturb Mr Simpson. Then she tapped softly and he invited her in.

'I've brought you some cocoa and biscuits. You don't have to have them if you don't want to.'

'Thanks, it seems a long time since supper. I need to talk to you about the envelope. Why don't you bring your drink in here?'

'No, I won't do that as I can't stay long, Dad's a light sleeper and wouldn't approve of me being in here with you so late.'

She put the tray on the bedside table and then moved to stand at the end of the bed. The door was still ajar. He couldn't risk what he was going to say being overheard.

'Close the door.'

She stiffened at his abrupt command and didn't move.

'Please, Ellie, when you read it you'll realise why your father mustn't know.'

Once the door was safely shut he handed her the sheet of paper; although he had read it several times he still had difficulty comprehending the contents.

He watched her read it and saw her expression change from interest to horror. 'This is so much worse than gangsters or robberies. Why would Joe have the names and signatures of the people who have joined Sir Oswald Mosley's fascist party? I can't believe he's a fascist.'

'Look at it again, Ellie. Don't you recognise some of those traitors? Can you imagine what would happen if this list became public? For Christ's sake, some of them are politicians, members of the aristocracy, important people in this country. I don't know how my uncle got hold of this, but you can be damned sure he's been using the information to fund his other business ventures.'

She looked at the paper more closely. 'This has been cut from a ledger. I think it comes from their membership book. Thank goodness we didn't put an advert in a newspaper. What are you going to do with it? I wish you hadn't opened the envelope or let me read it.'

Before he could answer the door opened and her father appeared, looking none too pleased, in his pyjamas. Ellie was holding the page and didn't have time to hide it.

'Secret meetings? What's that you got there, my girl? I'll read that if you don't mind.'

'Don't, Mr Simpson. You don't want to know the contents. It's a list of traitors. It's why I was shot.'

'If my daughter has read it then she's in danger. What were you thinking of, letting her get involved? What you going to do with it?'

'We were just talking about that when you came in. I think we must send it anonymously to Scotland Yard.'

'Can I have a look? Bit late to worry about anyone else knowing.' He didn't wait for permission but removed the paper from Ellie's fingers. He nodded as if unsurprised at what he saw. 'You can't do that, Jack, Ellie's grandfather is on here.'

'Did you already know about this?' Jack wished he was strong enough to take charge of the situation but he wasn't feeling great.

Ellie looked almost as bad. 'Which one is he, Dad? Mum never told me her maiden name or anything about her family.'

'Sir Reginald Humphrey. He's an MP, rich as Croesus, and thinks of the rest of the world as cannon fodder, or peasants to do his bidding. There were a lot like him in the last war. God help us if we get the same stupid buggers in charge when this next lot kick off.'

'Do I have cousins and uncles and aunts on that side of the family?'

'There were two sons, but both were killed in Flanders. Your mum is the only one left and you're that man's only granddaughter.' His colour had returned and he jumped to his feet. 'I should have worked it out myself. She's gone home – Humphrey told her if she was prepared to sever the connection to me he'd take her back.'

Ellie looked distraught. He didn't blame her – she'd just learned her grandfather was a fascist and her mother had chosen him over her husband and children.

'I need to think about this, Mr Simpson. We could always black out his name and then hand the list in, but there's no guarantee they couldn't work it out anyway.'

'And if they did,' she said, 'it might well lead them to us.' She headed for the door. 'I found some photographs and letters which were hidden in the suitcase up there, Dad. I don't really want to look at them anymore. I'll give them to you.'

He followed her from the room and neither of them said good night. Whatever they thought about Sir Reginald, Ellie and her brothers were a part of his family. Perhaps the best thing to do would be to burn the wretched thing and be done with it.

She returned almost immediately. 'I'm going to put the letter somewhere safer. Good night, see you in the morning.'

The gunman had been sent by somebody on that list and was no doubt ransacking the office at the airfield this very minute. It wouldn't take him long to discover Ellie's name. He could possibly find his way here sometime tonight.

Mr Simpson was a farmer – he was bound to have a shotgun somewhere on the premises.

*

Greg stayed the night in a seedy bed and breakfast in Romford, having had too much to drink to go back to London. He arrived home at midday to be informed there'd been a message from Wattisham telling him not to report for duty for another week.

He rather thought he would drift back to Glebe Farm and spend time with Ellie. That Reynolds chap, even though he'd denied it, was taking too much interest in her and he didn't want to be cut out before he'd really got to know her. He was caught up in family business until late afternoon but decided he would stick to his original plan.

Stupidly he ran out of petrol on the way there and had to walk five miles with his can to the nearest garage. He cadged a lift back to his MG and when it was mobile again returned to the same place to fill the tank. He didn't want to be caught out a second time.

It was now too late to turn up unannounced and he couldn't locate another B&B. He would kip down at the airfield and then arrive at breakfast time. He missed the turning and had to reverse into a field. He was about to pull away when he realised he could see the hangar from here. There was another vehicle driving down the track.

The aero club was in darkness – so who the hell was going there now? He turned the headlights and engine off and rummaged around in the glove compartment until he found his trusty torch. If he went across the field, he could reconnoitre and see exactly what was going on.

His night vision was excellent and his eyes adjusted to the darkness within a few minutes. He had the torch in his hand and thought it might be more useful as a weapon than for illumination.

The intruders had already broken into the office and were searching for something. They didn't seem bothered if anyone heard them. The amount of racket they were making meant he could creep up to the building and sidle along so he could peer through the window.

There were two men, both dressed in dark clothing with balaclavas over their faces. He couldn't tackle both of them. They were working in silence, tossing things from shelves to the floor.

'It's not here. They must've found it. Obviously, you didn't kill that man last night. We can't go back without it this time,' said one of the men in a surprisingly cultured voice. He'd expected them to be rough – not speak like him.

The other one replied, – also with an upper-class accent. 'We must go to this farm that's mentioned here a couple of times in their account book. If it is there, and I can't think where else it can be, we'll scare the information out of the girl. What was it called again?'

'Glebe Farm. We can hardly ask for directions so it might take time to find the bloody place.' The man pointed his torch at his wrist. 'Ten o'clock now – that means we've got a few hours before dawn. I don't want to be anywhere near when it gets light.'

Greg backed away from the window and then vaulted over the fence that surrounded the airfield and ran flat out to his car. He didn't know how long he had before those bastards turned up at Ellie's house. He had to be there before them. They had a telephone so he could ring the police as soon as he arrived. With luck they could barricade themselves in and remain safe until the local constabulary turned up.

It must have been Jack Reynolds who'd been shot – but if so why hadn't the police been called? Something so exciting would have been the talk of the village and he'd heard nothing this morning. Presumably Jack was in hospital somewhere; Ellie and her parents would be sitting ducks.

He found the turning to Glebe Farm easily. He switched off his headlamps and drove the remainder of the way in darkness. He was pretty sure he was there first, but he wasn't taking any chances. He thought the field where he'd parked last time would be an ideal place to leave the car. The gate was open, thank God. He switched off the engine and sat for a moment listening. Nothing untoward – just the sound of owls and other night creatures.

He swung his legs over the closed door of his car, slipped the heavy torch into his jacket pocket, and made his way stealthily to the house. He paused and scanned the yard. His breath hissed through his teeth. The house was dark, no sign of the would-be burglars.

It wouldn't be a good idea to hammer on the door – this would mean lights would come on and these would be seen by the men who couldn't be far behind him. He needed to get in silently and then find Mr Simpson and let him know what was going on.

The yard encircled the back door; no point in trying here, this would be locked. Maybe there was a window left open somewhere. He did a circuit of the building trying every window with no success.

<u>Eleven</u>

Jack found the gun and collected a handful of cartridges. He would sit on the stairs and wait. As he reached the door the latch lifted. The hair on the back of his neck stood up. Someone was outside and trying to get in.

His heart pumped heavily and his fingers tightened around the stock of the gun. He moved slowly to the back door and pushed the bolts. They moved without a sound. He stepped out and quietly closed the door behind him.

He didn't want to kill the bastard – merely disable him – and do this with as little noise as possible. He reversed the weapon so he was holding the barrel. His pulse steadied. He was calm. He owed this bugger a good thumping but would have to settle for knocking him out. Pressed up against the wall as he was, he would be invisible to anyone coming around the side of the house. He was glad of the support it gave him.

There was a faint sound. He raised the gun and felt a shaft of agony in his right side. He'd get one chance to stop this bastard so he'd better make his blow a good one.

A man stepped into view. He began to swing. The distinct sound of a car approaching distracted him. The man he'd intended to knock unconscious grabbed the gun and they struggled silently.

It was an unequal contest and he lost his grip. The car had stopped but he could hear the engine purring in the darkness. Who the hell was coming here at this time of night?

He was grabbed roughly by his injured shoulder. He couldn't stop the yelp of pain. 'Good God! Is that you Reynolds? What the devil are you doing out here?'

The pain and dizziness subsided. 'Inside, quickly, they'll be here in a minute.'

Whoever it was didn't argue and Jack was relieved when the door was bolted firmly behind them. There was a slight sound and then the flicker of a torch.

'Sod me! What the hell are you doing here, Dunlop? You can tell me later. Can you use a shotgun?'

'If I have to.'

'Now, for God's sake keep your voice down, I don't want to wake Ellie or her father if I can help it.'

'A bit late for that,' she said from the top of the stairs. Greg shone the torch up and Jack saw she was, like him, in her pyjamas. 'Greg, what on earth are you doing here? I heard a car just now – in fact I thought I heard two cars.'

Jack beckoned her down and quickly explained why he was prowling about with a shotgun. Dunlop told them how he came to be here. 'You do understand why we can't call for backup, why we have to handle this on our own?'

'I think you're wrong but I'll do what I can to help you tonight. Ellie, why don't you get dressed? We've probably got a few minutes or so before they try and break in and you're no good to either of us in your night clothes.'

Jack waited for the girl to refuse, to object to this man telling her what to do. Instead she vanished upstairs without a word.

'She shouldn't be involved in this, Dunlop. She could get hurt.'

'You're in no fit state to repel invaders and I'm sure Ellie can handle a shotgun better than either of us.'

This was a ridiculous state of affairs. To be arguing about something so trivial when at any moment two murderous bastards could smash their way into the house.

'There's one more gun – I'll go and get it. I'll see if I can find another torch at the same time.'

They'd been talking in whispers and he was pretty sure Mr Simpson wouldn't wake up unless there was a full-blown fight. If there was, he doubted he'd be much use. This Greg bloke seemed to know what he was doing despite obviously coming from a long line of posh blighters.

With the single beam of the torch he led them to the small room, more a large cupboard really, where the guns were kept. It obviously also served as a makeshift office, but as it had no windows it wouldn't be pleasant working in here.

He grabbed hold of the door frame to steady himself. The torch flashed over his face and down his arm. 'You're bleeding. You shouldn't be on your feet, old man, you should be in hospital.'

Jack collapsed into the single chair that stood in front of the small deal table. 'I reckon you're right. I'm going to stay here for a bit. Don't worry, if I'm needed I'll be ready.'

Greg took down the gun and loaded it efficiently. 'That reminds me, the two men outside aren't your usual sort of burglars. I overheard them speaking and they're definitely public-school.'

This merely confirmed what Jack already knew. 'There's not time to explain everything now, but when this is over we'll fill you in.'

Greg put the gun under his arm, barrel pointing to the floor, and left without replying. He took the torch with him leaving Jack in the dark. He closed his eyes and took several deep breaths hoping the dizziness and nausea would pass.

Whatever was happening elsewhere he'd be a liability at the moment so he might as well get a bit of a kip until things kicked off.

*

Ellie had never dressed so quickly. She hesitated outside her dad's room not sure if he would be better off asleep or downstairs helping. She decided to leave him where he was. Greg seemed to know what he was doing although she would rather have Jack, if he was fit, in charge.

Using the narrow beam of her torch to guide her, she retraced her steps. Greg was waiting and handed her a shotgun and four cartridges. He put his finger to his lips and gestured with his thumb towards the back door and then the front.

This must mean there were two men attempting to get in. They were most certainly armed as one of them had shot Jack last night. Her hands were shaking so much she doubted she would be able to use the weapon she had under her arm. She prayed – to a God she didn't think existed – that she wouldn't have to.

There was a light touch on her arm and she pushed her fears to the back of her mind. Greg drew her into the sitting room and then whispered in her ear.

'Would gun shots attract any attention?'

'No. Farmers shoot rabbits and foxes at night.' Her heart was thumping so loudly she was surprised he couldn't hear it.

'They don't know anyone is up. If we start making a racket and shouting about calling the police and then fire our guns out of the window I think they'll take off.'

'That will wake Dad but it can't be helped,' she whispered back.

The sitting room ran the width of the house and he pointed to the back window. She crept to the front and lifted the latch and then pushed it open a few inches. She dropped cartridges into the barrels and closed the gun. She heard him doing the same thing behind her.

'On the count of three,' he said quietly.

One – two – three. She shoved the gun out of the window and pulled the trigger. The simultaneous explosions echoed into the night. The room stank of cordite.

'Call the police. Someone is trying to break in. I'll get the bastards,' Greg yelled.

She pulled the trigger a second time and then he did the same. As the sound died she saw two dark shapes fleeing up the track. Moments later an engine burst into life, headlights lit the scene and then the car roared away.

'What the effing hell is going on down here? God Almighty – I nearly had a heart attack.' Dad was standing in the doorway. He'd not stopped to put his slippers or dressing gown on. She couldn't remember ever seeing his bare feet before.

Then Jack staggered in looking equally shocked. 'I'm going to make a nice cup of tea whilst Greg explains what just happened.'

Her hands were shaking and she almost dropped the kettle as she filled it at the kitchen sink. She quickly riddled the range and threw half a hod of coal into it. It would soon come back to heat.

Doing something ordinary allowed her to recover her composure. By the time she'd got everything ready she was almost calm. There was something bothering her and it had nothing to do with the men who'd tried to break in.

She leaned against the table and screwed up her eyes. Then she remembered. Jack was bleeding again. Jimmy had left an emergency medical kit for such an eventuality. She was about to grab it and run through the house but stopped to think more clearly. She must wash her hands, collect boiled water and clean cloths if she was to be of any use.

When she shouldered her way in carrying the tray with everything that would be required it was as she feared. Jack was stretched out on the sofa and both her father and Greg were at his side. 'I've got everything we need to sort this out. Which one of us is going to do it?'

Dad moved away as if Jack was on fire. 'Not me, love, I'll leave it to you young ones. I'll have the tea ready when you're done.' The door banged behind him.

'I've checked and two of the stitches have broken. I need to wash my hands before I attempt to repair the damage.'

'There's no need. I've already done mine. The doc explained how to do it and I've got everything I need in here. Hopefully he'll stay unconscious until I've finished.'

Greg didn't argue. 'I've been pressing on the wound. I'll keep my hand here until you're ready to start.'

Sewing skin couldn't be much different to sewing material and she'd done plenty of that. Jimmy had left two needles already threaded. All she had to do was push each one through and then knot the ends.

Jack's eyes remained closed throughout the procedure but she was certain he was awake as she'd seen his fists clench. When the fresh dressing was bandaged into place he looked at her.

'Thank you, Jimmy would be proud of you.' His voice was weak and so was his smile.

'Why don't you help Jack sit up, Greg, and then he can drink the tea that will be coming in a minute.'

She dashed out and barely made the downstairs cloakroom in time before she was horribly sick. She pushed herself upright and pulled the chain. She hoped she'd never have to do anything like that ever again.

She emerged from the scullery after washing her face and rinsing her mouth to discover the kitchen was empty. She would much rather go to bed and try and forget about the past hour. But the others would be waiting for her and she'd no wish to worry them by disappearing.

The door was half open, lights on everywhere, and from the racket more than tea was being drunk in the sitting room.

*

Jack had swallowed a couple of the strong painkillers Jimmy had left for him and followed that up with a mug of sweet tea liberally laced with whiskey. He was feeling a lot better now – in fact tickety-boo.

'Let me get this straight. You drove down from London in the middle of the night to see Ellie.' Seemed strange to him that this bloke was prepared to go to such lengths for a girl he'd only just met.

'I did. Once I'm attached to my squadron I don't know if I'll get the opportunity to gad about the country seeing young ladies.'

Jack held out his mug and Mr Simpson – no, he was to call him Fred now – tipped in another generous measure of alcohol. 'Why don't you help out at the airfield until you do? I'm not going to be much use for another few days.'

'You can stay here, Greg, there's a spare bed in Jack's room. I'm sure he won't mind you sharing,' Fred said helpfully.

'I've not got an instructor's licence so can't see how I can help.'

'You can accompany nervous flyers as you don't need one for that. Both the Swallow and the old Tiger Moth are dual control. Also, I don't think Ellie should be there on her own at the moment.' This clinched it.

'You're right. I'm still waiting to hear why those men came here and why you didn't want the police involved.'

Fred explained but Greg didn't look convinced. 'So you're not intending to send this paper to the appropriate authorities because of the family connection? I think you should, regardless of the consequences. Until you do someone on that list is going to continue to try and recover it and next time you might not be so lucky.'

The argument became noisier and at this point Ellie came in. She marched over and removed the mug from his hand. 'The doc told you not to drink alcohol with those painkillers. I should think half the countryside can hear you shouting about things that should remain private.'

He could see why Greg was keen. Tonight she looked rather attractive. Too fond of bossing people about for his taste; he preferred his birds less angular and more biddable.

'Thanks for sewing me up, Ellie, you did a good job. Greg, can you give me a hand to get up? I'm for my bed. That reminds me, could someone collect my kit from my lodgings tomorrow?'

'I doubt I'll have time until the evening. You'll just have to manage until then.'

Jack's head spun as Greg and Fred heaved him to his feet. He wasn't sure if it was the alcohol, the medication, or his injury that was causing him to feel so bloody grim.

Somehow he made it to his bedroom – well not really his anymore as Greg would be dossing down in here as well for the next few days. They dumped him unceremoniously into bed and then left him to it. His borrowed pyjamas were stiff with dried blood and he could do with a drink of water.

He heard Fred returning to his room and Greg went back downstairs. With some difficulty he unbuttoned the top and slid it from his injured arm. He'd sleep with just the bottoms until he got his own belongings tomorrow evening.

The room was in darkness, they hadn't bothered to put on the light when they brought him in, but the door was still half open so he could see perfectly well. He couldn't arrange his pillows himself so slumped back as they were.

That Greg bloke was right. They had two choices: one – hand it over to the police; and two – post it back to Ellie's grandfather. Neither of these was ideal as both would have repercussions, but the alternative could well be far worse. The thought of Ellie or Fred being shot wasn't a happy one.

He must have dropped off because when he came to there was the soft sound of someone else breathing in the other bed. The house was silent, not even a clock ticking. It must be getting on for dawn and as soon as it got lighter he would go for a leak and then find himself something to drink.

Although wide awake he thought it would be unwise to attempt to clamber out of bed in the dark. He didn't want to wake Greg, or anyone else for that matter. His head was clear, no more than a dull ache coming from his injury, he reckoned he was perfectly capable of making himself a cup of tea, even one-handed.

The heavy curtains had been drawn across and let little light into the room. Dammit! He couldn't wait any longer. He had to get up and use the bog. Slowly he pushed back the covers and dropped his feet to the floor. Tentatively he stood – pausing for a moment to see if he was in full command of his legs.

The man across the room continued to sleep – at least he didn't snore. The door was on the opposite side of the room and as Jack's night vision came into play he could just about see it. He edged his way across, lifted the latch and stepped out into the corridor.

Now he was on his feet he decided to use the restroom downstairs and not risk waking everyone up. He was pretty sure Fred would be up with the lark as he had to see to the cows before breakfast. He wondered why Glebe Farm didn't have a dog or two, but perhaps because they had no sheep they didn't need one. Once his bladder was empty he was ready to make himself a hot drink.

As he stepped into the kitchen something hard was pushed into the small of his naked back. 'Make a sound and you're a dead man.'

Twelve

Ellie jerked from deep sleep, instantly wide awake, and for a moment disorientated. Something was wrong. She sat up and listened but could hear nothing untoward. Perhaps she'd been disturbed by an owl. Then she heard someone coming out of the room in which Jack and Greg were staying.

One of them needed the lavatory – nothing to worry about. Now she was awake she also needed to pee but would wait until whoever it was had returned to his room. She slid out of bed and groped for her dressing gown and shoved her feet into her waiting slippers.

That was strange. She hadn't heard anyone go into the WC. As she quietly opened her door there was the sound of someone using the facilities downstairs. She swallowed a giggle. From the sound of it, he'd been desperate.

Still smiling she headed for the upstairs loo, then froze. Her bladder almost emptied. The men they'd chased away had come back. She sidestepped into Jack's room but didn't dare call as every sound was travelling through the sleeping house.

Jack was in the bed on the right and she tiptoed across the boards. She didn't need light to find her way. Her knees bumped the end of the bed and immediately she knew it was empty.

'Greg, Greg, wake up. They're in the house and I think they've got Jack,' she whispered as she shook his shoulder.

His hand came up and covered hers. 'I'm awake. I'll get dressed. Sit on the other bed.' He mouthed the words into her ear and she nodded.

It took him seconds to pull on his trousers and then he was beside her. 'What did you hear?'

She told him and he was silent. 'Stay in here. I'm going down. We left the cartridges and shotguns in the sitting room. If I can get hold of one, we've got a chance of coming out of this unscathed.'

He didn't wait for an answer, just assumed she would do as he said. If there were two assailants, then it would be better if there were two of them as well. She didn't hear him leave but felt a slight draught as the door opened and closed.

Should she get dressed before she went down? Would the time it took to put her clothes on prove critical? Her dressing gown was cumbersome and flapped about her ankles. With this off and wearing her slippers and pyjamas she was perfectly decent and able to move about freely.

Greg hadn't put on his shoes – he would want to be as quiet as possible. She slipped through the door and pressed herself against the wall expecting to hear shouting or shots – but the house was eerily silent. Edging closer to the stairs without making a sound was more difficult than she'd thought. Several floorboards creaked when you stepped on them and she had to keep pausing, trying to remember which ones they were.

She was halfway down the stairs before she could hear voices coming from the kitchen. There was a knot in her stomach and her legs were trembling. Where was Greg? She didn't want to bump into him if he was carrying a loaded shotgun.

The sitting room door was across the hall to her left, at the bottom of the stairs. To access the kitchen and dining room you stepped into the central passageway which led to the back door. The man who had captured Jack must have been standing there when she'd heard him.

There was only one weapon – Greg must be ahead of her. She picked it up and from the moonlight filtering in through the open curtains she found two cartridges and dropped them into the barrels. The smell of cordite still lingered in the room as an unpleasant reminder of what had taken place in here earlier.

Something made her decide to exit via the window and not creep through the house. Instead she would make her way around the outside where she was less likely to be heard and would have a better chance of surprising the attackers.

With the cartridges back in her pocket and the gun safe to carry she scrambled over the windowsill and dropped into the flowerbed that ran directly underneath. The quickest route to the kitchen was to go past the front door and turn right. She would have to crawl almost immediately if she wasn't to be seen.

She paused beside the window to listen. Someone was talking quietly and she recognised the speaker as Greg. For a second she was unable to breathe. How had they taken him captive so easily and so silently? She edged back until she was at the front of the house again. These men now had two hostages and at least three guns and she only had the one.

However, she had the advantage of surprise. Her heart was racing, her palms damp. She couldn't think straight. Then her head cleared and she had a brainwave. There was a box of fireworks in the barn and she was pretty sure there were bangers amongst them. They were several years old but that shouldn't be a problem. She only needed a couple for her plan to work.

*

Jack instinctively raised his hands. The press of cold metal on his naked flesh was more than enough to make him cooperate without argument. The gun barrel dug into him, forcing him to move towards the kitchen.

All he could think was that he didn't know where Ellie had hidden the envelope. They'd have to fetch her and he didn't want her downstairs with these two bastards.

He stubbed his toe painfully on the wooden doorstep and stumbled into the kitchen and would have crashed to his knees on the flagstones if his capturer hadn't grabbed his shoulder. Luckily, it was the left one.

There was sufficient light from the room to see where he was going. The second bloke must have been waiting inside to close the door behind them.

The pressure in his spine continued. Why didn't one of them speak? If he was fit, he would have risked disarming the bugger with the gun but now had no option but to obey. He pulled out one of the chairs from under the table and swung it round so he could sit.

It was a relief to have his back safely pressing against the back of a chair. 'I don't want anyone else to be hurt. You can have the bloody paper but I don't know where it is. Someone hid it whilst I was asleep.'

'Did you read it?'

Jack hesitated, not sure if it would be better to admit they all knew the contents or deny having looked at it. Sod it! 'I know it's a page from the membership book listing the treasonous shits who are members of the fascist party.' The atmosphere changed. He ploughed on regardless. 'If I'd wanted to give it to the authorities I'd have done so already. That bastard Humphrey happens to be Ellie Simpson's grandfather. So family comes first and you can have the bloody list and bugger off.'

The light was switched on and he blinked in the glare. The two men pulled off their balaclavas and dropped their handguns on the table with a clatter.

'We were sent by someone else on the list and didn't know there was any family connection. This is an unmitigated disaster and our employer will not be happy that we broke into the house of Sir Reginald's granddaughter.'

The speaker, not much older than himself, seemed genuinely upset. What had been a life-threatening situation now seemed to be something else entirely.

'Which one of you bastards shot me?'

The other guy turned to face him. He looked the tougher of the two. 'It was me. I apologise wholeheartedly. But I can assure you if I'd meant to kill you, you would have been dead. It's only a flesh wound.'

The door swung open and Greg stepped in. He was holding a shotgun but it wasn't pointed at anyone. 'Good God! Timothy Harkness, how the hell did you come to be involved in this nonsense?' He addressed this remark to the man who'd just admitted to shooting Jack.

'By all that's holy, Greg Dunlop. I've not seen you since Oxford.'

Things had gone from tragedy to farce. Might as well ignore the two long lost friends and put the kettle on, which was what he'd come down to do in the first place.

He glanced at the second bloke who was looking equally bemused. 'Do you mind if I make a cuppa?'

The man shrugged and pulled out a second chair and flopped into it with an audible sigh.

Jack listened with growing incredulity to the conversation between Harkness and Dunlop.

'I worked in the city for a bit and then decided to join the RAF. They're going to need hundreds of pilots when we go to war with Germany.'

Harkness looked less friendly. 'If the government would listen to us there'd be no need for a war. Hitler has agreed to Britain remaining neutral in any forthcoming conflict.'

Jack riddled the Aga noisily hoping to defuse the tension. It worked. 'Don't make so much noise, unless you want Ellie and Mr Simpson down here to join in the tea party,' Greg said sharply.

'I'll have to wake her up as she's the only one who knows where the envelope is. I don't suppose your mates will leave without it.'

'I'll go and get her. You stay here and make the tea. You shouldn't be prowling about anyway; you should be in bed resting the doc said.'

Being given orders as though he was a skivvy by some posh gent didn't please Jack, but there was nothing he could do about it at the moment.

Both unwanted visitors were now sitting at the table, apparently relaxed, waiting for him to hand them a mug of tea. No doubt they'd want cake to go with it. He wasn't inclined to make conversation with a couple of Mosley's lot so he kept his back to them.

Dunlop had sensibly unloaded his shotgun before propping it against the dresser. There were two revolvers in the centre of the table – a grim reminder of what might have happened if Ellie's grandfather hadn't been on that list.

There was a scuffle on the roof just above him. It didn't sound like a squirrel or a rat but something larger. Puzzled but not alarmed he carried the kettle to the sideboard where he could see the teapot standing. Then something rattled down the chimney and there was a God almighty explosion.

He threw himself to the floor. The room was full of smoke. Then everything went black.

*

Greg discovered Ellie wasn't in his room – she must have gone back to bed. He tapped on her door but received no answer. He opened it and switched on the light. It was empty. She must have ignored his instructions and come downstairs.

Then the hair on the back of his neck stood up as he remembered there was a second shotgun and cartridges in the sitting room. Ellie didn't know nobody was in danger and might think she had to rescue them both.

Ignoring the need for quiet he hurtled down the stairs and checked. He was right. There was an open window so she must have gone out that way. He unbolted the front door and ran out. He was about to call her name when there was a deafening noise from the kitchen.

It didn't sound like shots but as if something had blown up. What next? Someone in the neighbourhood would be here to investigate and God knows what would happen then. As he rushed towards the noise he saw Ellie, a shotgun under her arm, kick open the kitchen door and yell for everyone to put their hands up.

He could barely see her through the smoke that poured from the open door. Then Jack and the other two staggered out coughing and spluttering and she followed them.

The back door was opened and the smoke began to clear. His eyes were stinging – God knows how the others were coping.

'What happened? Is the house on fire?' Mr Simpson tried to push past him but Greg held him back.

'I'm not sure – but I don't think so. I can't hear any crackling coming from the kitchen.'

He was right. There was the devil of a mess, every surface in the room was smeared with soot but apart from that there appeared to be no serious damage.

He quickly explained what had been going on whilst his host had been asleep. 'Bugger me! It's a good thing the missus wasn't here. I can hear them outside – I'll get started on the clean-up. I suppose you'd better take them all into the front room.'

Greg could hear him muttering under his breath about not being happy to be making tea for burglars. The front door was open and the through draft had driven the remaining smoke out through the back door. He had trodden on something sharp on his first foray and was reluctant to wander about outside in his bare feet for a second time.

'Greg, there you are. What a lark! Miss Simpson almost blew us up in her rescue attempt.' Harkness said as he came in from the dark. 'I've never met a girl quite like her.'

'Mr Simpson, as you might expect, is now up as well. He said everyone can go into the sitting room.'

Jack limped in next. Considering what he'd been through in the past twenty-four hours he looked surprisingly well. He grinned, his teeth white in his blackened face. 'She's told me where the paper is and I'm going to get it. I never got my cup of tea and I doubt the bloody range will work after what happened.'

A cheerful voice called from the kitchen. 'Don't worry, son, I'll soon have the kettle boiling. I've just got to give the mugs a bit of a wipe and everything will be tickety-boo.'

Jack hobbled past and went upstairs and then Ellie and the other erstwhile burglar came in. He was relieved to see she was holding the cartridges in one hand so the gun was no longer loaded.

'As soon as Jack's found the envelope you can go.'

'Don't worry, Miss Simpson, once we've got what we came for we'll leave you in peace,' the man replied.

She glared and pointed to the front door. 'Wait out there. I don't want you in this house a moment longer. Take your nasty friend with you.'

Harkness was standing at the foot of the stairs. He took one look at her face and the shotgun and did as she asked without comment.

Once they were out she closed the door in their faces. 'Jack, do you want me to come and find it for you?'

'No, I've got it. I'm just putting on a shirt and some shoes. I'll be down in a minute,' he yelled back.

'Ellie, why don't you give me the gun and the cartridges? I'll collect all the weapons and lock them up in the cupboard again.'

'There's no need, thank you, I'm quite capable of doing that myself. If you want to make yourself useful, Greg, why don't you help my dad in the kitchen?'

He snapped his heels together and saluted smartly. 'Yes, ma'am, on my way.'

As he hoped she smiled at his nonsense. She really was a remarkable girl. His family would be horrified when they found out he intended to marry her at the earliest opportunity. About time a member of the Dunlop family decided to marry someone not already vaguely related.

Keeping it in the family had another meaning amongst his set. Most of his peers were related to him in some way – since time immemorial the upper crust married their own class. Jack returned with the envelope. He'd removed the grime from his face. The dark circles under his eyes were not from the soot but from fatigue. The sooner he was back in bed the better.

Greg stepped forward and removed the envelope from his hand. 'Why don't you go and sit down? I'll give this to them and make sure they actually leave this time.'

'Fair enough – after all, they are mates of yours. Tell them to sod off. They won't get off so lightly if they show their faces here again.'

Ellie was about to argue, but Jack shook his head and she nodded. 'Greg's right, we don't need to be involved anymore. I'll go and help in the kitchen if you promise to take it easy.'

The torch was still in Greg's pocket, but he didn't need it. Harkness and his friend were waiting a sensible distance from the house. He had no intention of crossing the gravel in his bare feet.

'I've got it.' He waved the envelope in the air and they both hurried towards him. As he handed it over Harkness spoke to him.

'Sir Reginald will find out what happened here. Don't be surprised if the Simpsons get a visit from him.'

'I don't see why he'd want to come here now when he's ignored the family for the past twenty-five years. However, I'll tell Ellie and her father to be prepared, just in case.'

He waited on the doorstep until he heard the sound of their car and saw the headlights flashing as they drove away into the night.

Thirteen

When Ellie explained to her dad exactly what she'd done he was impressed rather than angry. 'Clever girl, you weren't to know what was going on. Never mind about this mess, Mrs B will take care of it when she gets here later.'

Amazingly the old range worked fine once they'd fished out the spent bangers from the chimney. The mugs were a bit smeared, but the tea was hot and the cake had suffered no ill effects as it had been in its tin.

'I'm not happy we had to hand over the list, Dad, it seems a bit like betraying our country.'

'Family comes first, love, and your brothers would be caught up in it if the authorities got hold of the information.'

'I don't see how. Why should they connect us to Sir Reginald Humphrey? Mum doesn't even live here anymore. We can pretend we know nothing about it.'

Greg spoke from the door. 'They've gone. Harkness warned me your grandfather might put in an appearance when he hears about what happened. Even more likely,

I'd say, now that Mrs Simpson has gone to live with him.'

She handed him his tea and a slice of cake on a reasonably clean plate. 'I hope he doesn't. In fact, I'm going to write to him before I go to sleep and tell him what happened. Once he knows that we have no wish to be associated with a traitor that should do the trick.'

'Take Jack's tea and cake, love, I'll be along in a minute.'

Greg had already gone ahead of her. The crockery rattled on the tray and for a horrible moment she thought she might drop the lot. She leaned against the wall for a second or two hoping the trembling would stop.

Then the tray was taken from her hands. 'You look shattered, Ellie, almost as bad as Jack. I'll take this through for you.'

With some difficulty she straightened and made her way to the sitting room. Jack looked as if he was asleep in the chair but his eyes opened when they came in. He managed a lopsided smile.

'Just what the doctor ordered. I'm going to down these and then hit the sack. What time is the first booking today?'

'I have to be at the airfield by eight o'clock.' She glanced at the mantelpiece and was shocked to see she only had six hours. 'Golly! I didn't realise it was so late

165

– or should I say early? Dad will have to be up to milk the cows in a couple of hours.'

She gulped down her tea but ignored the cake. 'I'm going up – I'll see you in the morning.'

Greg stopped her. 'I'll drive you down. Remember, I've agreed to help out until Jack's on his feet again.'

'Thank you. Good night.'

There was no sound coming from the kitchen and when she looked in it was empty. Dad must have seen the time and gone back to bed as well. Heaven knows what Mrs B was going to think when she saw the mess she had to clear away before she could get on with anything else.

Although they had a real bathroom, with hot and cold running water, all the rooms still had a washstand and large china jug and basin. She made good use of that before tumbling into bed.

*

When she went down just after seven the next morning the place was spotless and the new housekeeper beamed as she came in. 'What a palaver! These old ranges can be very temperamental. Your dad's had his breakfast and gone off to do the milking.' Her ample frame was enveloped in a yellow, floral wraparound apron and her frizzy brown hair was hidden under a headscarf.

166

'I'm sorry you had all this to do before you started today. Did my dad ask if you wanted to live in?'

'He did and I'd be right grateful. Just until your ma comes back, of course. Be ever so helpful living here and I can do all the bottling, jam making and pickling for you. Pity to waste all the soft fruit and vegetables from your veg garden.'

'Nothing cooked for me, thank you, I only have toast and marmalade.'

'No wonder you've got no flesh on your bones, Ellie. You should eat more. Cooked breakfast would do you good.'

Greg wandered in and Ellie introduced him. 'I couldn't help overhearing, Mrs B, and I'd certainly like whatever you're cooking. It smells delicious. Jack's still asleep. I expect he'll come down later.'

Half an hour later they were on their way and she felt strangely comfortable in his company. She supposed having shared so much over the past few days meant they were closer than they would otherwise be.

She glanced sideways and he smiled. He really was a very attractive young man. She much preferred corn coloured hair and blue eyes to red hair and green eyes.

'I've been thinking about Jack's Uncle Joe. He must have known what was in that envelope and I'm thinking that's why my dad allowed him to set up his airfield here and even lent him the money to buy the new de Havilland Tiger Moth.'

'Blackmailed him, you mean?'

'Something like that. When you think about it there has to be something fishy – otherwise why would someone from the East End come to Glebe Farm and not go somewhere else? Too much of a coincidence, if you want my opinion.'

'You could be right. No point in worrying about it now as the airfield belongs to Jack. You can always ask your father if you really want to know.'

'I'm not going to mention it. He would have done it to protect my mum. With him family is more important than anything else. I just wish she was as loyal as he is.' Something nasty occurred to her. 'Do you think she's a fascist too? I do hope not. Don't turn down the track, I want to go into the village and post this letter to my grandfather before we go to the airfield.'

*

Mrs B was the only one in the house when Jack eventually found the energy to get dressed and go downstairs. She greeted him with a friendly smile and the offer of a cooked breakfast which he declined.

He could do with his car back but couldn't think of a way to get it unless he cadged a lift into Romford and caught the train to London and collected it himself. There was no point in borrowing old Fred's truck as then someone would still have to drive it back from the station. He was wearing togs borrowed from Greg and needed to get his own things some time today, perhaps he could use it for that. He'd ask him when he came back for lunch. Ellie had offered to go this evening, but he didn't want to wait that long.

He wandered outside into the sunshine and spotted Ellie's bicycle leaning drunkenly against the wall. It was only a couple of miles to the village – surely he could manage that even with one duff arm? There was a large wicker basket attached to the front handlebars and a rack over the back mudguard.

He should really put the saddle up but, apart from not knowing where to find the necessary spanner, he only had one good arm so wouldn't be able to do it anyway. He found it strange riding a lady's bicycle but soon got the hang of it.

His landlady handed him his belongings and closed the door as if she couldn't wait to be rid of him. He'd had the forethought to bring a couple of lengths of string with him and, with some difficulty, finally achieved his objective. The suitcase was tied to the back and the kitbag balanced in the front basket.

This meant his vision was obscured and he had to peer over the top of his luggage in order to be able to see where he was going. The last half a mile was downhill so he could allow gravity to do the rest.

Fred was in the yard with two blokes who must be his labourers. He was greeted with a wave. 'Go on in, lad, we'll bring in your stuff. You shouldn't be peddling about the place, not in your condition.'

'I'm all right, thanks. I'm bushed, but nothing a bit of lunch and a cup of tea won't put right.'

*

After lunch he was left to his own devices. Unpacking didn't take long and he had the rest of the afternoon to kill. He kicked off his shoes and stretched out on the candlewick bedspread. Jimmy had told him to rest as much as possible and he'd done the exact opposite so far. If he wanted to be back at work before Greg had to leave he'd better start taking care of himself.

Fred had said they were working on the far side of the farm this afternoon – something to do with hedging or fencing, he hadn't been listening too closely. Mrs B had finished her chores, cleaned out the rooms she would be occupying, and gone home to collect her clothes.

The house was quiet and he stretched out and dozed off. He was roused by a thunderous knocking on the front door. He sat up; it took him a moment to clear his head. He rolled out of bed and went to the head of the stairs.

'Hold your horses. No need to make so much racket. I'll be there in a minute.' Whoever it was must have heard him yell because the noise stopped.

Jack took his time putting his shoes on, washing his face and running his fingers through his hair before he went down to answer the door. He was pretty sure he knew who was out there. His mouth quirked. Of course, it could be the rozzers and not Ellie's grandfather – but he doubted it.

He pushed the bolt back and opened the door. A large, uniformed chauffeur with a belligerent expression was standing on the doorstep. There was no sign of Humphrey but he supposed he was sitting in his car until he could come in without being kept standing about.

'Can I help you?'

'Sir Reginald Humphrey is here to see his granddaughter.'

'Sorry, he's out of luck. Miss Simpson and Mr Simpson are out for the rest of the day. Tell him he's free to wait in his car until they come back.' Jack shut the door but remained behind it expecting the chauffeur to bang again and demand entry for his master.

After a few minutes of silence Jack locked the door and went to the kitchen to see if there was any grub lying around in the pantry. He'd better check the back door was locked as he didn't want any more surprise visitors. Last night's intruders had come in through the scullery window but this was now definitely latched.

Mrs B, if she returned before Fred, would have to knock. Better that than allowing the fascist bastard outside to get in the house without an invitation.

He found bread and cheese and made himself a sandwich which he took to the table. He'd just sunk his teeth into it when the knocking began again. He ignored it for a few minutes but it continued until he had to get up.

He didn't bother to go to the door but shouted from where he was. 'I told you, I'm not letting you in. You will have to wait until Mr Simpson or Miss Simpson return. I'm a guest here and it's not up to me who comes in.'

This time the response was from a deep, plummy male voice. 'Open this door at once. I'll not be kept waiting like a tradesman. I've more right to be in this house than you have.'

'Sod off, you fascist bastard. I'm eating my lunch. There's a pub in the village. Go there and come back this evening.'

*

The day at the airfield was like any other. Gladys, who was now running the office, noticed nothing out of the ordinary in there. Both she and Sid accepted Ellie's explanation, that Jack had sprained his ankle, without comment. Greg went up twice with nervous pilots and she took the rest of them.

She was in the office having just signed a log book and said goodbye to a pupil when Jack rang. 'I thought I'd better let you know that your grandfather and his chauffeur are outside. I told them to sod off to the village to wait but I don't think they have.'

'Don't let him in – let him sit in his car. I'm not coming back just for him. We'll be finished here in a couple of hours; can you hold the fort until then?'

'Can do. Take your time – I can always give him both barrels if necessary.' He sounded as if he was eating his lunch. He swallowed noisily before continuing. 'Helped myself to some bread and cheese – hope you don't mind.'

'Of course not. What does Mrs B think of all this kerfuffle?'

'Fortunately, she's gone home to collect her things. She said she wouldn't be back until four.'

'I've got to go – we'll be home about six o'clock.'

'Hang on a minute. There's no need for you to go to my old digs, I borrowed your bicycle and fetched everything myself.'

He hung up not giving her time to reply. He was supposed to be taking things easy not cycling all over the place. There was nothing she could do about it so she might as well get on with the afternoon.

*

Greg was a good driver but Ellie still flinched every time they hit a pothole. Her stomach was churning and she wasn't looking forward to the inevitable confrontation with her unwanted relation.

'Do you think my mother knows he's here?'

He looked at her blankly for a second and then nodded. 'Your grandfather? I doubt it – he wouldn't want the daughter he's only just been reunited with to know what you know. If he's anything like my father he will come and go as he pleases and not bother to inform anyone of his whereabouts.'

'I'm hoping that she doesn't know what he's really like. She might be a bit of a snob but I'm certain she's not a fascist. I've heard her talking about Hitler with Dad and she always agreed with him that the man is a monster.'

They turned onto the lane that led in one direction to the village, and in the other to her home. They would be at Glebe Farm in five minutes and she needed to get herself ready. As far as she was concerned Sir Reginald Humphrey was nothing to do with her and she intended it to remain that way.

'It won't be so bad, Ellie, with Jack and I at your side he can't do anything you don't like.' Greg patted her on the knee and the warmth and strength of his hand was reassuring.

'As long as this is the one and only time I have to meet him then I can deal with it. But Dad and I are then going to have to decide if we're going to tell Mum. She's just got back the life she always regretted leaving – she will be devastated to lose it again so soon'.

They turned into the yard and he was forced to slam on the brakes; only his arm braced across her chest stopped her from crashing painfully into the dashboard.

'The Bentley must be his car. The other one is Jack's – his friend must have brought it back for him. I'm glad Jimmy's here – safety in numbers and all that.'

Greg expertly manoeuvred his sports car into a small space to one side of the Bentley. 'Your dad will have to park his truck in the field when he gets back.'

She scrambled out, not bothering to open the door, and headed for the back door. 'I'm hoping all this will be over before he gets back. He's had more than enough to deal with recently.'

'It must be a relief to him that everything is in the open. Having that hanging over him for years must have been miserable.'

'I wonder if he was doing it for me or for my mum? I'd like to think it was for her and then there might be the chance they'll get back together again.'

His hand was resting in the small of her back and she didn't shrug it off. 'After the war Neil's going to take over the farm…' She stopped and swallowed the lump in her throat. 'It's inevitable, this war with Germany, isn't it?'

'Fraid so. Let's not think about that right now. I've just noticed the Bentley's empty – Humphrey must have

175

taken his chauffeur in with him.' He stepped around her. 'That's not the done thing. Staff wait outside. I'll go in first, if you don't mind.'

She didn't mind at all. She'd had more than enough daring-do in the past twenty-four hours and was quite happy to let him take charge. Jack was injured and Jimmy wasn't a big man – Greg was.

Mrs B opened the door as they approached. One look at the housekeeper's bleached complexion was enough to warn Ellie that things weren't going well indoors.

'I'm ever so glad you're back, miss, there's a horrible man in the front room and there's been a lot of shouting and carrying on. I wouldn't have come to work here if I'd known this was going to happen.' She sniffed again and reached for the handkerchief from her sleeve to wipe her eyes. 'I had the nasty chauffeur in here with me until Mr Reynolds fetched him. It's not right him being in the house – he should have waited outside.'

'Mr Dunlop will take care of things, Mrs B. I promise you it won't happen again. Shall we go in and let the men get on with it?'

Ellie put her arm around the distressed woman and guided her into the welcoming warmth of the kitchen and closed the door behind them. The wood was thick, as were the ancient walls, and the sound of raised voices was no longer audible.

'Have you settled in? Do you need any bed linen or towels and things?'

'I found everything I needed, thank you. I could do with a few of my bits and bobs that I couldn't carry. Do you think Mr Simpson would fetch them in his truck?'

'I'm certain he will. Now, I can smell something delicious – have you made steak and kidney pie for tonight?'

'That I have. There's new potatoes from the garden and carrots and peas as well. I made a rhubarb crumble for afters. No need for custard as you've always got plenty of cream.'

'Will there be enough for Doctor Hunt? He's driven down from London to return Mr Reynolds' car.'

Mrs B sniffed. 'As long as I don't have to feed the other two nasty bits of work, there'll be plenty to go around.' Her colour was better and Ellie thought the chance of their new housekeeper changing her mind had been averted.

Fourteen

Not long after Jack had spoken to Ellie he heard the familiar sound of his own car in the yard. Jimmy had brought it back for him. Not the ideal time – but having another bloke around would even the odds.

He opened the kitchen window and yelled. 'Front door, mate, make it snappy. Don't want the uninvited guests to barge their way in.'

His friend waved and was out of the car and sprinting towards the house before either the chauffeur or his master had time to react.

'Come in, I'd better tell you what this is all about.'

Jimmy was suitably impressed by his tale. 'Exciting life you're leading, old son. Exactly what are you planning? If they've been outside for a couple of hours already they're obviously not intending to leave before they've spoken to someone.'

'Ellie told me to keep them outside until she and Greg get home.' He looked at his watch. 'Another hour at least.' Something was moving behind the hedge at the top of the track that led to the farm. 'Bloody hell! It's the housekeeper, Mrs B, coming back. She's going to have to walk past them.'

'Don't want the old biddy scared witless – better invite them in. If we keep them in the sitting room and ply them with tea and cake that should keep them quiet for a while.'

'Do me a favour, Jimmy, you're one of them. Would you tell Humphrey he can come in? He's less likely to kick off with you. Blokes like him don't like ordinary folk like me.'

His friend looked dubious. 'He doesn't know me from Adam – can't see why he wouldn't be just as rude. I'll give it a go. Whilst I'm talking to them you can let the housekeeper in and get her to put the kettle on.'

They watched from the window until Mrs B came into view and then Jimmy nipped out smartish. Jack saw him speak to the housekeeper and point in the direction of the front door which meant she didn't have to walk past the Bentley.

Jack had the door open when she arrived, red-faced and puffing after her long walk. 'Sorry about this, Mrs B, it's to do with Mrs Simpson. If you'd make us some tea and a bit of that fruitcake would go down a treat too.' He took one of the large suitcases from her hand and dashed through the house and dumped it in her new lodgings. She followed with the other one. 'No rush with the tea and things – get yourself sorted out first.'

'Thank you, sir, I'll do that. I'll be along with a tray in half an hour.'

He closed the door firmly behind him in the hope that she wouldn't hear if there was further shouting from Ellie's grandfather.

Sir Reginald burst into the house via the front door closely followed by his chauffeur. The man's appearance matched his temperament and politics. He was about the same height as Ellie, had brown hair like her, but there the resemblance ended. He had small, beady eyes set behind metal-rimmed spectacles, and red veins on his cheeks – the tell-tale sign of a heavy drinker.

'I don't appreciate being kept outside like a lackey. When Charlotte told me what she'd had to endure over the past twenty years she failed to mention that her husband had taken in unsavoury lodgers.'

Jimmy peered around the man's shoulder and pulled a face. Jack couldn't prevent his smile. This further enraged the unpleasant visitor. He seemed to swell and his face turned an interesting shade of beetroot.

'Don't you smirk at me, you oaf. My man will not stand for such insolence.'

The chauffeur surged forward with clenched fists but Jack moved more quickly and shot into the sitting room. His friend stepped around the spluttering idiot and stood shoulder to shoulder with him.

'Sir Reginald, this will not do. Servants do not enter through the front door, but by the back. Kindly send him on his way.' Jimmy's cut-glass accent was sufficient to stop the chauffeur in his tracks. He shifted uncomfortably and glanced at his employer.

'Go, Johnson, but remain within call.'

The man slunk off. 'I am a house guest here, Sir Reginald, a personal friend of the family. Doctor Hunt is my personal physician and also a friend of the family. In the absence of either Ellie or Mr Simpson you have no option but to be entertained by us.' Jack couldn't quite match Jimmy's accent but thought he sounded posh enough to impress.

He moved to one side and gestured towards the sitting room. 'Would you care to come in and sit down? The housekeeper will be bringing tea and cake in a while.'

As soon as he said this he realised the chauffeur would be banging on the door and expect to spend the next hour or so in the kitchen. She wasn't going to like that one bit.

The baronet marched past him, ramrod straight, bristling with annoyance. He reckoned the man was ex-military to have a bearing like that. He spoke quietly to Jimmy. 'I'd better warn Mrs B to expect company. She won't be pleased and I don't blame her.'

Fortunately, he was able to speak to her in her rooms before the chauffeur arrived and was able to explain the situation. 'I'll not leave him in here with you any longer than necessary, Mrs B. I need to speak to Sir Reginald without him being present.'

'Very well, sir, I'll give him a cup of tea. But I've got to get on with my work and if he gets in the way he'll have to go outside. I'm not having him in there without me present so he'll have to kick his heels outside until I'm done here.'

'Keep him hanging about as long as you want, Mrs B.'

Jack hurried back to the sitting room hoping that Jimmy would have been able to smooth things over, but the atmosphere was frigid.

Humphrey was standing in the centre of the room and looked ready for a fight.

*

'It's quiet enough at the moment, Greg, I hope this is a good sign. I'm not looking forward to this at all. I hate arguments and loud voices.'

'There's four of us and only two of them – that's if you count his chauffeur – so you've nothing to worry about. I can assure you we can eject both them if we have to, and without recourse to the shotguns in case you were wondering.'

She hesitated outside the door. Then, taking a deep breath, she pushed it open with rather more force than she'd intended. It slammed against the wall and the four occupants reacted as one would expect.

Jack laughed, Jimmy shook his head, the uniformed man, standing to attention by the window, jumped as if stuck with a hatpin. The elderly man shot to his feet and glared at her. She glared right back.

He was about to rip into her but she was having none of that – not from him – and not in her own house. 'I apologise if I startled you. Would someone mind explaining what that person is doing in my sitting room?' She pointed an accusing finger at the chauffeur. She drew herself to her full height and stared down her nose at her aristocratic relative. For the first time glad she was so tall.

'I don't know how things are arranged in your home, Sir Reginald, but here the servants know their place and it isn't in this part of the house.' She pointed at his driver. 'You – go back to your car. You won't have long to wait.'

The man sloped off and she was sure she heard him muttering "make up your bloody mind why don't you" as he left.

'Don't be uppity with me, young lady, I drove all this way…'

'Actually, you didn't. You were driven. I've written you a letter which you will receive tomorrow. I've no wish to speak to you in person. In fact, I never want to see or speak to you again. I hope when my mother realises what you are that she comes home to the people who love her.'

He looked ready to explode. His nostrils flared and his eyes bulged. She raised a hand imperiously to stop him speaking. 'Please leave now. There's nothing you have to say that I want to hear.'

'You're going to regret this. I intend to contact your brothers. Charlotte assures me that they will be delighted to meet me. You obviously take after your father.'

'My brothers have joined the RAF to fight for King and Country. They already know you are a member of the fascist party and a supporter of Hitler. I hardly think they will want to acknowledge that there's a traitor lurking in the family.'

His look was venomous but he said nothing and stalked out. She held her breath until the front door slammed behind him.

'Well, that was fun! Unpleasant aristocrat routed by a commoner,' Greg said approvingly.

'We've had to put up with his ranting and raving, threats and so on about what would happen to us and our families if we ever spoke about what we know,' Jack said with a smile. 'After a bit we just ignored him. I'm surprised he spoke so freely in front of his man.'

The sound of the Bentley driving away at speed was a relief to all of them. 'Why was the chauffeur in here?'

'I think he's more of a bodyguard – I sent him to the kitchen but Mrs B wanted him out so we had to let him come in here again.

'Serves him right for working for someone so obnoxious. Jimmy, I hope you can stay for supper?'

'I'd love to. The last train leaves from Romford at nine thirty – as long as someone gets me there for that, as I'm operating tomorrow.'

She left the men talking and dashed upstairs to wash and change into something less utilitarian. Now that Mum had gone there was no one to comment on her clothes but, having three unattached gentlemen here at the same time, she owed it to herself to make an effort.

There was a pretty, navy blue, cotton dress with white spots hanging in her wardrobe. It had never been worn and now seemed the ideal opportunity to show it off. She had a strip wash standing in the bath and did the best she could with her short hair.

She was still dressing when Jack yelled up the stairs that the food was ready. She'd not heard Dad come up to change so he must have washed the day's grime from his hands and face downstairs. Something he never did when Mum was in residence.

Satisfied there was nothing more she could do to improve her appearance, Ellie ran down to join them. It was too warm for stockings and she rather liked the feel of the early evening air on her bare legs. 'Sorry if I kept you waiting.'

Jack whistled his appreciation and Greg smiled. He nodded towards Jack. 'I'd have changed too, but that chap is wearing my only clean shirt.'

'That's true and I've no excuse as I've got my own togs now. Fred hasn't bothered and he's waiting in the dining room. Seems Mrs B intends to serve all our meals in there in future.'

*

The evening came to a close when Greg offered to drive Jimmy to the station. Something prompted her to offer to accompany them. 'In which case, Jack, can we use your car? No room in the back for a passenger in mine.'

'Go ahead. I'm going up anyway, feeling a bit rough.'

Immediately Jimmy became professional and stepped over to place his hand on his friend's forehead. 'No fever – and your arm's healing nicely despite having been re-stitched. Try and take things a bit easier tomorrow, no cycling all over the countryside for you.'

'I want to get back to work so will rest for a couple of days. Thanks for bringing the car back, Jimmy.'

It was still light enough to drive without the headlamps on. She sat in the back and let the men chat about football and cricket – not something that interested her particularly. She transferred to the front seat after Jimmy had departed.

'It's a beautiful evening – seems a pity to go home so soon. Would you like to have a drink with me somewhere?'

'I don't drink alcohol but would love a lemonade. Would you mind very much if we didn't go to the pub in the village? There must be somewhere in Romford that isn't too rough.'

'You're the local girl, I'd have thought you would know where we can go.'

'To be honest, I can't remember the last time I was here at night. Mum didn't approve of girls going out in the evening.'

*

'In which case, let's give it a miss. We've got a busy day tomorrow,' Greg said with some reluctance. Spending time alone with Ellie this evening had reinforced his determination to claim her for himself. Once war was declared he'd have no time. Having a fiancée, having someone of his own to fight for, would make what was coming a little easier to bear.

She was quiet beside him in the car and he couldn't see her expression in the darkness. He wasn't used to girls that didn't feel the need to fill every second with sparkling repartee but were content to be still. Would she fall in with his plans? Could he convince her before he left?

Certainly, his own crowd thought he was a good prospect. He was personable, came from the top drawer, and would inherit a fortune one day. Would this be enough to convince her? Maybe he would speak to her father before he spoke to her – surely Fred would see the advantages for his only daughter. By the time they arrived at the farm he was convinced she'd fallen asleep.

'Wake up, Ellie, we're home.'

'I'm wide awake, I was just thinking. Do you think that man can actually cause this family any harm?'

'Can't see how. He's got more to lose than you have. I'm sure he understands you wouldn't hesitate to inform on him, regardless of the consequences.'

'Thanks, it's reassuring that we have come to the same conclusion. I intend to forget about him and hope he does the same for us. One thing does puzzle me, the reason he came thundering down here in the first place. It doesn't make sense that he just came here to threaten us.'

'Possibly he just wanted to see where his daughter had spent the past twenty-five years, see if he could persuade you to leave Glebe Farm too.'

'I doubt it. There has to be something else behind his visit and we just can't work it out.' She opened the door and ducked out. 'The house is dark; everyone has gone to bed including Mrs B. I'd no idea it was so late.'

He left the keys in the car and followed her to the back door which fortunately had been left open. He didn't fancy having to wake someone to let them in. He'd hoped to get a chance to kiss her but she was already inside. Maybe the opportunity would present itself at the airfield – fat chance of getting her alone here as Jack was always about. He appeared to have taken on the role of older brother where she was concerned. As long as Jack wasn't interested in her as a girlfriend, things should be okay.

'Night, Greg, see you at breakfast. Make sure you don't wake Jack; he needs his rest.'

'Thanks for a delightful evening, Ellie, you must let me take you for that lemonade before I leave.'

'Actually, if you want to take me out, I'd love to see *Gone with the Wind*. I noticed it was playing at the cinema this week. If we go straight from the airfield we should just make the last performance.'

They were now standing at the bottom of the stairs talking in whispers.

'It's a date – but I'm not taking you in your overalls. You'll have to take a change of clothes with you.'

'I'm not a complete idiot, you know. And it's not a date – it's just two friends going to the pictures.'

She vanished upstairs and he heard the latch on her door as she went into her bedroom. Ellie might think it wasn't a date but by the end of the evening he was sure she would have changed her mind. His lips curved. He would really push the boat out and buy her some fish and chips when they came out – how could she resist him after that?

He crept into his bedroom and almost tripped over his feet when Jack spoke to him from the darkness. 'You took your time, Dunlop. Remember Ellie's inexperienced, she's a sweet young girl and not ready to have a serious relationship with anyone, and especially someone who reminds her of her obnoxious grandfather.'

The bed creaked as Jack turned over. The one-sided conversation was finished. Greg wanted to tip him out of bed but thought better of it. However, he would put Jack straight about a few things at the earliest opportunity.

Being told he couldn't have something, and by someone like Jack Reynolds, hardened his resolve. He didn't bother to find his pyjamas, just stripped off his outer garments and got into bed in his underclothes. He'd only been here a couple of days and already standards were slipping. He bit back his chuckles as he slid under the sheet. Glebe Farm and its inhabitants were changing him and he hoped it was for the better.

Fifteen

No more was heard from Sir Reginald and by the end of the week Ellie was convinced the matter was over. She removed the stitches from Jack's arm, following Jimmy's detailed instructions, and he was ready to return to work.

Saturday would be Greg's last day and she was going to miss him. They'd been out twice together and she let him kiss her on the second date. Things had changed after that and he now had an annoying, proprietorial manner where she was concerned.

Greg was taking the de Havilland for a last jaunt when Jack arrived. He strode towards her looking serious. What now? Just when she was beginning to relax.

'Fred said that Dunlop has asked for permission to marry you.'

For a moment she was too surprised to think of a sensible answer. This would explain why Greg had changed, but it didn't explain why Jack thought it was any of his business.

'I'd no idea. This is the first time I've heard about it. I can't see why you're so interested unless you're jealous.'

He smiled. 'Don't be bloody ridiculous. I think of you like the sister I never had. You're a damn good pilot and you shouldn't give that up for someone you've only just met.'

'I've no intention of giving anything up. Greg hasn't spoken to me about getting engaged and if he did I'd refuse. I don't think one kiss is sufficient reason for him to consider that I'm his property. Don't worry – I've no intention of leaving here unless the government stops civilian flying. Then I'll help on the farm as one of our men has already said he'd volunteer if there's a war.'

'Good, I'm relieved to hear you say that. I'll join the RAF, if and when, but not until I have to. They didn't make me feel very welcome when I enquired. I think I'm not posh enough for them. Not officer material – I don't know if anyone from the ranks can be a pilot – certainly can't be at the moment.'

'As you're here, you can see the books. Gladys finished early and is going to the bank on her way home.' He followed her into the office and she pointed to the appointment book. 'Chock-a-block, and we still have a waiting list. I wish we had some girls on our books. I can't understand why they're not interested. It's something women can do as well as men as it doesn't rely on strength.'

'Girls like you are rare. Most young women are only interested in finding themselves a decent husband and setting up home. I take it that doesn't appeal to you. Greg's rich, good-looking, reasonably intelligent and would make a good husband. I'm surprised you're not even considering it.'

'If I was going to get married in the next few years then he would definitely be in the picture. I'm sure I'll take the plunge eventually but it's not on the agenda at the moment. I'll tell him when he comes down.'

Jack was suitably impressed by the figures but left, saying he had business in Romford, an hour before Greg came in to land. She wasn't looking forward to this conversation. In fact, she wasn't sure she could bring the subject up as Greg hadn't actually mentioned anything about them getting engaged.

She had no further pupils, Sid had gone home; she would be alone with the man who had taken it upon himself to discuss her future with Dad without having the courtesy to speak to her.

He landed perfectly and taxied the aircraft to its usual place. He climbed out and strolled confidently towards her swinging his helmet and goggles nonchalantly in one hand.

Perhaps it would be better to wait until they were home before she confronted him as she didn't want to walk back if he took umbrage.

'I'm done here. Mrs B's doing a special farewell meal for you tonight and I want to put on my glad rags in honour of the occasion so, if you're ready, I'd like to leave immediately.'

'It's a good thing I popped home to replenish my wardrobe. Are Jack and Fred going to wear a jacket and tie?'

'I think so. I'm going to miss you, Greg, it's been fun having you staying with us. You seem like one of the family now.'

His expression changed and her stomach lurched. This was quite the worst thing to have said in the circumstances – did he think it gave him the necessary encouragement to speak? It would ruin the evening for all of them if he proposed and she refused him.

'Can I drive? You promised I could have a go with your MG and this will be my last opportunity.'

The thought of her behind the wheel of his precious car was enough to distract him and the danger was averted. 'Not today, sweetheart, but I give you my word, next time I visit you can drive her.'

'Spoilsport! That mightn't be for weeks. Never mind, Jack's happy for me to use his Austin whenever I want and that's probably more my speed.'

'Good move Ellie. I can hardly refuse now, can I? You can drive home but promise not to go too fast. I don't think my nerves can stand it. I've never been driven by a girl before.'

'If you're happy to be a passenger when I'm the pilot then I can't see why you're nervous about sitting next to me in a car.'

The MG was a dream to drive and she was sorry when the short journey was completed. 'Thank you, that was lovely.'

Jack's car was back; his business couldn't have taken him very long. If she wanted to have a bath she needed to get in first or there'd be no hot water left.

*

Fred was relieved to hear his daughter's plans didn't include marriage. 'Thanks for speaking to her, Jack, I'll not worry about it anymore. Is anyone talking about what happened here?'

'No mention of it. Latest gossip is that the barmaid's in the family way and several of the customers were waiting to have the finger pointed at them.'

'That Mabel is a generous girl; no money involved, you understand, but takes pity on the men who make eyes at her.'

'Have you heard anything from Neil and George?'

'Not a dickie-bird. Ellie wrote to both of them so they know what's what.'

'Did she write to your wife as well?'

'No idea – but I doubt it. Charlotte will ignore any unpleasantness and pretend things are how she wants them to be. I'm expecting to hear from her solicitor that she wants a divorce.'

'Don't see how she can get one as she has no grounds. Mrs B wants us all to change tonight. I'd wear my suit if I still had one – I don't own anything more respectable than a blazer so that will have to do.'

'Good God, son, I'm not going that far. Far too hot – a wash and a clean shirt will do me.'

Jack decided he'd follow Fred's example. He was looking forward to having the room to himself again and wouldn't be sorry when Greg departed tomorrow morning for his base.

*

The evening was tedious but the meal worth the effort of changing. Greg was particularly charming and not just to Ellie. When he suggested the two of them went for a moonlight walk Jack was surprised that she accepted immediately. She must know a proposal was on the cards and he would have thought she'd do everything to avoid that.

His bedroom overlooked the garden and he said goodnight to Fred and dashed upstairs. The windows were already wide open – all he had to do was sit on the window seat and he'd be able to hear what was said. Eavesdropping deliberately left a sour taste in his mouth but he was curious to know how she was going to handle the tricky situation.

As expected their voices carried clearly to his position.

'I've enjoyed having you here, Greg, thank you so much for helping out. I hope you'll visit us again one day, although I expect you'll have better things to do with your time.'

'It's been my absolute pleasure. And I'm rather hoping I'm going to see a great deal more of you in future.'

Here it comes – Dunlop was about to pop the question.

'No, Greg, don't spoil things. You know I've no interest in anything apart from flying and I intend to keep doing that as long as I can. As far as I'm concerned you are a friend of the family. I hope you understand.'

There was a long silence. Jack smiled in the darkness unsurprised that she'd taken the initiative.

'I see. I suppose your father told you my intentions.'

Jack tensed. Was she going to reveal who actually informed her?

'I'm not blind, Greg, I noticed you were treating me differently since we kissed the other night. If I'd gone to bed with you that would be different – you might feel you have to do the gentlemanly thing. But a kiss? I hope I get the opportunity to kiss quite a few attractive men before I settle down.'

Bloody hell! She wasn't as naive as he thought. He waited to hear what the response would be. If it had been him he would have made love to her right there in the garden. There was an uncomfortable tightness in his groin at the thought. This wouldn't do. Tomorrow he'd find himself a willing bed-mate – if he was reacting to Ellie then he must be desperate.

He'd heard quite enough and moved away from the window and switched on the light. He drew the curtains noisily letting them know he was there. If he was honest he felt a bit sorry for Dunlop, he quite liked him, but Ellie wasn't right for him. It would be the same situation as her ma marrying Fred, but in reverse. Better that folk stuck to their own kind, in his opinion.

When the door opened shortly afterwards he pretended to be asleep. There was no need to rub salt in the poor bloke's wounds.

'She turned me down. Comprehensively. But, in case you're interested, Reynolds, I'm not giving up. She's agreed to correspond with me and I have an open invitation to visit if I get any leave.'

Jack pushed himself up on his elbows. 'Good for you, mate, but I don't hold out much hope for your success. She's made it very plain marriage to you, or anyone for that matter, doesn't feature in her plans.'

'So she discussed it with you?' He didn't sound too pleased and Jack didn't blame him.

'Fred told me and I told her. I needn't have bothered as she'd already guessed. You'd be better off sticking with some classy debutante, she'd fit in better with your family than Ellie would. It didn't work out too well for her mum, marrying beneath her, did it?' Jack heard the other bed creak.

'You could be right. But don't they say that, "love conquers all"?'

'I reckon they do, and it could be right. Goodnight.' He turned over and fell asleep immediately.

*

When Ellie came down for breakfast Greg had already left. Jack greeted her with a wave of his bacon-laden fork.

'He left you a letter, it's on the dresser. Will you be ready to go in twenty minutes? If not you can cycle.'

She glanced across and saw the envelope but ignored it. 'Unlike you I don't stuff my face every morning. It's too hot to use my bike so I'm ready when you are.'

He nodded towards her new work outfit. 'Much better – you can do your job just as well in slacks. I'm glad to see the back of those overalls.'

'I'm wearing these because of the weather, not because I want to look smart. When I have my flying kit on nobody can see what's underneath anyway.'

*

On the drive to the airfield she thought it safe to ask a question that had obviously been bothering her. 'Have you heard from Joe?'

'My aunt said he's still helping police with their enquiries and she's not been able to see him. They took away several boxes from the attic but she's no idea what they are intending to charge him with – if anything at all.'

'I'm finding it hard to accept that Joe isn't the man I thought he was. I'd always wondered why he came to Glebe Farm and why my dad agreed to let him have these fields and barns. Knowing that Joe blackmailed him is horrible.'

'I'm not exactly happy with it either. I spoke to Fred about this, asked if he wanted me to move out, but he said no. He thinks that he's actually gained more from the arrangement than he lost. You wouldn't be a pilot and neither would your brothers if Joe hadn't set up here.'

'I suppose you're right. If Dad isn't bothered then I'll forget about it. Do you think your uncle was blackmailing other people as well? Was that what was in the boxes the police took?'

They bumped to a standstill in his usual parking place. This wasn't a conversation they could continue when they might be overheard and Sid was already busy in the hangar.

'I'd always thought he was a fence, never actually got his own hands dirty, just handled the stolen goods. Now I'm not so sure. I'm trying to figure out how he came to be in possession of that list. I can think of only one feasible explanation – he was a member and tore the page out himself. How else could he have got hold of it?'

Ellie was glad she hadn't eaten any more than a slice of toast as her stomach lurched uncomfortably. 'That makes sense and I don't know why I didn't think of that too. What doesn't add up is why no one attempted to recover the evidence until now.'

'It has to be something to do with the police investigation. But I agree, why wait until now to get the document back?'

Sid would wonder why they were still sitting talking in the car and not getting on with things. 'I don't want to think about it now. Shall we talk about it after Dad goes up tonight?'

'Let's forget about it. Matters have moved on and it's out of our hands now.'

*

He was right. It was far more important to continue to train as many young men, who could afford the £2 an hour, as possible. The country would need hundreds of pilots if the truce with Germany collapsed. This way she could do something valuable and would feel less bothered about not having passed on the information to the correct authorities.

Jack was slowly becoming part of the family and he had developed an interest in farming much to her dad's delight. Neither Neil nor George had ever expressed any interest in continuing the family business.

Simpsons had been farming this land for generations and over the years more land and other farms had been added. There were four farms leased to tenants and a dozen or more cottages rented out, and these didn't include the tied cottages for the farmworkers.

They didn't live as though they were wealthy, which was the reason Mum had been so miserable. She suspected Dad was one of the biggest landowners in the area and could easily afford to build himself a grand house if he wanted. Finding the money for the new aircraft would have been easy for him.

Now she came to think of it, she and her brothers had gone to the most expensive schools and he'd never quibbled about paying for extras. Perhaps she could have been a debutante and swished around in silk gowns if her mother had had her way.

She'd not given Greg a second thought until Mrs B gave her an envelope several days later.

'Ellie love, didn't you see this from Mr Dunlop? It's been on the dresser since he left.'

'Thanks, I'd forgotten all about it. Been far too busy at work.'

She took the letter to her bedroom where she could read it in private.

She went to the window seat to read the letter:

Ellie

I thought it best if we didn't speak to each other this morning. I understand why you didn't want me to propose and I respect your views.

There's a war coming and when it does anyone flying an aircraft will be vulnerable. I thought that having you in my life would give me something tangible to fight for – a reason to stay alive.

I imagine that you're shaking your head and frowning, thinking I'm trying to manipulate you into doing something you're not comfortable with.

You're wrong, sweetheart, I love you and I should have said so last night. I'm pretty sure you don't reciprocate my feelings at the moment, but you are attracted to me, and that's a start.

Would you do me a favour? Write to me occasionally and maybe invite me to visit? I'm not going to pressure you into doing something you don't want. I'd love to be able to take you out to dinner or dancing in Town, introduce you to my friends, but with no strings on either side.

We enjoy each other's company. The fact that I love you isn't a problem. All I want is to be able to spend time with you.

Take care of yourself

She put the letter down and wiped her eyes. He was right; she was attracted to him and might enjoy being escorted to nightclubs and smart restaurants. Tomorrow she would discuss this with Dad. If he was happy for her to go out occasionally with Greg then she might actually consider it.

Sixteen

The weeks slid by and towards the end of August Ellie decided to go to London to buy herself some new clothes. Elizabeth and Anna, the only two girls she'd kept in contact with after leaving school, were going to meet her at Liverpool Street. She had more than enough in her bank, since Jack had been paying her the same rate as himself, to buy what she wanted without asking her dad for a handout.

He'd been quite happy for her to have the occasional date with Greg and so she'd written back telling him this – which was why she needed a couple of new outfits. Her first invitation was to dinner and then to a party in Mayfair. He'd suggested booking her into the Savoy, which was reasonably close to the station, but she didn't want to stay in a grand hotel on her own. Instead she would stay at his London home.

Jack insisted on driving her to Romford station on his way to work on the Saturday morning. 'Make sure you catch the four thirty train. I don't want to hang about waiting for you this evening.'

'Don't worry – if I don't get off that train then I'll get a taxi home.'

'I'll go for a pint.' He grinned. 'But I warn you, I'll not be in the sunniest of tempers.'

'Even more reason for you not to come and let me make my own arrangements.'

'Stop arguing, Ellie, the only taxi you're getting in today is this one.'

'Are you going to put up the Anderson shelter that arrived the other day?'

'Fred's getting a couple of blokes from the village to do it and giving them a quid each.' His expression became grim. 'We've had those bloody gas masks for months, evacuation plans for the children have been made and Mrs B has put up the blackout curtains. That bastard Hitler is about to march. I just hope we're going to be ready.'

'The last time I spoke to Greg he said Britain began rearming in the spring and new planes are arriving all the time. Whatever the Prime Minister is saying about peace with Germany, I don't think he believes it any more than we do.'

The car ground to a halt outside the station and she hopped out. 'Thank you, see you just after five o'clock.'

Although the train stopped at every station the journey was completed in half an hour. She rushed towards the barrier, ticket in hand, and was relieved to see her two friends jumping up and down waving from the other side.

'Right on time, Ellie, we only just arrived ourselves,' Elizabeth said after having hugged her enthusiastically. Her friend was a head shorter but in her high heels she looked almost as tall.

'I like the new hairdo, very fashionable. In fact, the two of you make me look like a shabby provincial miss.'

Anna didn't go in for physical signs of affection but smiled warmly. 'Which is exactly what you are, Miss Simpson. We've come to render you our able assistance. I promise you, that when you go home tonight your family won't recognise you. It's just a pity you have your hair so short, but never mind, we've booked you in for a manicure and make up in the West End.'

'I'm not glamorous like either of you and I don't think a lot of lipstick and rouge would suit me. I just want a couple of smart outfits and an evening gown – plus all the bits and bobs that I need to go with them.'

Her friends exchanged a smile and her heart sank. She was very fond of the pair of them but, lovely as they both were, she had no desire to look like either of them. They were the epitome of what her mother thought was right for a young lady from a good home but wouldn't suit someone who flew for a living in a man's world.

'We are both impressed that you've managed to snag such a prestigious catch as Gregory Dunlop. He's often seen in the fashionable magazines with a beautiful young deb on his arm,' Elizabeth said as she slipped her hand through Ellie's arm.

'We're just friends, nothing else. I told you I met him through Neil and he helped out at the airfield for a bit.'

Anna was walking at her other side as if she thought Ellie might want to escape from them. 'That's what we thought. You're not his type, he'd never marry someone like you. He's just doing you a favour.'

Before she could stop herself, Ellie blurted out the truth. 'Actually, he did ask me but I turned him down. I believe he's hoping to persuade me to change my mind.'

Anna stopped dead and a pinstriped businessman cannoned into the back of her sending her flying in a most undignified heap. By the time the apologetic gentleman had helped her friend to her feet and brushed her down a small crowd of interested spectators had gathered.

'I apologise again, my dear, you must allow me to pay for your shoes to be repaired.' The man dipped into his wallet and handed over a five-pound note. Ellie was astonished Anna took it – she certainly wouldn't have done.

'That's very thoughtful of you, sir. I shall get the heel repaired immediately.'

Only then did Ellie notice the heel of Anna's shoe had snapped off leaving her strangely unbalanced. 'There's a cobbler's over there. Are you going to take the other one off or try and walk the way you are?'

'The way I am. If I hang onto your arms I won't overbalance again. Look at this – I've got a big hole in the knee of my best silk stocking.'

'Well, you've got more than enough to buy yourself several pairs of stockings and a pair of shoes.' Ellie was still shocked that Anna had accepted so much money from a complete stranger. The only people who did that worked in quite a different sort of profession.

'Don't be so stuffy, Ellen Simpson, why shouldn't we have a delicious lunch paid for by someone with more money than we'll ever have. I wouldn't have taken it if he'd been an ordinary sort of person.'

'Come on, let's not hang about here anymore, I'm beginning to feel a bit conspicuous.'

'Talking about conspicuous, don't the shop windows look hideous now they've been taped up. I can't see it making any difference if a bomb did drop on the street,' Elizabeth said.

'It's supposed to prevent the glass flying out over passing pedestrians but we won't know if it works until the Germans drop a bomb on London. I don't want to think about that, not today, I've come up here to spend time with my best friends and enjoy myself.'

*

The last pupil of the day had driven away on his motorbike at two o'clock. Jack finished up in the office and locked the door. Sid and Gladys hadn't been working today and he'd quite enjoyed being on his own for a change.

The two men from the village had finished digging out the foundations for the shelter. He would have liked to give them a hand but his arm was aching unpleasantly and he thought it would be better to give it a rest for the remainder of the weekend.

Mrs B was talking on the telephone when he walked in. She beckoned him frantically and he hurried over to take the receiver from her. She held her hand over the mouthpiece and whispered. 'It's someone from the Ministry – but I'm not sure which one. Will you speak to him?'

He took the phone. 'Jack Reynolds speaking, how can I help you?'

'Good man – just the person I wanted. I believe you're the owner of Glebe Farm flying school, is that correct?'

'It is. Who am I talking to?'

'Sorry, should have introduced myself. Charlie Rotherham – attached to the Air Ministry. I've been hearing good things about your school. We've already got half a dozen pilots who trained with you. We need you to cancel your civilian clients and instruct the RAF bods instead.'

'I'd be delighted to help out with the war effort. However, the instructor who trained most of those pilots is Ellen Simpson. You blokes okay to officially employ a girl instructor?'

'No problem at all. Miss Simpson has already proved her credentials. We'll be sending you the first half a dozen on Monday.'

'Do we get paid for doing this or is it considered our patriotic duty?'

Rotherham guffawed. 'Good God, old chap, you will be well remunerated for your trouble. Just keep turning out well trained pilots and the RAF will be happy to pay. We're going to need as many young men as we can lay our hands on. Someone will accompany the trainees with the necessary paperwork. Toodle-pip.'

The phone disconnected. Mrs B was lurking at the end of the passageway waiting to hear why a government official had been ringing him.

She was as thrilled as he was when he told her. 'Well I never! Imagine that! There will be brave RAF boys protecting this country because of our Ellie. Fred will be ever so proud.'

'She doesn't know yet. I hope Ellie will still be able to take time off. A young girl like her shouldn't have to spend every waking minute working.'

'When the war starts everyone will have to do their bit and I'm sure Ellie will be happy to do whatever she's asked. A fine young man like you, Mr Reynolds, will be volunteering yourself I expect.'

'Not initially, my job is to train pilots. I'll be doing far more good for the war effort turning out half a dozen every couple of months.'

'Will you have to teach them all the technical things as well?'

'I don't know until I meet up with the men in charge on Monday. Good job I brought back the appointment book – I've got to cancel everything in here.'

It took him the remainder of the afternoon to get messages and speak to everyone. One or two had been disgruntled, but mostly they'd understood that the defence of the country came first.

The blokes doing the Anderson shelter had finished so he thought he'd go and have a look at where they might be spending a considerable amount of time in the not too distant future. From what he'd heard Romford was close enough to both London and the RAF base at Hornchurch to be considered in danger from bombing when it started.

Fred had been talking about the leaflets he'd been getting on a regular basis from the Ministry of Agriculture telling him what he should be doing to prepare. Every spare bit of land was to be ploughed and planted with cereal crops or vegetables of some sort – especially potatoes. The fact that all his farms now had tractors would make things a lot easier.

Jack glanced at his watch. He had an hour before he needed to leave to meet the train. He could do with a pint and had plenty of time to visit the boozer near the station.

The door to the Anderson shelter had been left open but the daylight didn't penetrate the dismal, dark depths. There were wooden benches running down either side, and one at table height across the back. Presumably this was for candles and flasks of tea.

He stood at the top of the three steps but didn't venture any lower. He'd ask Mrs B to make sure there were blankets and pillows stored by the back door. There would be no point in leaving them down here as they would soon become damp and mouldy. Probably be a good idea to have a bucket with a lid just in case anyone wanted a pee. The thought of either Ellie or Mrs B using it made him smile. They would have to be bloody desperate.

Tea was being pushed back and replaced by supper – a cold meal tonight – as neither he nor Ellie would be back before five thirty. Fred was visiting one of his tenants after he'd finished work so had been quite happy with the arrangement.

Later at the pub he took his pint outside and sat on the wooden bench in the bit of scrubby grass that grandly called itself a garden. The interior of the pub was filled with miserable sods moaning about shortages, being called up, the bloody war and so on. It was far more pleasant to sit in the early evening sunshine and sip his warm beer and enjoy his own company.

Ellie enjoyed her day out with her erstwhile friends but came to the reluctant conclusion she no longer had anything in common with them. Although she'd been a qualified pilot while still at school she had kept that side of her life quiet. Mainly because her mother had only agreed to her being at the airfield if nobody else knew.

Elizabeth and Anna wanted only two things – to enjoy themselves and find a rich husband. Neither of those was of any interest to Ellie. As she'd already agreed to go to London and meet Greg – and had spent a lot of money on suitable clothes to go in – she wouldn't cancel this arrangement. However, she would make it perfectly clear she wouldn't be seeing him again.

She travelled in a ladies-only compartment and was relieved that nobody else got in with her. She'd deliberately chosen to come home before the rush hour. Tramping about shops and trying on clothes wasn't her idea of fun but at least she now had a lovely evening gown in oyster silk and two pretty cotton dresses.

The train steamed into the station on time and she was waiting at a door with the boxes containing her new purchases, plus her handbag hanging over her arm. She'd require the help of a porter to get everything off the train and she hoped Jack had bought a platform ticket and would be waiting to meet her.

Opening the carriage door was going to be tricky. This required her to put down the boxes in order to unhook the leather strap and lower the window so she could lean out and turn the handle on the outside. At least if the carriage door was open the train wouldn't depart with her still inside.

She was halfway through her tricky manoeuvre when he appeared in front of her. 'You're making a dog's dinner out of that, Ellie, let me help.' He lifted her out of the train as if she was a child and then stretched in and collected her parcels.

'I would have managed, eventually, but I'm glad you came onto the platform to help me. As you can see I've had a successful day's shopping.'

He grinned, making him look younger. 'Are we getting a fashion parade later?'

'Absolutely not. I can't tell you how glad I am to be back, I'm really not a city girl. If I hadn't already agreed I wouldn't go to London again.'

He tossed the boxes onto the back seat and climbed into the front leaving her to make her own way around to the passenger side. She had barely slammed the door before he engaged the gears and the car moved forward smoothly.

'I had a phone call from some guy in the Air Ministry, you'll be pleased when I tell you what he said.'

After he'd explained she could hardly believe it. 'Does this mean we will be able to stay open after the war's declared?'

'Certainly does – but I doubt any training will be done so close to London once the Luftwaffe arrive.'

'I don't want to think about that. As long as I can keep flying for a few more months I'll be happy. Do you think they'll commandeer our aircraft?'

'Very likely. A Tiger Moth is perfect for training – easy to fly but hard to fly well. Thank God we don't have to do more than teach the blighters to be pilots. They can learn to navigate and so on somewhere else.'

'I'm okay with a compass and map but have had no instrument training at all. You just peer over the side in our planes, but they can hardly do that in a plane with a closed cockpit.'

'I'll stay until the airfield is closed down. I'm hoping to be a fighter pilot rather than bomber or coastal command – but it's not up to me.'

The first thing they saw as the car drew to a halt in the yard at the back of the house was the humped mound of the Anderson shelter. 'I'd forgotten that was going up today. It seems strange to have this in the yard, and gas masks, when war hasn't even been declared.'

'Let's hope we don't have to use it. I shouldn't bother to investigate; it will only depress you. Mrs B is in charge of getting things ready in the event of an air-raid.'

The housekeeper was in the kitchen when they walked past. 'Did you have a lovely time, Ellie? Fred isn't back yet so you've plenty of time before supper.'

'I'm just going to put these away and change into something more comfortable and then I'll come down and give you a hand. And yes, I had a good time, thank you.'

'Go away with you, my girl, it's not your place to help me. I'm here to help you. I picked a whole basin of raspberries from the kitchen garden so we're having those for afterwards.'

Jack followed Ellie into her bedroom and dropped the boxes onto her bed. 'I'm going to sit in the garden until your dad gets back – why don't you join me when you're ready?'

The evening gown now seemed too glamorous for her, she should never have allowed her friends to persuade her to purchase it. The summer dresses were perfect, she'd not feel uncomfortable wearing either of those.

She pulled on a faded cotton skirt and an equally disreputable blouse, removed as much of the make-up from her face as she could – there was little she could do about her primped hair until she washed it. She was ready to join Jack in the garden. He'd made no comment about her new, sophisticated look – perhaps he'd not noticed. Greg would have paid her a compliment, but then he was interested in her and Jack wasn't. This was a good thing as she couldn't work with him if he started looking at her in that funny way men had when they wanted to kiss you.

Seventeen

The first six RAF trainees arrived at seven o'clock in the morning in a canvas covered truck. They were all young men, not much older than Ellie, and she thought that a couple of them would have been extremely rude to her if they hadn't been in the company of an officer. These two were offended at the thought of having a young woman instruct them, but this wasn't a problem as they ended up on Jack's list.

Instructing the three well-spoken, intelligent young men she was given proved to be a lot easier than teaching the mixed bunch that usually signed up. When they weren't flying they were studying manuals and textbooks. The Flight Lieutenant who'd accompanied them on the first day tested them on what they'd learnt and she picked up quite a lot of interesting information by just being in the vicinity some of the time.

'I say, Miss Simpson, how are your three bods progressing?'

'They are all doing okay, no problems so far, Flight Lieutenant.'

'Good show. We want them solo ASAP so they can log as many hours as possible before the next lot arrive.'

'We thought they would be here for several weeks – isn't that the case?'

'I'll be for the high jump if I didn't get them moved onto the next stage of their training in three weeks. I'm assuming you will use the de Havilland as well once they can fly solo.'

'Yes, of course we will. Excuse me, I'd better get on.'

*

Extra fuel was delivered without being ordered and the trainees brought their own packed lunches so all Gladys had to do was make endless pots of tea. Mrs B baked biscuits or made a cake every day for their pupils which added an almost festive atmosphere.

Ellie was logging more hours than she'd ever done before. The average needed for someone to go solo was around a dozen hours so this meant the first six achieved this by the end of week one. Then came the hard part. Virtually anyone could fly a Tiger Moth or Swallow when only required to do circuits but either she or Jack had to now make sure they could find their way using landmarks, a compass and map.

By the end of the second week all six trainees were ready to learn how to control the plane if it stalled, do aerobatics and land without the aid of an engine. So far no one had come to grief but Ellie was both physically and mentally drained.

'I'm supposed to be going away for the weekend. We're expected to work on Saturday so I'm going to ring Greg and cancel.'

They were driving home when she mentioned this to Jack. 'You deserve a couple of days off. It's already arranged. The Flight Lieutenant and I can deal with your three. As we don't work on Sunday, thank God, you'll be fine. Just make sure you get back here by Sunday evening.'

'I will. To be honest, I don't really want to go, I'm far too tired. The thought of gallivanting about town mixing with Greg's friends doesn't appeal.'

He patted her knee affectionately. 'You sound just like one of them when you want to. Pretend you're in a film, swan about in your new clothes and don't let them know who you really are. If you mention flying, don't say you're an instructor, just that you fly for pleasure.'

'I used to love drama at school so I think I could do that. I'll have to warn Greg; he'll think he's taking out a complete stranger otherwise.'

'What time is he coming to pick you up tomorrow?'

'Nine o'clock – I can have a lie in and listen to you and dad going off to work. Then I'll have a leisurely bath and get ready. Pretending to be a lady of leisure will make a pleasant change.'

She didn't pack her overnight bag until half an hour before Greg was expected. The least time her evening gown spent rolled up in tissue paper the better. She applied a little rouge and a smudge of lipstick, ran a brush through her hair, and she was ready.

The smart navy-blue dress with wide shoulders, matching belt and buttons down the front was, she believed, just right. The low-heeled shoes, also in navy, and matching handbag completed the ensemble.

'I'm going now, Mrs B, see you tomorrow evening,' she called as she dashed out with her case in her hand.

'Have a lovely time, Ellie, you deserve it.'

Greg met her at the door looking dashing in his RAF uniform. She dodged past and threw her case into the back of the open sports car before he had time to kiss her.

'You haven't told me where we're going, is it somewhere very grand?'

'I'm taking you to our London house in Hanover Square, then I thought we could have tea at the Ritz. We're meeting my friends for dinner at La Coquille and then we're going on to the 400.'

'The 400? I've never heard of that.'

'It's a nightclub. It's in cellars next to the Alhambra Theatre in Leicester Square. It's where everyone goes nowadays.'

'It all sounds very jolly. I'm not looking forward to meeting your parents as I'm sure they won't approve of me.'

'Relax, sweetheart, neither of them is in Town at the moment. Both my older sisters are married and busy bringing up a load of squalling brats and I rarely see either of them.'

'I'm sure they both have perfectly adequate nannies and don't have to spend time with the children if they don't want to. One thing my mother did tell me was that wealthy families spend as little time as possible with their children.'

'A bit harsh, Ellie, but more or less correct. But then you and your brothers went to public school, didn't you? I noticed that you don't always speak like your father.'

His implied criticism of her beloved father made her reply less than friendly. She spoke in a crystal-cut accent. 'Are you implying, Gregory, that my father is somehow inferior to you? I do hope not, because if that is the case then I shall insist that you return me to Glebe Farm immediately.'

His reaction was unexpected as he ignored her question. 'That's absolutely perfect, Ellie. Talk like that and no one will suspect...'

She interrupted him, no longer in the slightest bit amused. 'Suspect what exactly?' She shifted as far away from him as possible in the sports car and stared at him icily.

He finally grasped his error. She watched his neck, and then his face, turn an unflattering shade of beetroot. Instead of answering he swerved dangerously and screeched to a skidding halt on the side of the road much to the annoyance of the vehicles behind him.

He ran his finger around his collar and cleared his throat noisily. For the first time since she'd met him he wasn't in control of the situation. 'I'm sorry, I'm a complete ass, wide open mouth and both feet straight in.' He swivelled so he was facing her and she glimpsed moisture in his eyes. 'Please, will you forgive me for being so crass? I think the world of Fred; I wish he was my father. I love you and I'm sure my friends will too.'

He looked genuinely upset and she couldn't bear to see him like this. She reached out and touched his hand. 'It's all right, I'm just a bit touchy at the moment.' Then she remembered what she and Jack had been discussing last night. 'Actually, I think it might be a good idea if I do pretend to be from the top drawer. I won't be seeing any of them again and I don't want to put a damper on what will be my only jaunt around London.'

'You really don't have to – just be yourself.'

'Admit it, Greg, if they think I'm one of them, things will go more swimmingly, won't they? In fact, you need to fill me in on all the things I'd already know if I was a debutante.'

'That won't work, if you were on the circuit they would know who you are. If we're going to do this, let's think of a spiffing story.'

On the remainder of the journey to Hanover Square they came up with her new identity. She was Miss Ellie De Wolfe, recently returned from America where she'd been living with her grandparents.

'I've learned a few Americanisms from Jack which I can throw into the conversation.'

'I shouldn't do that, sweetheart, I doubt anything you've heard him say would be acceptable in company.'

*

They drove through an impressive archway into the courtyard at the back of his London home. He whisked her through the magnificent Georgian house and almost pushed her into the room she would be using that night.

'I expect you want to powder your nose and hang-up your evening gown. The bathroom and lavatory are at the far end of the corridor but you have a sink in your room.' His eyes crinkled endearingly at the corners as he smiled before continuing. 'Don't try and pee in it. A young lady, who shall be nameless, tried and the sink collapsed. I won't go into details but you can imagine how embarrassing it was for her.'

She couldn't repress a giggle. 'I promise I won't. I suppose the gentlemen can do so with impunity.'

'It's not something I've ever asked them – but I can assure you that I don't do it. Now, hurry up as I want to take you to a couple of exhibitions before we have tea.'

*

The afternoon was far more enjoyable than she'd expected. His interest in art surprised her, but then she scarcely knew him really. Tea at the Ritz, which included champagne, was delicious. She hadn't taken much persuading to drink a couple of glasses despite her usual avoidance of alcohol. When they jumped out of the taxi at his house she was more than a bit tiddly.

'I'm so full I don't think I'll be able to eat dinner tonight. I've enjoyed myself, thank you so much.'

He put a steadying arm around her waist. 'You shouldn't have had that second glass, Ellie, it's gone to your head. We don't have to be at the restaurant until nine o'clock. I suggest that you have a sleep for a couple of hours. I'll wake you in plenty of time to get ready.'

It was a good thing he guided her to her room as she'd never have found her way without his assistance. 'I only brought one evening gown – I hope I won't be overdressed.'

'I'm wearing a dinner jacket, so it won't matter what anyone else comes in. It's true, sometimes the ladies go home and change after dinner but only if they live nearby.'

'Don't you have to wear your uniform?'

'I should, but I doubt anyone from my station is going to see me. I'll have to wear it every day soon enough.

*

Greg pushed her gently onto the bed. As soon as she was prone her eyes closed and she fell asleep. He removed her shoes and loosened the belt of her dress. He was tempted to sit and watch her sleep but he thought that might be a bit much.

He left the door ajar and retreated to his own domain. He had a suite of rooms but still had to share the single bathroom. The servants had their own facilities on the ground floor but there were more of them than there were family. The way things were going families like his would have to do without live-in staff. Already the two parlour maids had left, as had the footman. He'd joined up, was now in the army, but he'd no idea why the girls had gone. Perhaps they too had become part of the growing armed forces.

He thought he might as well stretch out on the bed – he had nothing else to do. He rarely stayed in this house as it had been the sole domain of his unpleasant pater. Now he had bought himself a flat in Kensington he no longer used this place and no doubt he was now living there with his current mistress. The less he saw of any of his family the better – he had little in common with them. He had been brought up with the proverbial silver spoon in his mouth, had enjoyed the trappings of wealth, but if he was honest, found most of his so-called friends shallow and boring. As he drifted off to sleep he was smiling – Ellie and her family were far more interesting and likeable than his own.

*

He was roused from a light doze by the sound of the telephone ringing. Why didn't someone pick it up? By the time he reached the hall where it stood it had stopped. As he turned away it started again. His chest constricted and he was reluctant to lift the receiver.

'Dunlop speaking.'

'Thank God! It's Jack. Ellie must come home at once. Fred has had a stroke.'

'How awful – is he in hospital?'

'I'm ringing from Old Church Hospital in Romford. I couldn't find contact details for Neil or George.'

'I can get hold of Neil and he will know how to find his brother. We should be with you in an hour and a half.'

He pounded up the stairs and crashed into the bedroom. It was empty. For a moment he couldn't think why she wasn't there and then realised she'd properly gone to use the facilities. He could hardly bang on the lavatory door so would have to wait until she got back.

Her packing was done when she wandered in. 'Your dad's had a stroke and is in hospital. I've got to ring Neil. Come down when you're ready.'

She looked confused as if she hadn't taken in this information. Then she straightened and the bewildered look vanished. 'I'll be down in a minute. I'm fine – it was just a shock. Dad's always been so healthy.'

It took only a minute or two to be connected to Neil's Wing CO. Greg explained the circumstances and was told that his friend would get compassionate leave and would be at the hospital as soon as it could be arranged.

Ellie was on her way down as he tore up again. 'I'm just going to grab my kit bag. I'll need to return to base from the hospital. Good thing I didn't get out of my uniform.'

They'd been travelling for a quarter of an hour before he remembered he hadn't let his friends know that they wouldn't be joining them tonight. Bad form, but it couldn't be helped.

'I should never have come. I almost cancelled because we're so busy. Grandpa died from a stroke and he was in his eighties and Dad isn't even sixty yet.'

'My uncle had a stroke in his forties and is still going strong thirty years later. He made a complete recovery within a few weeks.' He squeezed her knee and she put her hand in his. 'I'm sure Fred will be up and about in no time.'

She didn't answer and when he looked there were tears trickling down her cheeks. He hated to see a woman cry but it was far worse watching Ellie. She left her hand where it was until they arrived at the hospital.

He put his arm around her waist to escort her inside. The overwhelming smell of disinfectant and boiled cabbage was unpleasant but everywhere looked pristine and the nurses were immaculate in their uniforms.

The receptionist directed them to the emergency department. She pulled away from him and ran forward when she saw Jack hurrying towards them.

She threw herself into his arms and for a moment Greg thought there was something between them. Then he arrived at their side and could overhear what was being said.

'It's not as bad as they thought, Ellie. He's come round and is able to speak clearly and doesn't seem to have any weakness in his limbs. I'm sorry I ruined your weekend.'

'I'm so glad that you were there for him. Greg is going to stay with us – and to tell you the truth I wasn't really looking forward to meeting his friends. I'd much rather spend time with him here.'

Greg offered his hand and Jack shook it vigorously. 'Good to see you, mate, but wish it was in better circumstances.'

'Can I go in and see him?'

'He's in there. He's going to be transferred to a ward in the morning.'

She dashed off leaving Greg with Jack. 'What's going to happen with the farm whilst Fred's incapacitated?'

Jack shrugged. 'I'm sure something will be arranged. I'm hoping his tenant farmers will look after things until he's better. I'll go now you're both here. I'll get Mrs B to leave out something on a tray for when you get back. I need to get things organised for tomorrow. The pigs will need feeding and the cows milking and I can't do that on my own.'

'I don't have to be back on base until late afternoon so if you've got some old togs I can borrow I'm happy to give you a hand. I've mucked out enough horses to know the right end of a shovel.'

Jack slapped him on the shoulder. 'Right – that means we can do the pigs so all I've got to do is find someone who knows how to milk a cow.'

'I can do that,' Ellie called from the door. 'I've helped dad hundreds of times. He's told me to go home so I know he's feeling better. If he has his way he'll get himself discharged tomorrow.' She turned and said goodbye to her dad and then came over to join them.

'I still think it would be a good idea, Jack, to speak to his tenants. We can manage Sunday but we will have to be back at work the next day so we'll have to have something in place by then.'

Stepping out into the bright sunshine after the gloom of the hospital made him realise there was still time to take Ellie out to dinner.

'We'll see you back at the house later. No need for Mrs B to do anything for us, we can get something to eat before we come back.'

With a casual wave Jack strode off without a backward glance. 'I don't want anything fancy, but I am hungry. What about fish and chips?'

'Perfect – although not quite what I had in mind when I planned this weekend. Is there somewhere nearby we can get a drink to go with our supper?'

'We can eat them in the garden at the pub – the landlord is quite happy for customers to bring their own food as long as they buy a drink or two.'

<u>Eighteen</u>

By Monday everything was under control at Glebe Farm. Dad was making such excellent progress he was going to be allowed home in a few days and the consultant was hopeful he would be back to work the following week.

Greg had mucked in, literally, and seemed less bothered by being up to his elbows in pig manure than Jack, who'd proved surprisingly squeamish. Anyway, Ellie was happy the livestock had been taken care of satisfactorily by the three of them.

She'd been sorry to see Greg go and when he'd kissed her goodbye she'd responded enthusiastically. He was going to visit when he had another twenty-four-hour pass. He was now officially her boyfriend and she was happy with that – as long as he didn't pursue the idea of marriage she would continue to go out with him. She rather liked the idea of having a handsome RAF officer as her beau.

*

Everything changed on September 1st as Hitler invaded Poland. She and Jack returned home, after hearing the news, in a sombre mood.

'I knew there was going to be a war with Germany, but always hoped it wouldn't happen. It's inevitable now, isn't it?' Ellie said.

'The sooner it starts the sooner we'll have that bastard beaten and things can go back to normal. Remember Flight Lieutenant Jackson said it doesn't change anything for us at the moment. We'll find out what's happening on the nine o'clock news tonight.'

Her dad was back at work but only doing a half-day. He seemed to be enjoying having the extra leisure time.

He was sitting on a deckchair reading the paper when they got in as if he hadn't got a care in the world, as if the world wasn't going to change irrevocably in the next few days. How could he be so calm when Neil, George and Greg would soon be in deadly danger?

'I suppose you two heard about Poland. Greg rang and said to tell you all leave is cancelled indefinitely so he won't be here for a while. Not heard anything from your brothers.'

'I don't think either Greg or George will see much action initially; it's going to be fighter pilots who are needed first,' Jack, beer in hand, said and prepared to sit in a deckchair that had been left folded up against the wall.

'No, not that one…' Too late. There was the sound of tearing canvas followed by a stream of extremely rude words as Jack ended up on his backside with the remains of the chair surrounding him.

'I tried to warn you.' She could barely speak through her giggles and her dad was also laughing too much to do more than splutter. When she recovered her breath, she continued. 'It was folded up because it is torn.'

'Ha bloody ha! It's not the first time I've had a sore arse, but if I'd dropped my beer I'd be really cross.' He extricated himself from the ruined deckchair and stood up. 'I'll sit on the grass if there aren't any more chairs. Do you intend to join me or continue to stand there sniggering?'

'I'll get the rug and find myself a cold drink and then I'll happily join you both.'

When she told Mrs B the housekeeper didn't laugh. 'He's been having a lot of pain in his arm, Ellie, I hope this didn't make it worse.'

'I've forgotten about his accident. He's not mentioned it to me but I'll ask him about it. It might have been all that heavy work he did the other week in the yard.'

'It's a salad tonight, why don't you eat it outside?'

'We will, but only if you agree to join us. You're part of the family now and I'm really not comfortable with you eating on your own in the kitchen whilst we sit in splendour in the dining room.'

'Fred said the same the other day so I'll be happy to join you. If you give me a hand, we could put up one of the trestles so we don't have to eat from our laps.'

As neither of the men could help, the shifting and carrying was left to Mrs B and Ellie. If you worked in a man's world it was only fair that you didn't expect them to run around after you when you were at home.

Whilst she put the finishing touches to the impromptu dining table she was watching her dad and Jack deep in conversation. She couldn't remember either of her brothers talking to him like that. If Mrs B could be considered an honorary Simpson, then so should Jack. He fitted in so well – was like another brother to her. She could talk to him about anything and not feel a bit embarrassed. If it wasn't for his fiery red hair she might actually believe she was related to him in some way.

They gathered in the sitting room to listen to the nine o'clock news. When the bulletin had finished she got up to turn the wireless off.

'War hasn't even been declared and we've got to use the blackouts from tonight. It's a good thing I've got everything ready. I'll go round and draw the curtains now,' Mrs B said and she dashed off to comply with the regulations.

'I can't believe thousands of little children are going to be sent into the country without their parents. I think it's really unkind.'

'Ellie, don't be daft,' Dad said. 'It's better they're homesick than killed by German bombs.'

She shuddered. 'I know you're right but imagine how many families are going to be miserable tomorrow. I suppose the RAF will be the first involved in any action. I'm not going to think about the young men we've got to know over the past few weeks. Worrying about Neil, George and Greg is quite enough for me.'

'None of the guys we train will be ready for action for a year or more – they just get the basics from us, then have to learn all the technical stuff and do the training for whatever aircraft they're going to be flying in future.'

'Your brothers joined up two years ago and have only just qualified,' Dad reminded her. 'I reckon it takes a long time to turn out the sort of blokes the RAF wants to fly their planes.'

'So people joining up now mightn't be active until the war's over. I just hope we've got enough trained men to do what's necessary over the next months.' Ellie didn't want to talk about it anymore. Her brothers and Greg could well be in action in the next few days and that was too dreadful to contemplate.

*

Greg had completed half a dozen circuits and bumps with his crew to make sure they were comfortable together. He'd also flown in formation with the other bombers in his squadron doing what was essentially a dry run for when they were ordered into battle.

He had been in the Officer's Mess when the Prime Minister made the solemn announcement that Britain was at war with Germany. This had been expected, but what wasn't was the order to attack German warships off Wilhelmshaven two days later somewhere he'd never heard of. Thank God all he had to do was fly the kite, Bobby Telford, his navigator would get him there.

The CO warned them that on no account should civilian establishments, either houses or dockyards, be bombed. The entire squadron set off at a run to the crew room and scrambled into their kit to wait for the lorry to drive them to the aircraft.

After a decent take-off he took the Blenheim to cruising height. 'Exactly where are we going, Bobby?'

'Across the North Sea, skipper, almost to Denmark. The warships are supposed to be in the Elbe estuary somewhere.'

'The weather's bloody terrible, I'll be surprised if any of us find the target, let alone hit it,' Greg replied gloomily.

At some point during the flight a squadron of Wellingtons joined them, but he only had their word for it as he could see sod all. Surely with over thirty bombers on the raid some of them would be successful?

This was the first time any of them had flown a genuine sortie and after the initial chatter the kite fell silent. Well – not exactly silent as noise from the engines filled the interior. The rain hammered against the fuselage and the occasional gusts of wind made the aircraft shudder.

The radio crackled into life reminding them to stay in formation. The navigation equipment was untested under genuine battle conditions and he hadn't the foggiest where they were. He just hoped Bobby was as good as he thought he was.

He glanced out of the cockpit window and was reassured to see Blenheims on either side of him. If he was lost, then so were they.

The flight commander's tinny voice told them they were approaching the target. They had orders to drop their bombs at will and preferably on a German warship and not in the drink.

Bobby and Jimmy, the rear gunner, remained calm, working efficiently together. Through the murk he spotted the warships. 'I think the battleship is the Admiral Scheer,' Jimmy, yelled over the intercom.

Greg held the kite steady. 'Let it go when you're ready, Bobby.' He waited for the lurch which would indicate the bomb had gone and instinctively corrected the kite.

Unfortunately, the Germans spotted them at the same time. Tracer fire from the fleet's anti-aircraft guns rent the sky. The flak was concentrated and he heard shrapnel clattering along the fuselage.

He peered through the perspex blister on the starboard side of the cockpit but saw no explosions beneath him. Suddenly the Blenheim lurched sickeningly to one side and he lost control. The bloody aircraft fell into a screaming dive and he thought they'd had it.

Somehow, he managed to pull the stick back and get them level again. 'Everyone okay?'

They responded that they were unhurt. 'There's a bloody great hole in the starboard wing, skipper,' Jimmy said cheerfully.

'Bobby, I need the course for home. We've done our bit so let's get the hell out of here.'

Squadrons stayed in formation on the way to the target so the fighters could protect them more easily. However, you made your own way back once you'd dropped your bombs. He hoped some of the others had had better success than him. It looked like bloody chaos out there.

Despite the hole in the wing the aircraft continued to respond to Greg's control almost normally. The return journey was more relaxed than the outward had been. Bobby handed him a spam sandwich whilst slurping his lukewarm tea from one of the thermos flasks.

'Take something to Jimmy – he needs to stay alert in his turret and a hot drink will help. I don't think we'll meet any German fighters in this rotten weather. But he's got to keep his eyes peeled just in case.'

He brought the crate in and touched down safely and then taxied it to the hangar. He wasn't the first back and he waited in the hut with the other aircrew for the rest of his squadron to arrive.

'My bomb was a dud, it hit the bloody target but didn't explode,' one of the pilots complained.

'I'm not sure I was anywhere near the target – although according to the equipment I was directly overhead,' someone else said.

'It was a bloody shambles, if you want my opinion,' the most recent arrival said. A chorus of agreement rippled around the already overcrowded shed.

'Let's get on the bloody lorry, the last bods are approaching the runway now. Let's see what's said in the debrief,' Greg added as he made his way through the fog of cigarette smoke to the door. He'd given up smoking himself as Ellie didn't like the smell of tobacco.

He squashed himself on the bench at the far end to allow room for everyone else to crowd in. The vehicle creaked and groaned as the last aircrew jumped aboard.

Bobby and Jimmy were crushed next to him. 'Imagine doing this at night in the middle of winter. It was bad enough in daylight.'

'I'm pretty sure I saw a Wellington crash into one of the warships, skipper. That lot have gone for a Burton,' Jimmy said glumly.

'It was a monumental cock-up, but at least our squadron all got back safely, if not entirely intact,' Greg replied.

The adjutant told them to stow their kit and then get a hot meal – the debrief would be in the lecture room in an hour. The atmosphere in the canteen was jolly. Nobody talked about the poor buggers who'd lost their lives in the other squadron, they were just pleased to be alive themselves.

The general consensus of opinion was that although several of the bombs had been duds, and that the navigational equipment was pretty useless, lessons had been learned. Hopefully the next time they were sent out on a mission these things would have been rectified.

His Blenheim wouldn't be airworthy until the hole in the wing had been repaired. Greg wasn't sure if this meant they wouldn't be on call or if a spare kite would be found from somewhere.

His brush with death made him think of Ellie and he joined the queue at the one telephone available so he could ring her. Hearing her voice would be enough to restore his faith in humanity. He was going to ask her to send him a couple of photographs – one he would pin in his cockpit, the other he'd keep in his wallet.

*

It seemed wrong that war had been declared on a Sunday but Ellie supposed it didn't matter what day of the week it was to Hitler. Most people would have been at church when the announcement was made but no doubt the news would have percolated into the congregation before the end of the service.

She wasn't a churchgoer, wasn't even sure she believed in the existence of a supreme being, but it couldn't do any harm to say a few prayers just in case. Next week she'd definitely go to matins even if it meant putting on a frock.

Mrs B had taken over the role of poultry keeper which meant Ellie's mornings were far smoother. Her trusty bicycle had been handed over to the housekeeper so she could pedal into the village or to the local shop when necessary.

Monday was like any other day and she and Jack set out for the airfield without mentioning the fact that Britain was now at war.

Gladys greeted them with a worried smile. 'My Bert says he heard that all civilian aircraft have been grounded. Does that mean I'm out of a job?'

'Nothing's changed here,' Jack told her. 'We're part of the war effort and they want us to continue to give the new recruits basic flying skills. When things kick off it will be different, but don't worry about it now.'

'My Bert says it will all be over by Christmas, so he doesn't know what all the fuss is about. He did his bit in the last lot but he volunteered for the ARP. He don't think he'll have much to do apart from making sure everyone's blackouts are working.'

'I reckon there'll be more accidents from people stumbling about in the dark now the street lights are turned off and the cars can't use their headlights,' Sid chimed in as he dropped his bicycle against the wall of the office.

'I'm just glad he's not going to be conscripted. My sister Vera says her Tommy has had his call-up papers and he's just had his fortieth birthday.'

'I don't think they'll want him, Gladys, it's just a precaution. The reservists for all the armed services and the young men will be wanted first,' Ellie reassured her.

'I'll get the kettle on then, I can hear the lorry coming down the track and the boys always want a good brew before they start.'

The RAF transport was, as always, on time and neither the cadets nor the Flight Lieutenant behaved any differently than they had the previous week. All six were now reasonably competent; this would be their last week at Glebe Farm Aero Club before they were sent on their way.

This week the trainees would be doing more than circuits and bumps – they would be staying up for a couple of hours and using a compass, map and landmarks to find their way. The Flight Lieutenant was going to accompany one of them and she and Jack would go up with two others.

The remaining three had to spend the time studying their textbooks. All six of them would be examined on what they'd learnt before they could go onto the next stage of the two-year training. A soldier received a few weeks learning to drill and follow orders instantly as well as how to use his weapon but would be ready for battle after that.

She didn't know how long it took for a sailor, but she doubted it would be much longer than that for a foot soldier. The RAF was the elite service and only took the best recruits.

On Wednesday evening she was sitting in the garden enjoying the evening sunshine when Mrs B called her to take a phone call. 'It's your young man, Ellie, he's ever so nice. You've fallen on your feet there, my girl.'

'Greg, I'm glad you called. I haven't heard from Neil or George and I really want to know what's happening.'

'I don't know about either of your brothers, but I don't think there's been much action in the air so far. My squadron has flown one mission and we all returned safely.'

Her stomach somersaulted. The thought of him having already faced the enemy when war had only been declared three days ago was quite horrid. 'I'm glad you're all right. I won't ask you what happened as I know you're not allowed to talk about your missions. Suffolk is a long way from Romford otherwise I'd borrow Jack's car and come and see you.'

'There's no need to do that, sweetheart, it's possible we're going to get leave after all. At least if nothing else happens over the next few days, we will. It's only a couple of hours in the MG and at the moment we can still get petrol on the base. I'm pretty sure it's going to be rationed soon which will make seeing you a bit tricky.'

'I could catch the train to Colchester, then you would only have to come halfway. In fact, as I'm not working at weekends anymore, I could come to Ipswich – that's not very far from Woodbridge is it?'

'How come you've got Saturdays off as well?'

'We've got this first lot of cadets ready to move on in a week less than they anticipated. So, unless things change, Jack and I have the weekends free in future. Even if you can't get more than a few hours we could still see each other.'

'That's spiffing news. I don't have to stay on the base unless there's a flap on, as long as I report in the morning and evening. Actually, I rang to ask if you've got any spare photographs of yourself you can send me.'

'Sorry, I haven't. We don't go in for photographs in this family, I'm not sure there's even a camera in the house.'

'You must have taken pictures of your aircraft for your brochures – I bet there's a camera at the airfield. Get Jack to take a couple of snaps of you in your flying gear; even better get some of you in the cockpit.'

'Wouldn't you rather have me looking glam in a pretty frock?'

'When I first saw you, you were wearing scruffy dungarees and still looked beautiful. You're not a silk stocking sort of girl and I want my photos to look like you and not someone else.'

She wasn't sure if she was offended or pleased by his remark. 'If we can find a camera I'll get Jack to take some of each and then you can make a selection when we meet.'

'I should have asked earlier, is Fred doing well?'

'Yes, he's itching to get back to full-time work but his doctor says he mustn't overdo it for another few weeks. It wouldn't matter, but the Ministry of Agriculture is demanding that all farms produce a lot more food but we're not getting any extra labour to help with this.'

'Britain imports a lot of our food and that's going to be difficult with the U-boats patrolling the channel. I bet they'll set up the Land Army again and then you'll be able to get some girls to help out.'

She heard someone talking to him and then he was back. 'I've got to go, there's a queue of bods waiting to use the phone. If I can get a twenty-four-hour pass I'll come to you, if not I'll see you in Ipswich for lunch. I'll let you know in the morning if I can meet you.'

The line went dead and she replaced the receiver. Being at war had changed everything – including her feelings towards him. Was it because he could be killed the next time he flew on a mission? Under normal circumstances she would have kept the relationship casual but now she thought she might be a little bit in love with him.

Nineteen

The second cohort of RAF cadets were as enthusiastic as the first and Ellie's life settled into a well-ordered pattern. Unfortunately, Greg had been unable to get away to meet her, but they spoke on the telephone a couple of times a week.

Jack had borrowed a camera and taken a roll of film, mostly of her in her work outfit as well as something a bit more elegant. He'd also taken a few shots of the RAF boys and the aircraft. She had been a bit uncomfortable asking him but he'd laughed at her hesitation. He'd said that they were like siblings and therefore she could ask him anything she might ask Neil to do for her.

Someone in the village had a dark room and the prints would be ready in a few days and Mrs B had volunteered to collect them when she next went to the shop.

At the end of the month Greg finally got a weekend pass. 'Now petrol's rationed I'm not sure how often I'll be able to drive down to see you after this. Nothing's happening here and we're all mooching about with nothing to do. The adjutant has told us we can have weekends free until further notice.'

'That's wonderful. Neil is coming Saturday so you'll be able to catch up with him. George has got himself a girlfriend too and is going to stay with her family. I feel sorry for the families of the soldiers and sailors. There are quite a few homes without their sons at the moment. It must be horrible knowing that if your boy is a sailor his ship could be torpedoed like the Athenia. Imagine deliberately targeting a passenger ship like that.'

'From what I've heard the army is having a grand old time in France. They've not seen any action either – it's mainly at sea. Chamberlain thinks we can blockade Germany and stop food getting through but it works both ways.'

This was a depressing conversation and she didn't want to think about Britain doing the same horrible things to German civilians. 'What time will you be here on Saturday?'

'Before lunch – if that's all right? I'll share with Jack like I did before. It's a good thing there's no food rationing yet or Mrs B might find it difficult to feed two extras.'

'I don't think we'll ever be short of food here, one of the advantages of being on a farm. I'm helping out at the weekends and so is Jack to try and make Dad take it a bit easier.'

'I'll do whatever you want. A bit of physical exercise will do me good. After the initial training RAF chaps don't do any square bashing or PE.'

'It seems so long since I've seen you, I'm really looking forward to Saturday. By the way, I've got the snaps you wanted – you can choose two when you come. Have you got one of you in your uniform I can have?'

'I think so, one of the bods took some last week.'

*

Ellie was busy cleaning out the cowshed when Greg turned up. 'Gosh, I didn't expect you before breakfast. I see you've changed into overalls – have you come to give me a hand?'

In some way she was relieved he had arrived when she was busy; they had become so close over the phone he would probably expect to kiss her whenever he wanted. She recalled her mother saying that well-bred girls didn't indulge in any sort of intimacy until they were formally engaged. Mum had been gone for months, and if she was honest, they were all much happier with Mrs B in charge. But the rules of etiquette were ingrained in Ellie's brain and however much she tried to ignore them they kept popping up at the most inconvenient moments.

'I'll do the sweeping now, you hold the hose,' he said and removed the stiff broom she'd been using from her unresisting fingers.

'You're lucky I've already mucked out, hence the manure all over my gumboots. Did you bring yours with you?'

'Don't own a pair, I borrowed the overalls and boots. I hope whoever owns them doesn't mind.'

'They're George's, which is a good thing as Neil will want his tomorrow.'

With both of them working the task was soon completed. She cleaned her boots and then did the same for him. Everything was ready for when the cows came in for milking that evening.

'Dad and Jack are doing the pigs – we got off lightly today.'

She and Greg had washed their hands and arms and when they'd stepped out of their overalls and wellingtons were clean enough to go inside for breakfast.

'Good morning, I hope you're all hungry, there were a dozen cracked eggs today that need to be eaten,' Mrs B said as they sat down.

'I'm starving; all that hard work gives a chap an appetite,' Greg replied.

There was a definite whiff of pig when her dad and Jack joined them. She was used to it but she wondered if Greg would wrinkle his nose. Instead he stood up and shook hands with both of them. 'Thank you for inviting me, Fred. It's good to see you Jack. I must say that both of you look tickety-boo.'

'There's no need to stand up for us, lad, you get on with your breakfast before it gets cold.'

Three chairs scraped against the flagstones as they sat down. Everyone was too hungry to chat and it wasn't until they were all on their third cup of tea that conversation started.

Ellie was about to ask what a Spitfire was like to fly when a car pulled up outside. She jumped to her feet. 'I'll go. Are we expecting anyone, Dad?'

'No, love, no one.'

She rushed outside and skidded to a halt. It was a police car. Two men in plain clothes emerged. Before she had time to take in what was happening a second car pulled up and the yard was full of uniformed constables.

*

Jack dropped his cutlery and surged to his feet. 'Another car's arrived. Something's up.' Ellie was still standing in the doorway which was a bad sign.

'Two police cars, Jack, what do they want here?'

'We're about to find out. One of the detectives is brandishing a paper – it could be a search warrant.'

Greg arrived beside them. 'I should leave this to us, Ellie, make yourself scarce.'

She remained exactly where she was.

The man with the paper strode up to them. He flashed his warrant card. 'Chief Inspector Dutton. I have a warrant to search these premises.'

'Why?' Ellie stepped forward and held out her hand but he ignored this gesture and just waved the document in front of her.

'Stand aside, miss, we intend to search these premises.'

The three of them stepped to one side and the detectives and uniformed men poured into the house. She waited until they'd gone before speaking again.

'Joe has told them about the envelope. They must have gone to the airfield and discovered it's no longer there.'

'It seems a bit odd they already had a warrant to search here.'

'I just got a glimpse and could see it was genuine but I didn't have time to see anything else.'

'I'm going to demand to read it,' Jack said, 'I think they're trying to pull a fast one. The warrant will be for the airfield not here.'

'I'll stop them searching, you get hold of the warrant and see if you're right,' Greg replied.

She glanced towards the kitchen where her dad and Mrs B were waiting. 'I'll take care of Dad, I don't want him involved so soon after his stroke.'

Dutton was about to go into the office. 'Hey, hang on a minute. You're not going anywhere until I've read that warrant,' Jack said loudly.

The policeman tried to bluster his way out of it but Jack insisted. He was right – the paper referred to the airfield not Glebe Farm. 'This is an illegal search, Chief Inspector, I demand that you and your henchmen leave this house immediately. I can assure you there will be a complaint made to the Chief Constable about this. There might be a war on but that doesn't mean you can break the law yourselves.'

'This is a matter of state security, sir, that overrides common law.'

'Quite possibly, but you barged in here under false pretences. Until you come back with the correct paperwork you can sod off.' Up to that point he'd been rather proud of his self-control, but now his anger had made him less polite.

The detective and his entourage slunk out and the three of them went outside and watched them drive away. He turned to Greg.

'Thank goodness Ellie kept Fred out of this. The shock might have given him another funny turn.'

Greg nodded. 'Mrs B will have seen everything. What are you going to tell her?'

'That it was a mistake?'

'That won't wash. She will have heard you throw them out. Remember she was here when Sir Reginald kicked up a stink a few weeks ago – perhaps we can say it was something to do with him.'

'That's a good idea. I'll tell her that fascist said we are communists or something and they were looking for evidence.'

'As Russia is now allied to Germany, that would make sense.

Ellie joined them and had been listening to the conversation. 'I told Dad to go outside until the police had gone. Jack, do you mind speaking to Mrs B? Greg and I have so much to catch up on.'

'Right. You go off. I'll take care of this.'

Greg put his arm around her shoulders. 'Shall we go for a walk, Ellie?'

They wandered off hand in hand leaving Jack to sort things out. As the whole bloody mess was caused by his uncle this was only fair. Mrs B accepted his explanation with a shrug. Fred had vanished somewhere.

'He might be someone important but he was a nasty bit of work, if you want my opinion.'

'I've got to go down to the airfield for a bit, but I'll be back in time for lunch.'

The other two had obviously forgotten that the office had been searched. The lock was probably smashed and the place ransacked. Good thing the RAF bloke took their paperwork home with him.

Sure enough the door to the office hung drunkenly from its hinges and inside lived up to his worst expectations. Even the safe had been opened – presumably Joe had given them the necessary numbers. The bookshelf, with the piles of newspapers where the envelope had once been hidden, had been tipped face first onto the floor.

If Uncle Joe had told them the numbers to open the safe then surely he would have said the envelope was in the newspapers? Jack hadn't been able to speak to his uncle or aunt since he'd been shot. He'd tried ringing a few times but the number was now disconnected. He could only think that his aunt had moved away. He had been reluctant to contact the police in case it drew attention to himself.

Today everything had changed. He no longer felt guilty about not passing on the incriminating list to the proper authorities. If they behaved like this then they were as bad as the fascists.

It took him a couple of hours to repair the damage. He dumped the old newspapers in the back of his car. Mrs B could use them to light the fires when winter came. Paper of any sort was going to be in short supply pretty soon.

He was disgusted to see that the petty cash tin had been emptied. This was another thing to go on the long list of complaints he intended to send to the Chief Constable of Essex. He knew exactly how much had been in the tin as Gladys kept impeccable records. He couldn't prove one of the constables had filched it. No doubt he would be told that an opportunist could have stolen it. However, if they hadn't left the safe door open then nobody else could have taken it. So whichever way you looked at it, they were culpable.

The door was fully functioning and he doubted Gladys would even notice what had happened. It certainly looked a lot tidier now the piles of newspapers had gone. Satisfied he'd done everything necessary, he locked the office and drove back to the farm.

He was just in time to pull on his overalls and go out and feed the pigs. From the sound of it Greg and Ellie were helping out with the milking.

*

Neil arrived the following day just as Mrs B was laying the table for the evening meal. Ellie rushed over and threw her arms around him.

'Thank goodness you're here, I was beginning to worry you weren't coming after all.'

He returned her hug, lifting her off her feet as he'd always used to when she was little. 'I would have stopped at a telephone box and given you a call if there was a problem. I had to wait until the chap who lent me this car got back. As Greg and Jack are here before me, does that mean I'm sharing with one of them?'

'You've got George's room. Everyone's changed tonight, including Dad. I don't suppose you noticed how smart I'm looking?'

'I can't remember the last time I saw your legs, little sister, but very pretty they are. You should wear a frock more often.' He lowered his voice. 'I take it that you and Greg are now officially going out together?'

'I suppose we are. I don't want to get engaged or anything like that, but if we're still together after the war then I might well marry him.'

'I should bloody well hope so. You can't keep the poor chap hanging on for years…'

'Don't say that, Neil, I couldn't bear to think it might continue for as long as the last one.' She'd heard quite enough of this depressing talk. 'As the weather is still so wonderful we've been eating outside. Dad and Jack set up one of the trestles that were used for the party. The vicar has lent us half a dozen old chairs from the village hall so we don't have to keep carrying them in and out every night.'

She slipped her arm through his and led him out to join the others. Greg stood up to greet his friend but Jack just waved his glass of beer and Dad did the same. Mum, if ever she returned, would be horrified at how her high standards had slipped in her absence.

'Welcome, son, there's a bottle of beer in that bucket of water waiting for you.'

Neil removed his jacket and tie and hung them over the back of a chair. 'I'll wear something more practical to help out tomorrow, Dad.' He gestured towards Greg. 'The uniform might be smart but it's too hot in this weather.'

'Are you as bored in Wattisham as I am at Hornchurch?' Neil asked Greg.

'Certainly am. At the moment we can't even do training flights for reconnaissance as the navigation system is being upgraded.'

'Are you up to strength?'

'Absolutely, what about you? I think fighter pilots are going to be in high demand when this lot gets going.'

*

The evening passed pleasantly enough but the men wanted to talk about the progress of the war – or lack of it. She didn't want to hear about the U-boat going into a bay in Scotland and sinking one of their ships. She tried to change the subject by waving the War Emergency information and instruction booklet that had arrived that morning in the post.

After attempting to read them a few bits from it about identity labels, evacuation, and so on she was told to find herself a book if she was bored.

'I'm going to help Mrs B with the chickens. We lost a duck last night to a fox and we want to make sure we get all the chickens in before it comes back again.'

Greg jumped up. 'I'll give you a hand. Are we going to try and catch the ducks and put them in the barn as well?'

Dad laughed. 'Good luck with that, son, the pond's four feet deep in the middle.'

'I'm happy to sit up with a shotgun and see if I can shoot it for you,' Neil offered, but he didn't look too enthusiastic.

'Don't worry about it. What we need are a couple of outside dogs – they would keep foxes away.'

Ellie was surprised but delighted by Dad's suggestion. 'I bet there are plenty of strays in London that need good homes, especially with so many families moving out of the city last month. We could go to Battersea tomorrow and find two that come from the same home so will already be friends.'

'I'll leave it to you then, love, but don't get anything vicious. But as they can't come in the house there's no point in getting soft dogs.'

She was bubbling with excitement. Having dogs at Glebe Farm would be a welcome distraction from what was going on in the world.

Most of the chickens were already in the barn and it didn't take long to shoo the rest in. The ducks were all safely settled on the small island in the centre of the pond and should be safe from attack tonight.

'I'll have to take Dad's truck to London. I can hardly put them in the back of your MG.'

'It might not be open on Sunday,' Greg said.

'I'll give them a ring in the morning. Someone has to be there every day to look after the animals and I bet

Sunday is one of their busiest days as most people get the day off from work.'

'Where will they live if they can't come in the house?'

She pointed towards the empty stables. 'In one of those – they'll be lovely and warm even in winter. Come on, I'll show you.'

Although the loose boxes hadn't been in use since the shires were sold they were still weatherproof and ideal to use as a kennel. She unhooked the top half of the door and hastily closed it again. The sudden scuffling inside had made the hair on the back of her neck stand up.

'There are rats in here. Battersea has cats as well – I think I'm also going to bring back two of those. Mum wouldn't have domestic animals on the premises. I'm pretty sure it was her that insisted the horses went as well. Strange really, coming from her background one would have thought she would want to go out with the hunt, but as far as I know she didn't ride.'

He didn't answer. He was standing so close she could feel his breath on the back of her neck. A wave of unexpected warmth surged around her. Then his arms encircled her and she forgot all about rats, cats or dogs. His kiss was different this time, harder, more demanding and she responded. She was breathless when he eventually raised his head.

'Ellie, darling, you know I've fallen in love with you.'

She rested her face against his shoulder until her breathing steadied, unable to respond immediately.

'God! I'm sorry. I'm rushing things…'

'No, Greg, you're not. I think I'm beginning to feel the same.'

His arms tightened but she raised her hands and pushed against his chest. Instantly he released her. 'Please don't rush me, this is all new to me. I've never even had a boyfriend before, I need time to get used to these feelings.'

He dropped a kiss on the top of her head. 'I'll wait as long as you want, sweetheart. Now I know I'm in with a chance, that you're not falling for Jack, I'm happy.'

'Jack? Good grief, I've not even considered him in that way. I like him a lot, but he's just another big brother to me, nothing more.

<u>Twenty</u>

Ellie returned from Battersea delighted with the animals she and Greg had chosen. 'I can't believe we were able to find two cats and two dogs that had come from the same home.'

She turned and peered through the grimy window at the back of the cab. The two female cats, both black and white, were curled up with the two long-haired brown mongrels as before.

'We were lucky as the chap in charge said they don't usually let animals out until they've been given a proper check by the vet. As we wanted all of them he made an exception.' He was driving as Ellie wasn't confident enough to find her way through London.

'They come from a good home. It's sad that the family has been split up like this. The children have been evacuated and their dad is with the BEF in France. The mum has taken a job in a factory and doesn't have time to look after them anymore.'

'The fact that the dogs are called Jack and Jasper might well prove amusing – or possibly confusing. Which reminds me, sweetheart, is Jack Reynolds a permanent fixture in your house? I'm surprised he hasn't found himself different lodgings now he's recovered.'

'It's convenient having him with us. I get lifts and Mrs B has my bicycle. He and my dad are thick as thieves and Jack's been a godsend since Dad had his stroke.'

Greg squeezed her knee and she glanced across at him. 'I'm glad he's there. He can take care of himself, and you, if the need arises. I don't think we've heard the last from that police inspector. He was a thug and he'll be back at some point with the proper papers.'

'Jack said they wrecked the office – they'd better not try that in my house. I think the letter we sent to the Chief Constable might put them off for a bit; he should get that tomorrow or the next day and hopefully will reprimand the inspector.'

'I shouldn't be too sure about that, Ellie, there's a war on and the normal rules and regulations no longer apply. If they know what was in the envelope, that it contained the names of possible traitors, they'll tear the place apart trying to find it.'

A flicker of unease ran through her. 'I should have realised that. If there's a black mark against our name for any reason then this could be the end of my brothers' careers in the RAF.' She swallowed the lump in her throat as something else occurred to her. 'Do you think we'll still be able to work with the RAF?'

'I've no idea, but I doubt anything will happen for a few days. You'll have to talk to Jack.'

'In which case I can think of only one solution. Being raided by the police again might cause Dad to have another stroke.'

*

The cats, Sooty and Spot, purred when she lifted them out of the truck. The two dogs bounded after them and immediately ran to the bushes to relieve themselves. She had no need to call them back as they were bouncing around her feet minutes later.

She dropped the cats in the stable and the dogs dashed in behind their feline friends. She hastily closed the bottom half of the stable door. 'The man at Battersea said we should keep the cats shut in for several days, but I don't think they'll run away as long as the dogs are here.'

Neil and Jack had heard them arrive and came to inspect the new arrivals. 'Isn't Dad coming to see them?'

'He's asleep, seemed a pity to wake him. Jack and I are going to do the milking tonight. Will you and Greg feed the pigs?'

'Of course. Before we go inside there's something we have to talk about.' She led them to the far side of the yard and into the barn that had been used as a bar the last night her mother had been at Glebe Farm.

'I've come to a decision and I hope it's the right thing to do. Neil, our mother abandoned us without a second thought to go and live with a traitor. I don't think we owe her anything. What's important is to protect Dad from any unnecessary shocks. Do you agree?'

'I do. I think I can guess what you're going to suggest but I'll leave you to tell us in case I'm wrong.'

'I didn't tell any of you but I made a copy of that list before I hid it. I'm not sure why I did, but I thought it might be important later.' She looked from one to the other and they were all watching her intently.

'I think we should get in touch with someone in authority and tell them exactly what's happened. Give them a copy of the names on the list. I know it's not an ideal solution, and might well have unpleasant repercussions, but it's the only thing that will protect Dad.'

Jack looked dubious, not surprisingly, as his family was up to their necks in the conspiracy. Greg moved until he was standing directly behind her; his solidity was a comfort.

Neil broke the silence. 'Good God! You can't do that, Ellie. This could ruin us.'

'It won't do anything to us financially, and I don't see why any muck will stick. Nobody around here is aware that we're related to Sir Reginald; even if it does get in the national papers it shouldn't make any difference.'

'You're naive if you think a nosy journalist won't ferret out that George and I are related to him.' Her brother's eyes were hard – he looked like a stranger.

Instinctively she leaned back and Greg's arms encircled her waist giving her welcome reassurance. However, it was Jack who stepped in with further bad news.

'I've not had the opportunity to tell you that the RAF cadets won't be coming to us anymore. As of today, Glebe Aero Club is done. It has nothing to do with the other business as far as I know, it's a directive from the War Office. I'm arranging to sell the aircraft and I've already told the staff. They will be coming in tomorrow to collect their last pay slip and wages.'

She turned into Greg's embrace and rested her wet cheek on his shoulder. The dream was over. Civilians couldn't fly anymore and from now on she would be a farm worker.

*

Jack hated seeing Ellie cry, but it wasn't his responsibility to comfort her. He hadn't told her the worst – that was his problem not hers. His aunt had written to him saying that his uncle had been charged with blackmail and receiving stolen goods. He'd pleaded guilty and been sentenced to five years. It was unlikely he'd ever hear from either of them again as she'd failed to provide a return address on her letter.

He didn't think he could remain at Glebe Farm and he had nowhere else to go. The money from the sale of the aircraft would be sufficient to keep him solvent until he joined the RAF. Although he wasn't sure the nephew of a convicted criminal would be welcome in the elite branch of the armed forces.

'I'll move out as soon as I've sold the aircraft….'

She wrenched herself away from Greg and rushed over to him. 'Please, Jack, you can't go. Dad needs you to help him on the farm. Won't you stay until you join the RAF? I heard on the wireless that only reservists, volunteers and men between twenty and twenty-one are needed at the moment. You should be able to stay for another few months.'

He couldn't refuse her tearful appeal. 'I'd love to stay but you and Fred had better decide after you hear the rest of my news.'

Over a much-needed cuppa he told them and was surprised that they sympathised rather than condemned.

'I don't care about Joe Cross, lad, as far as I'm concerned you're one of the family. You stay with us as long as you want to – you're a natural when it comes to farming and I'd be sorry to see you go.'

This compliment didn't go down too well with Neil and Jack didn't blame him. The inference was that Fred's sons were somehow lacking and that he favoured a stranger.

Ellie, who was sitting next to Greg on the sofa, endorsed her father's remark. 'There's no need to look so po-faced, Neil, you know that neither you nor George are at all interested in farming. You've made it very clear that you intend to make flying your career. You should be pleased Jack's taking an interest and is prepared to help out. In case you haven't noticed we're already shorthanded, and with more land under cultivation it's going to get even more difficult.'

Her brother almost smiled but he still didn't look happy. 'Now you can't fly anymore you can work here – you know more about farming than either George or I do.'

They all assumed he was going to stay and that he didn't have any plans of his own. Jack supposed he could hardly refuse after what both Fred and Ellie had said. Now Greg looked less than delighted. Bloody hell! Whatever he decided to do was going to upset someone. He decided to change the subject completely to give him time to make up his mind.

'Is anyone going to tell Fred what you're planning to do, Ellie?'

*

Before Neil could prevent her, she told her dad everything, including that she thought they should hand over the list of names before the police returned.

'As it happens I had a letter from a solicitor this morning acting for your mother. It seems she wants to

269

divorce me on the grounds of cruelty. I've never raised my hand to her so I'm not sure what that's all about.'

'Dad, how dreadful. What are you going to do? Will you contest it?' Ellie asked.

'The marriage is over; I don't want her back and she'll be happier with her own sort. Doesn't do to marry out of your class, Ellie, you need to remember that.'

There was an uncomfortable silence but Fred seemed unaware that he'd dropped a clanger. Fred carried on oblivious to the embarrassment he'd caused his daughter and her boyfriend.

'If I agree then I don't have to pay any maintenance, make a settlement or pay costs. Seems fair enough to me.' He nodded and looked better than he had for weeks. 'You go ahead and do what you think's right, love, it's nothing to do with us now.'

'I'll do it, if you like. Might be better coming from me as it was my uncle got us into this mess.'

'Jack, would you? I'll go and get the list for you. Perhaps you could do it from the telephone at the airfield?'

'Good idea, Ellie.' He stood up and was collecting the empty mugs when Mrs B put her head around the door. 'As you weren't here for a proper Sunday lunch, Ellie, we're having it now. In the dining room tonight as it looks like rain.'

No more was said about the police or the divorce which was a relief. Greg and Ellie went out to see to the new arrivals and Neil was on the telephone talking to his brother.

This gave Jack an opportunity to speak to Fred alone. 'When I give this list of names to the proper authorities they might still decide to prosecute all of us for not handing it over when we first had it. We could be charged with treason...'

'Don't be daft, Jack, it won't come to that. They'll be so glad to have these names that they'll forget it's taken us a few weeks to pass them over.'

Jack left him to his cocoa. Despite being told that he was one of the family, tonight he felt he was intruding. Things would be easier when Greg and Neil went back to their bases tomorrow morning.

*

Ellie didn't want to go to the airfield but Jack persuaded her. 'You've been working with Sid for years; you owe it to him to say goodbye.'

'All right, I'll come. It's going to be unbearable seeing the planes and not being allowed to fly them anymore.' She swallowed the lump in her throat as they pulled up for what would be the last time outside the office.

The place was deserted – no sign of Sid or Gladys. 'This is very strange, they are usually here by now,' she said.

'I went to see them yesterday morning so they already know what's going on. I told them to come at ten o'clock to collect their wages and have a final cup of tea with us.'

She was clutching a cake tin and put it down on the packing case. 'In which case, we've got an hour to take everything out of the office. I'm surprised you have buyers for the aircrafts as no one can use them until the war's over.'

'The Swallow is going to be locked in the hangar – but the two Tiger Moths are being bought by the RAF. They're sending a couple of blokes over to collect them sometime today.'

The thought that one of the aircraft would remain was a comfort. When this wretched war was finished she'd be able to fly again.

'I'd like to buy the Swallow, Jack, how much do you want for it?'

'I've signed everything over to Fred; he was cheated by Joe and this is one way of putting things straight.'

'I hope The Ministry of Agriculture doesn't insist that the strip's ploughed up to grow potatoes.'

'It's possible, but hopefully they won't realise it's part of the farm.'

*

Saying goodbye to Sid was difficult, but he promised to come back when things were back to normal so she could start the flying club again. Gladys was tearful but resigned.

'My Bert says I can get decent money working in a factory, but I think I might try the telephone exchange. What are you going to do, Ellie? Join the WAAFs?'

'I wouldn't be let anywhere near an aircraft so I'm going to stay at home and help my dad with the farm. He's got the pamphlets about the Land Army which will be starting up again in the New Year so I'll not be the only woman working on the farm.'

'I've been asked to work at Hornchurch – I'm a bit long in the tooth – but ground engineers are in short supply so I'm going to be working in a civilian capacity. Johnny has joined up,' said Sid.

'I'm glad everyone that worked here has found something to do. Jack's staying at the farm for the moment but will join the RAF eventually.'

Jack was in the office sorting out the necessary papers to transfer ownership of the two Tiger Moths so wasn't part of the conversation. In fact, he'd been in there most of the morning making calls and she supposed that one of them was about the list of names.

Just after one o'clock everything was done. Jack checked the hangar was secure and she did the same for the office. He solemnly handed her the keys. 'This is all yours now, Ellie. Something to look forward to.'

She was too upset to answer, just nodded and scrambled into the car blinking back tears. He left her to sniffle and didn't speak until they pulled into the yard.

'It took a while but eventually I was connected to someone in intelligence. I had to go through everything that happened again. Then all I had to do was read out the list of names. They said as far as we're concerned the matter is over.'

She blew her nose loudly. 'Today's been the end of everything I love. I've lived for blue skies and Tiger Moths since I was a child and now it's all over. Mum has gone, the airfield has gone – from now on I'm just a farm girl.'

'Don't feel so sorry for yourself. You're young, healthy, have got plenty of money in the bank and whatever happens next, Glebe Farm is going to carry on as usual. When the bombing starts, I doubt anything will drop here.'

She glared at him. 'I'm not stupid, Jack, I know that. But, unlike you, Greg and my brothers will be in grave danger. Farming is a reserved occupation so you can hide away here for the duration of the war.'

Again, his reaction surprised her. Instead of being angry he laughed. 'I'll do my bit – don't worry about that. But I'm more use working here now than I would be hanging around at a base with a lot of snooty public-school boys.'

Twenty-one

Now that petrol was rationed, visiting by car became almost impossible. There was still fuel for the tractors but not enough for pleasure jaunts. Ellie met Greg most weekends in Ipswich, which she could reach by train quite easily.

Then the weather worsened and travelling anywhere became more difficult. At the end of November, after a particularly unpleasant journey on the train, Ellie had decided to tell Greg she wasn't coming again until the spring. He had abandoned his sports car in favour of the train himself.

The cinemas had initially been closed but the government had now reopened them as they believed the morale of the population was important. When they came out of the picture house after seeing *Wizard of Oz* they headed for the usual teashop.

They burst into the cafe bringing a gust of icy air behind them. The half a dozen customers glared at them and Greg hastily pulled the door shut.

'I think it's going to snow, it's certainly cold enough,' Ellie said as she removed her outdoor garments. 'It's horrible on the train. There's no heating and I never get a seat. The carriages are always crammed with men in uniform carrying bags.'

'Don't a lot of them get off at Colchester?'

'The soldiers do, but the airmen get off at Ipswich or stay on the train. There must be loads of bases in East Anglia.'

'Not that many, they're mostly in Lincolnshire. But freshly trained ground and air crew are arriving all the time. Although nothing much is happening, we all know it's coming. Don't forget we're sending our lot all over the Commonwealth to train and some overseas pilots have started to arrive in England.'

The waitress didn't need to ask for their order as they always had the same thing – scones, sandwiches and cakes plus at least two pots of tea. Ellie wondered how much longer these delicious treats would be available.

'Jack is leaving next week; did I tell you?'

'You mentioned he'd been for an interview at Lord's cricket ground and I can't see why they wouldn't be pleased to have such an experienced flyer.'

'He doesn't have to do the basic training so won't be sent abroad. Do you think it will take as long for him to be active as it did for you and my brothers?'

'I shouldn't think so – he's already got more hours in his log book than most of us. As he's done acrobatics he'll be ideal as a fighter pilot. I seem to remember him telling me he's got instrument training too.'

'He has. He's also qualified as a flight and ground engineer. He doesn't seem to mind what he does as long as it's aircrew.'

'Is something bothering you, sweetheart, you seem a bit quiet today?'

'I've decided I'm not coming to Ipswich again until the spring. I'm needed on the farm and can't really take a whole day off anymore.'

He reached across the table and took both her hands. 'I'm surprised you've come as often as you have, Ellie. I can still ring a couple of times a week and you can write to me. I've got Christmas free and was rather hoping I could spend it with you.'

'Of course you can, but don't you want to be with your family?' He rarely mentioned his parents or his older sisters and she didn't think he was particularly close to any of them.

'I haven't seen them since the summer. Ma has pushed off to America and Pa is doing something at the Home Office. Both my sisters have retreated to the country with their families so seeing them isn't an option even if I wanted to.'

'If your father is going to be on his own…'

'He'll be with his mistress. The last person he'd want to spend time with is his son.' Greg didn't sound particularly unhappy about this.

'Mrs B is already planning something special. Even the government is telling us to celebrate and not give the

Germans the satisfaction of seeing us frightened over the festive period. Which reminds me, I think that she and my dad are getting rather fond of each other. I wouldn't be surprised if they make a go of it when the divorce is finalised.'

'I'm hoping you might change your mind as well. I love you and want you to marry me.'

She withdrew her hands and put them in her lap. She hated to disappoint him but she wasn't ready to become anyone's wife at the moment. 'I promise I'll think about it. When I do want to get married it will be you who's top of my list. Now, can we talk about something else?'

His smile made her toes curl. 'Then I'll settle for that. How many on this list of yours?'

She smiled back. 'Oh, dozens, I'm a very popular girl. It's the smell of pigs that attracts men you know.'

His laugh turned several heads but they ignored the disapproving looks. No one seemed to laugh much nowadays. He raised her hands and kissed her knuckles. Then released her and carried on as if nothing momentous had just happened.

'Will Neil or George be home for Christmas?'

'Neil is coming but George is going to his fiancée's family. Jack thinks he might be able to get home as well. I hope so as he's part of the family now. He doesn't have anyone else and I think of him like another brother.'

'Do you have any family traditions I need to be warned about?'

'My mother disapproved of anything remotely frivolous so we never had a tree or decorated the house. This year is going to be different. I suppose we'll still go to church as it would look bad if we didn't, but apart from that I've no idea what Mrs B and Dad have planned for us.'

'What about gifts? Also, what should I bring to add to the feast?'

'Don't go mad; just bring something small for each of us that can go under the tree. If you can get hold of any chocolates, fancy biscuits or something like that, that would be marvellous. We always have a goose which Dad prepares. I don't mind doing anything on the farm apart from ringing the neck of any of the chickens, ducks or geese.'

'I should think not – it takes a strong stomach to do that. To tell you the truth, although I'm a good shot, I don't like killing anything which is one of the reasons my pa thinks I'm a disgrace to the family.' His smile faded and he looked away pretending to need something from his pocket.

There was no need to ask why he looked so sad. He was thinking that he was going to have to drop bombs on people, which would be far worse than slaughtering a game bird or two.

'Will you have enough petrol to drive down? Although even with the top on your MG is horribly cold.'

'It depends how much of my petrol ration I've got left. What I need is an old bike so I can cycle to the pub and not have to use the jalopy.'

'I'm sure there are a couple of dilapidated cycles somewhere on the farm. My brothers both had bikes and they certainly haven't taken them with them. I'm not sure how you'd get one to your base.'

'If I come on the train and you picked me up at Romford and then give me a lift back in your dad's truck, I can travel in the guard's van. It's only five miles from Needham Market station at the other end.'

The thought of having his own bicycle had cheered him up. Now she knew exactly what to give him for Christmas. One of the bikes could be renovated and would be an ideal present.

They walked hand-in-hand to the station and he waited until she boarded hers before crossing the line and catching his own train. Every time she saw him her feelings grew stronger and she thought if he asked her again to marry him she might agree. To be his fiancée – not to get married until the war was over.

She was squashed into a corner of the compartment by an overweight lady with what looked like a bowl of fruit attached to her hat. Watching this kept her amused until it was time to fight her way to the exit. The only good thing about being so crowded was that you hardly noticed the lack of heat.

The morning of Jack's departure arrived too quickly. Mrs B cooked an extra special breakfast and Dad came in from the fields to eat it with him.

'I'm going to miss you, son, even with Ellie working here full-time it's hard to keep up. It will be a bit easier when they send us a couple of land girls.' Dad waved his fork full of bacon in the air. 'I don't think I told you, love, that there's going to be some sort of hostel in the village and the girls are going to live there so we don't have to provide accommodation.'

'We've got plenty of room here, I wouldn't have minded them staying. I think we're too close to London to get any evacuees.'

Mrs B put a rack of hot toast on the table and they all helped themselves. 'When I was in the village the other day they were talking about evacuees. It seems that half of them have gone home again and they're going to have to re-open the schools in London after Christmas.'

'I've got to leave in twenty minutes, Ellie, if I'm going to catch the train. I've got to take a load of examinations in the next few weeks on navigation, instrument flying and so on. If I pass I can go straight to training in whatever capacity they want me.'

'If you had a choice, Jack, what would you prefer to do?'

'A fighter pilot, of course, and I'm keeping everything crossed that they agree I'm best suited for that.'

'You take care of yourself, my boy, and don't volunteer for anything – that's my advice.' Her dad dropped his cutlery and drained his tea in one gulp. 'I've got to get back to work. Goodbye, Jack, hopefully you'll be here for Christmas.'

He stomped out so quickly Jack didn't have time to reply. 'It's going to be hard for all of you having four of us in the firing line.'

'At least you're all based in England. The army in France is freezing in this terrible weather because they haven't got enough blankets. But even that's better than being a sailor.'

He flung his kitbag into the back of the car. 'Next time you see me I'll be in uniform. Take care of my car, no speeding.'

'It's very kind of you to leave it here for me to use. I promise I won't do anything silly. Aren't you going to drive?' He'd opened the passenger door.

'No, no point. It's yours for the duration.'

The car was quiet on the short journey to Romford as neither of them had anything more to say – it had all been said over the last few days.

She pulled up expertly by the kerb and twisted to say farewell. To her surprise he leaned across and cupped her face in his hands and then kissed her on the lips.

'Goodbye, Ellie, I'm going to miss you.'

Then he was out of the car and striding away laughing at her embarrassment. Several heads turned as he made his way towards the entrance of the station. Until he'd kissed her she'd not seen him as anything but an adopted older brother.

She ran her tongue along her tingling lips, not quite sure how she felt about him now. Why had he done it? Had he come to view her as a potential girlfriend and was letting her know she had two suitors? This idea was ridiculous – he'd just been teasing her. He was well aware she was in love with Greg.

The car skidded twice as the first heavy flakes of snow began to fall and she was glad to be home without anything worse happening.

The mood at church yesterday had been sombre. Despite the fact that nothing much had happened; everyone was expecting the Luftwaffe to arrive at any moment and drop poisonous gas on them. The women talked about shortages and the fact that rationing would be starting in January. Even those with husbands or sons at sea, or in France, appeared to be more concerned about the lack of basic food in the shops, than they were about the safety of their loved ones.

If Dad hadn't had his stroke a few months ago she thought she would've joined the Women's Auxiliary Air Force – WAAFs, but she wasn't going to leave him until she was certain he was completely fit. Anyway, being so close to aircraft but not being allowed to fly them would be upsetting to say the least.

Mrs B waved to her through the kitchen window and held up a cup. Ellie nodded. She could have a quick drink whilst she put on her overalls, thick socks and gumboots. She'd taken over the pigs. They were intelligent creatures and she enjoyed spending time with them. However, she was sure she never quite got rid of the smell however much she washed.

'It won't be the same with Jack gone, I expect you'll miss him too,' Mrs B said as she handed over a cuppa.

'I certainly will – but I think that my dad will miss him most. I wish he was as fond of Greg as he is of Jack.'

'Your young man is a bit grand for Fred, but he likes him well enough. Jack's more down-to-earth and just fits in better at Glebe Farm.'

'Everyone was moaning about shortages at matins. Mrs B, are you going to be able to get enough together to make it a memorable Christmas?'

'I've already made a cake and the pudding. We're lucky here, we won't go short. Fred got a letter from the Min of Ag saying all the produce has to go to designated shops and we can't sell from the door anymore.'

'I expect we'll have enough cracked eggs to keep us going and I'm sure nobody will notice when we take milk and cream. Last time I looked in the pantry there were two sides of bacon hanging up. I'm assuming we can keep those and just have to give up any future meat.'

'I should blooming well hope so, you're all working ever so hard, out in all weathers, and you deserve to eat properly.'

Ellie finished her tea. 'It's a good thing I've got several pairs of overalls. I'd hate it if I had to put on smelly ones.'

*

The weather continued to deteriorate and as soon as the snow thawed a fresh lot fell. The Spitfires from Hornchurch continued to fly over in formation and every time she heard them approaching her stomach lurched. Her ears were telling her these were friendly planes but all the talk of imminent bombing was making her nervous.

The week before Christmas Greg missed his planned evening call. 'He always rings at seven o'clock, Dad. I shan't be able to sleep tonight worrying about what's happened.'

'Don't fret, love, it won't change anything. We've got four young men to worry about and it's going to drive us daft if we panic every time there's a missed call. Believe me, we'll hear soon enough if anything's wrong.'

'I hate this war and it's hardly started yet. The Prime Minister keeps saying he's confident of victory, but I don't see how that's possible. I read in the Daily Sketch the other day that hundreds of civilians have been killed because of the blackout – far more than soldiers, sailors or airmen.'

'It's silly buggers going too fast when there's no street lighting or headlamps on the cars. I reckon that things will get better on the roads as petrol rationing gets tighter.'

Mrs B always joined them in the sitting room after she'd finished her chores. It was cosy in there with the log fire crackling away in the grate. Dad looked happier than she'd ever seen him and she was glad for him.

To give them some time alone in the evening she'd assumed the task of making the cocoa. After she'd taken their drinks into them she went to bed. Usually she was so tired she fell asleep immediately, but tonight she couldn't settle.

She was downstairs and getting the breakfast on the go before Mrs B appeared. At seven o'clock, her usual time for coming down, the telephone rang.

'I'll get it. No need for all of us to get cold in the passageway.'

Her heart was hammering as she lifted the handset, dreading what she might hear.

'Ellie, darling, sorry to ring so early but I guessed you would be worried. I won't be able to call you anymore as we're doing night flying training.'

'I don't mind if you don't call if I know you're safe. Dad's told me I've got to get used to not hearing from you so often and he's right. Just ring whenever you get a moment, if I'm not here you can leave a message with Mrs B.'

'Good show. I'll be home Christmas Eve. Neil and I have arranged to meet at Romford and will get a taxi so there's no need for you to come and collect us.' There was the sound of someone speaking in the background. 'Sorry, sweetheart, duty calls.'

She replaced the receiver and turned to see both her father and Mrs B hovering anxiously in the kitchen door. 'Night flying – he's absolutely fine.'

'Glad to hear it, Ellie love. I don't think any of us got much sleep last night. I'll give you a hand with the pigs this morning as I can't do anything in the fields until the snow goes.'

'When we've finished will you help me get the chain on Greg's bike? I've painted it in patriotic colours – I doubt that anyone else on the base will have a red white and blue bicycle.'

'I can do it after lunch, Ellie. One of the tenants has a problem with his roof and I said I'd go and have a look.'

'I managed to get the chain on Neil's but some reason I'm finding it hard to do it on this one.'

Mrs B beamed at her. 'I think it's a lovely idea, doing up those old cycles for your brother and young man.

They'll be ever so pleased with their Christmas presents. What colour have you painted the other one?

'I've just painted the frame red and left the rest in the original black. I'm so looking forward to having them both home. It's going to be a very special Christmas.'

Twenty-two

Ellie went up in the loft and after a lot of rummaging discovered a box of Christmas bits and pieces. She carried them downstairs and plonked them on the kitchen table.

'I don't think you'll find anything decent in there, Ellie,' her father said. 'They are the things that went up when I was a boy.'

'All the more reason to use them this year. We've got plenty of holly and even a couple of sprigs of mistletoe and Mrs B is a dab hand at making flower arrangements.'

'That I am, love, and I'm looking forward to doing it, I can tell you.' She put a second larger cardboard box beside the first. 'I've got plenty of pretty decorations in here, and two sets of electric tree lights. My hubby and I liked things to be jolly. I know they say that decorations are for the children, but just because we weren't blessed with any it didn't mean we had to do without.'

This was the longest speech Ellie had heard the housekeeper make since she'd arrived a few months ago. 'When are you bringing in the tree, Dad? I want to have it decorated before Neil and Greg arrive on Christmas Eve.'

'It doesn't do to bring it in too soon as the needles will drop before twelfth night. I got one with good roots and it's already planted up in a nice pot. If I put it back in the ground, we should be able to use it every year.'

Ellie was rummaging through both boxes. 'Look at these, Dad, they open out into bells and huge balls. I didn't know you could make things like this out of tissue paper.'

Mrs B smiled proudly. 'There's tissue paper chains as well, more than enough to make the dining room and sitting room look really pretty. I know there's a war on but I managed to get everything I wanted at Woolworths when I went into town. Apart from so many of our men being in France I don't think this is going to be much different from any other Christmas.'

Dad sucked on his pipe. 'The government's telling us to show a fighting spirit and not let that blooming Hitler see we're down-hearted. Prices went up in the beginning but I reckon things are about the same now as they were before.'

'I've only seen a Christmas tree with lights in other people's houses, and in Romford in the town square. We never had a stocking and Mum made sure we didn't believe in Father Christmas. This year it's going to be different. I'm doing a stocking for each of us as well as a gift to put under the tree.'

He chuckled. 'I hope you're not intending to bring the bikes in, Ellie.'

'Of course not. I've wrapped up a picture of their bikes and am going to put those under the tree.'

She began to collect little items to put in each stocking. Sugar mice and homemade fudge in pretty boxes would do for everyone but she needed different things for the men, Mrs B and Dad. The handkerchiefs embroidered with their initials had been a great find in the small haberdashers in the village. She had discovered a box of small, leather-bound books in the attic and selected one for each stocking.

As Greg had given up smoking there was no point in buying him a packet of five Woodbines for his. If she could knit she would make them all a warm hat but that skill was beyond her. There were suggestions in the newspapers for presents that could be made at home. Somehow a rubber duck made from an old inner tube didn't appeal, neither did a gas-mask case made from an old cereal packet. A trip to Romford market was out of the question as she was too busy on the farm. Then she found a box of bits and pieces in an old shoe box on top of the wardrobe Mum had used. There were garnet and onyx cufflinks which were perfect for the men and several bracelets and rings. None of these were valuable, made from gilt and paste, but ideal for a stocking gift for Mrs B.

The larder was groaning under the weight of festive food. Not only did they have a goose for the day itself but also a capon and a large gammon joint. Mrs B had been baking like a mad woman and there were biscuits, fairy cakes, pies and sausage rolls carefully wrapped in greaseproof paper and put in tins. It was below freezing in there so nothing should go off.

All three of them joined in with the decoration of the tree. Ellie had to balance on a chair to place the star on the very top whilst her dad steadied her with his hands on her waist.

'Doesn't that look a treat, Fred? Ever so lovely, and it fits in the corner just perfect,' Mrs B gushed. 'I don't reckon there's a better one in the neighbourhood. It's a shame we can't leave the curtains open so visitors can see it when they arrive.'

'Down you get, love, don't want you twisting your ankle, what with your young man, Jack and Neil coming tomorrow.'

'Now the tree's finished, I'm going to start on the other decorations. As most of them are yours, Mrs B, you decide where they're going to go and I'll put them up. I've got drawing-pins and sticky tape ready to go.'

When the house was finished it looked like something from a children's picture book. 'Dad, it seems a shame nobody else is going to see the house like this especially as it will probably be the one and only time. Why don't we have a bit of party on Boxing Day?'

'If Mabel is happy then you go ahead and organise it. Not anything fancy mind, just a few folks coming round for a drink and a bite to eat.'

When had Mrs B become Mabel? Everyone called *him* by his first name, he didn't answer to Mr Simpson unless forced to. But as far as she knew this was the first time he'd called the housekeeper Mabel.

'I'll go and ask her. Why don't you make a list of the people you'd like to come and then I can start ringing those with telephones and then drop a note into the others. I think it's safe enough to drive as there hasn't been any fresh snow for a few days.'

Mrs B was thrilled at the prospect of having a bit of a do on Boxing Day. 'We've got so much food that we'll never eat it all ourselves, not in a month of Sundays.'

'Dad's making me a list of those he wants to invite. Is there anyone you would like to ask? Perhaps some of your friends from the WI might like to come.'

'Ta ever so, Ellie. That would be lovely. How many do you think I can ask?'

'Well, there's six of us and I think that Dad will want to ask the men who work here and their families and probably his three tenants and their families.' She counted on her fingers and pulled a face. 'I think that will be about nine children, three babes in arms and ten adults.'

'This is a grand big house, Ellie. If we use the sitting room, dining room and the room with the piano that nobody goes in, there's ample room for fifty.'

'Golly! That's an awful lot of people to feed – have we got enough for them to drink as well?'

Her father joined them. 'Here you are, Ellie love, just the usual suspects.'

'Mrs B is going to ask some of her friends, that's alright, isn't it?'

'The more the merrier. I don't want you to spend all your time in the kitchen, Mabel. You're one of the family now and I want you to enjoy yourself.'

The housekeeper coloured. 'All three of my friends are on their own like me and they'll help me with the catering. The boys can take care of drinks. Mind you, it will have to be cordial or tea as there isn't nearly enough beer for everyone.'

'Don't you worry about that. There's still three cases of wine and one of what your mum called, "assorted spirits" in the shed. Jack said he's bringing a couple of crates of pale ale as his contribution, so there'll be plenty.'

She was making the cocoa when Mrs B came in with a small box piled high with oddments. 'I found these at my old cottage the other day, love, and thought some of the things would be prefect for your stockings.'

'Thank you, exactly what I wanted. With a couple of these in each they will be full up.' Impulsively she reached out and hugged Mrs B who returned the embrace enthusiastically. 'You take your drink, lovie, and go up to bed. Here's your bottle, all nice and hot.'

'I will, thank you again. It's so nice having you here. This will be my best Christmas ever.'

There was no need for Ellie to ring anybody the next day as Mrs B and her dad took care of that. She didn't go to bed early but stayed up so she could enjoy seeing the house decked out in its Christmas finery.

*

The weather worsened and Greg was glad of his thick greatcoat as he waited on the platform for his train to steam in. The station was busy and most people were huddling against the wall in a vain attempt to stay out of the arctic winds that whistled down the exposed platform. Many were dressed as he was, in RAF blue. He wasn't the only one going home for the holiday.

On the train, he wedged himself into a corner of the corridor and perched on his kit bag.

'Mind your feet, mate,' a surly erk said as he shoved his way past.

'That's, "mind your feet, sir," to you,' Greg replied to the Lance Corporal.

'Bleedin' 'ell – trust me to step on an officer's toes,' the man replied with a grin and a sloppy salute.

Greg laughed. 'Are you at Wattisham?'

'I'm with 110 Squadron, same place as you, sir.'

'I thought you looked vaguely familiar. Where do you get off?'

'Stratford, lived there all me life. Was a car mechanic so didn't take much training to look after your aircraft. You going all the way?'

'Romford.' Greg yawned. 'Night flying's a bugger, I'm going to get a bit of shuteye. Could you give me a kick when we get to my stop if I'm asleep?'

'Happy to. Not often I get the chance to kick an officer.'

Greg settled back, pulled his cap over his eyes and immediately dropped off. He was wakened with a jolt when someone grabbed his shoulder.

'Next stop is yours, sir.'

The train was already slowing down and Greg had to fight his way to the door through the crush in the corridor. 'Thanks, Merry Christmas.'

He almost fell flat on his face as he stepped from the train when his left foot slid out from under him. He only managed to keep himself upright by grabbing hold of a snow-encrusted pillar. A cascade of loose snow landed on his head and provided a bit of light relief to the watching passengers.

'This bloody platform is lethal. Here, let me take your kit whilst you brush yourself down,' a familiar voice said from beside him.

'Where did you spring from? I didn't recognise you in uniform.'

'I arrived a few minutes ago on the other platform. Neil was already here and has grabbed a taxi. We've got to stop at the pub and pick up the beer, hope that's alright.'

Greg followed Jack and was waved through by the ticket collector without having to produce his travel docket. He strode across and slapped his friend on the shoulder. 'It's good to see you, Neil, you look well. A bloody sight better than I do, I expect.'

'Life of Riley for me – not worth risking our kites on training flights so we're spending a lot of the time playing cards and reading.'

'I've been flying most nights for the past week. I'm surprised they haven't got you bods doing the same.'

They piled into the taxi, made a detour to the pub, and were then finally on their way to Glebe Farm. The car skidded violently and the driver muttered under his breath but continued.

Suddenly the cabbie lost control and the vehicle slid sideways ending up stuck in the hedge. For a moment no one spoke and then Jack laughed. The unexpected sound released the tension.

'That was fun. I reckon three strong blokes like us can push this free.' He grinned at the shaken driver. 'Okay with you, mate? We'll get you out of this mess and you take us where we want to go?'

'I ain't happy about this. But I need the cash and I don't suppose you'll still pay me if I leave you on the side of the road.'

'We certainly won't. We're paying double the usual fare and expect to arrive at our destination however difficult it is for you,' Neil said.

By the time the taxi was back on the road and facing in the correct direction they were all covered in snow but at least they were a good deal warmer.

'Ellie will be worried if we don't get a move on. She's expecting us to be there by three o'clock and it's already a quarter past,' Greg told the others.

The remaining couple of miles could have been walked more quickly, but he didn't blame the man as the lane down to the farm was treacherous.

He was first out of the vehicle and left the others to pay the fare – he would cough up his share later. He didn't want to waste another minute of the time he had to spend with the woman he loved.

Not a glimmer of light showed through the blackout curtains which had been drawn even though it wasn't quite dark. He was about to go to the back as usual when the front door was flung open and Ellie ran out and threw herself into his arms.

*

'I'm so glad you're here, now Christmas can really begin.' She tilted her face to receive his kiss. His lips were icy and there was snow embedded in his eyebrows and hair.

Someone shoved him and they were sent staggering backwards. 'Keep the canoodling for inside, you two, it's brass monkeys out here and we want to get in the warm.' Jack winked at her as he walked past carrying two crates of beer. No wonder he was eager to get inside as they must weigh a ton.

'Merry Christmas, Jack, Neil, sorry if we got in your way.'

'Blithering idiot! We could have gone right over if I hadn't been so close to the door,' Greg said. He hadn't found the incident at all amusing – maybe Jack had pushed them a little harder than was necessary.

She remembered his kiss when he'd left three weeks ago and thought maybe Jack had done it because he was jealous. In future, she would keep out of his way, make sure he understood she was in love with Greg.

The tree was admired as were the decorations. Neil drew her to one side whilst the others were devouring fairy cakes and sausage rolls in front of the sitting room fire.

'Things look pretty serious between you and Greg. I don't want to put you off, Ellie, but you'd be marrying into the upper classes. Do you think you can be the sort of wife someone like him expects? Remember, it didn't work out so well with our parents.'

'I love him, and if he asks me to marry him again, then I shall say yes this time. He might come from the same sort of background as Mum did but he's no different from you really. He doesn't see his family at all.'

'Is he independently wealthy, do you know? If he isn't, what will you live on once the war's over?'

'I wouldn't dream of asking him something so personal. Dad has already given him his blessing so he must think Greg's in a position to take care of me. Thank you for caring, but you don't have to worry. Even if we do get engaged I've no intention of getting married until after the war.'

Neil hugged her. 'That's all right then. I notice that Mrs B and Dad seem very chummy – is something going on there too?'

'I'm certain there is, and I'm happy for them both. Mum's no longer part of this family and I don't see why he shouldn't be happy after being miserable for the past twenty years.'

*

Going to midnight service was abandoned as by ten thirty there was a blizzard blowing outside. 'I don't think we'll be able to go to matins either, it's too far to walk and the lane will be blocked,' Dad said, trying to hide his smile of relief.

'I'm sure it won't matter just this once,' Mrs B said cheerfully. 'As long as it's cleared so folks can get here on Boxing Day afternoon for the party, it would be a shame if that had to be cancelled.'

'Don't fret, Mabel, I'll get out there with the tractor and do it in the morning. Neil, son, can you give me a hand with the milking in the morning? I've given the men the day off.'

'Be happy to. Presumably this means that Jack and Greg are doing the pigs.'

Jack pretended to scowl. 'What about Ellie? I suppose she gets a lie in.'

She smiled sweetly at him. 'Actually, I'm helping Mrs B. I'm going to feed the birds and then anything else she wants me to do.'

'Just make sure there's plenty of hot water. The four of us will need a bath before lunch.'

Dad chuckled. 'Hardly seems worth the effort as we'll have to go out again before tea.'

Mrs B choked on her cocoa. 'If you think you're sitting down to Christmas lunch in your overalls, Fred Simpson, you have another think coming.'

Dad was laughing so hard he couldn't answer. Mrs B left in a huff. 'That wasn't fair, Dad, you shouldn't tease her.'

Ellie hurried out and found the housekeeper banging about in the kitchen. 'Of course everyone will change for lunch, Mrs B. Dad was just joking. Please don't be upset.'

'I don't like being laughed at – never have, never will.' She paused in her clattering and turned to face Ellie. 'I suppose everyone thinks I'm a silly old woman now.'

'No they don't. Dad's very fond of you and didn't mean to hurt your feelings. I've never seen him so happy and it's all because of you.'

'You don't mind then, love, that Fred and I are getting close?'

'The closer the better. You're already one of the family. Is there anything we need to do tonight?'

'The vegetables are done and in basins of cold water in the pantry. The goose doesn't have to go on until nine o'clock. The pudding just needs another couple of hours in the steamer. Everything's ready, thank you, love.'

'In which case, why don't you turn in? I've got to put the stockings up before I go to bed, but apart from that I'm done too.'

When she returned to the sitting room only Greg was there. 'The others have gone up. Come and sit with me by the fire for a bit, we've not had the chance to talk in private so far.'

Was he going to propose again? Her pulse skipped and she joined him on the sofa knowing that this time her answer would be yes.

Twenty-three

Jack was still awake when Greg came to bed. He'd been reading *The Big Sleep* by Raymond Chandler, a book that one of the guys in his training group had loaned him. Reading an American book made him half-wish he'd not come back. His life had been less complicated and definitely less grim.

He put the book down on the bedside table. 'Am I to congratulate you?'

Greg's mouth tightened but then he smiled, but it wasn't very convincing. 'I've got the ring in my pocket, was intending to ask again, but something she said made me think again.'

Bloody hell! Had the silly girl told him about the kiss?

'It's none of my business, mate, you don't have to tell me if you don't want to.'

'I might as well, you'll hear soon enough in the morning.' He slumped onto his bed and rubbed his eyes. The poor bloke looked knackered as well as miserable.

'Ellie loves you and you love her so I can't see why there should be a problem.'

'If only it were so easy. Before I could pop the question, she said there were some things she wanted to ask me. Neil had been talking to her about the danger of marrying into a family like mine.'

'It's none of his business – just because their mother made all their lives miserable, and never fitted in, it doesn't mean that Ellie will be the same.'

'I tried to reassure her that I don't want her to change but she persisted with her questions.' He rubbed his eyes again before continuing. 'She asked me where we would be living when the war was over and what sort of employment I would be taking.'

This didn't sound particularly controversial – in fact these questions sounded sensible.

'However much I dislike my family and my father, when he dies I'll have to take over the estates. The damn things are entailed so I have no choice. Believe me, I'd cut myself off entirely if I could.'

'I can't see Ellie swanning around as lady of the manor. I take it she didn't react well to your answers.'

'It was the worst five minutes of my life. She was in floods of tears but nothing I could say would convince her that if we loved each other enough we could make it work.'

'Sorry to hear that, but I shouldn't give up just yet. When she's had time to think about it, realises that life without you would be a bloody sight worse than having to live in a stately home, she'll come around.'

Greg shook his head. 'I can't marry her knowing she might well be as miserable with me as her mother was with Fred. I love her too much. No, I've got to let her go.'

When he switched out the light he said quietly. 'With any luck I'll get shot down and she can get on with her life.'

'Don't be so bloody daft, man, that's no way to talk. If you go on a mission with that attitude you're bound to go for a Burton. You've got two blokes in that kite with you – think about them.'

The bed creaked and the light went back on. 'I need a drink. I brought a bottle of Courvoisier and Johnny Walker as my contribution to Christmas. I'm sure Fred won't mind if we open one of them.'

'I never say no to a drink.'

Neither of them had brought anything apart from pyjamas but someone had thoughtfully supplied what they needed. Jack shrugged into his dressing gown and pushed his bare feet into the slippers.

They crept along the passageway like burglars and he was sure neither Ellie nor Fred would have heard them. Greg went ahead of him to find the whiskey and he paused in the passageway outside her bedroom.

There was no sound of her crying so maybe she wasn't as upset as Greg had thought. He thought a mug of coffee would go down a treat with the whiskey, and maybe a couple of mince pies too.

'Where are you going?' Ellie spoke from right behind him and he almost fell down the stairs.

'Greg and I are going to have a glass or two of whiskey. He's devastated and wants to drown his sorrows.'

She was looking remarkably cheerful for a girl with a broken heart. 'I'm going to join you. I think I overreacted, which was a bit silly. There's no reason why we can't be engaged and see how it goes, is there?'

'None at all. I've changed my mind; you go down and I'll go to bed. You don't need me playing gooseberry whilst you make things up.'

Her smile was radiant and she stretched up on tiptoes and kissed his cheek. 'You're such a good friend, Jack, I'm so glad that you're part of this family now.'

He was glad for them, and if he was honest, also a bit envious. He doubted he would ever find a girl like her for himself.

*

Ellie was wearing her comfortable, but highly unflattering, flannelette pyjamas. She hadn't stopped to put on her dressing gown or slippers. When she'd heard footsteps outside her bedroom door she'd thought for a moment it was Greg coming to comfort her. When they'd continued past her door she'd come out to investigate.

Was Jack correct? Would she be able to put things right with Greg? As she scampered down the stairs her heart was pounding and her feet were already frozen from walking on the uncarpeted boards. Apart from the sitting room, which had a threadbare rug in the centre of the room, the other floors were flagstones. Not ideal for somebody with bare feet.

The kitchen was deserted – where was Greg? He must be looking for the whiskey which Mrs B had put in the scullery along with the other drink that had been left over from the last party. He'd never find it on his own.

She was so cold she might as well nip in and collect the whiskey for him. The best glasses were kept in the sitting room so that was no need for her to hang about any longer. With the precious bottle in one hand she dashed through the house desperate to get onto the carpet.

The room was unoccupied. Before she did anything else she was going to thaw out and she would need to stir up the fire to do that. She chucked a few bits of kindling onto the glowing embers and they caught immediately. Within a few moments there were welcome flames and she tossed a couple of logs into the blaze. The socks she had stuffed full of little gifts were hanging a safe distance from the fire. Each one had the name of the recipient sewn on.

Her teeth were chattering and she bitterly regretted her impulsive decision to come down in just her pyjamas. She put the bottle of whiskey on the sideboard and got out one of the cut glass tumblers from the cupboard and put it next to the bottle.

Greg must have gone back upstairs whilst she was in the scullery. If he came down again at least he would be able to get himself a drink. She pulled a pouffe in front of the hearth and settled onto it and stretched out her legs towards the fire. She wanted to warm up a bit before she went back to bed.

After a while she was sleepy and her feet were no longer ice blocks. The chiming clock on the mantelpiece struck twelve. Christmas Day – and no one to say Merry Christmas to.

The rattle of crockery startled her and she scrambled to her feet just as the door was pushed open and Greg walked in carrying a tray.

'I thought you could do with another cocoa and a fresh hot-water bottle before you go back to bed, sweetheart.'

'I thought you'd gone to bed, I couldn't find you anywhere.'

He put the tray on the sideboard before answering. 'I was looking for the whiskey in the music room and heard you come in here. You shouldn't have come down without your slippers.' He tossed over the hot-water bottle and she caught it and hugged it eagerly. He was being very matter-of-fact for a man who was supposed to be devastated.

'Thank you. I'll take my drink up with me and leave you to have your whiskey in peace.'

He turned. 'No, we need to talk. Sit over there. Do you want some of this?' He gestured to the bottle in his hand. She shook her head and nervously perched on the edge of the sofa, not sure if she liked the new, authoritative Greg.

He strode across and handed her a mug and a plate with two mince pies. She took them both. How was she supposed to deal with these at the same time? She couldn't put the plate on her lap as it was already occupied by the hot water bottle. She didn't want anything to eat anyway, her stomach was churning and she felt a bit sick.

This was hardly a romantic interlude. In fact, it was far more like being summoned to the principal's office. Not enjoyable at all. She pushed herself back and then put the plate down beside her. This meant he couldn't sit there, but she wasn't sure she wanted him to.

He carried on over to the side table and then returned for his glass, mug and plate. He didn't seem perturbed about the positioning of her mince pies and settled himself comfortably at the far end of the sofa.

'Why did you come down, Ellie? Have you changed your mind about marrying me?' His tone was even, as if he was speaking about the weather, not something so emotional as a rejected proposal.

'I have and I haven't.' Two could play this game and she wasn't going to allow him to boss her about. She took a sip from her cocoa trying to look nonchalant and hide the fact that her hands were shaking.

'For God's sake, don't speak in riddles. I was suicidal an hour ago and intended to drink myself into a stupor.' He no longer looked calm – in fact he looked desperate.

She put her drink down and launched herself towards him. 'I'm sorry, I do want to marry but not until after the war. I love you and can't bear to see you so unhappy.'

He met her in the middle, his face transformed by happiness, and pulled her onto his lap. She put her arms around his neck and when he kissed her his mouth was hard, demanding, his tongue pressed against her closed lips until she opened them allowing him access. Her skin was on fire and when he slid his hand underneath her pyjama top she didn't protest.

Then, abruptly, he raised his head. 'I'm squashing your mince pies, sweetheart, you'd better move before we ruin the sofa.'

He tumbled her from his lap and stood up. He peered over his shoulder and laughed. 'What a waste – they didn't deserve to be sat on.'

He carefully removed his dressing gown and together they scraped the mess into the fire. 'Your virtue was saved by a mince pie, darling, I bet there aren't many girls who can say that.'

'Good thing they were on a plate, there's nothing to see on the sofa. I didn't think I wanted one, but I'm hungry now so can I share yours?'

Solemnly he held out his plate and she resumed her place, but this time tucked her feet under her bottom. 'As we're now officially engaged, shouldn't I have a ring on my finger?' She waved her right hand at him.

'Strangely enough I didn't come down with it in my pocket. You'll have to wait until tomorrow.' His smile made her pulse skip. 'Merry Christmas, sweetheart. I don't care if we have a long engagement, as long as I know you're waiting for me, that's okay by me.'

*

Ellie overslept and when she eventually made it downstairs the house was empty – even Mrs B was absent. Hastily she pulled on her overalls and gumboots and ran out to see what she could do to make up for her tardy appearance. It didn't matter that it was Christmas Day, that it was still snowing, the livestock must always come first.

The cows were almost milked, the pigs happily rootling in their troughs, and Mrs B was just returning from feeding the poultry, geese and ducks.

'Merry Christmas, love, you go along indoors. No need to hang about out here as everything has been done.'

'I've never been late before. I'm so sorry that I wasn't here as I promised I'd help you today.'

They scraped the worst of the snow from their boots, kicked them off and then removed their overcoats. Ellie hung up her overalls hoping everyone else would be as forgiving as Mrs B about her laziness.

'I'll get the breakfast as you had to do my job.'

'There's no need, Ellie, it's boiled eggs and soldiers this morning. We need to leave room for our Christmas dinner.'

'In which case, Mrs B, I'll light the fires everywhere.'

The sitting room wasn't icy, the fire she'd revived in the middle of the night was still smouldering and clearing out the ash from underneath the grate and getting it burning merrily again didn't take long. The dining room and music room fires were laid and she just had to put a match to the newspaper scrunched up underneath the kindling.

There was enough woodland on the farm to keep them in logs all winter. Dad bought in coke for the Aga and coal for the house fires as this gave more heat than logs and kept the fires burning for longer.

She'd paid special attention to her outfit this morning, although she hadn't put on a frock. Greg loved her for who she was, she realised that now, and didn't want her to pretend to be something else. Therefore, she was wearing slacks, but they were very smart. Her blouse was cream and her cardigan a gorgeous bright red, perfect for Christmas morning.

As she was about to return to the kitchen she paused, there was something different about the sitting room and she couldn't think what it was. Her mouth curved in delight. She'd hung up five socks, but someone had put up a sixth, there was one made for her.

Loud voices echoed down the passageway from the back door. The men were back. On Christmas Day the pigs and cows weren't mucked out – but the milking parlour and dairy always had to be pristine. Tomorrow she would help with both unpleasant jobs to make up for her absence today.

Greg met her with open arms and a smile that made her hot all over. 'Good morning, darling, and happy Christmas.'

They exchanged a brief embrace, it wouldn't do to kiss in front of anyone.

The stockings were judged to be perfect. They agreed to not open the gifts under the tree until after lunch. Ellie was now wearing her engagement ring and had never been happier. As she was laying the table the telephone rang.

Neil answered it and he poked his head into the dining room a few minutes later. 'That was George, he offered his congratulations. He's promised to bring Fiona to meet you when the weather improves.'

'I thought it might be Mum. I don't understand how she can cut herself off from us all like this. We're still her children even if she doesn't love Dad.'

'Don't worry about it, little sister, you never really got on with her anyway. I expect Sir Reginald insisted she did so. I wouldn't be surprised if the divorce was his idea too. She's hardly going to be getting married again.'

'I don't see why not, she can't be more than forty-six, that's still quite young. I'm certain Dad and Mrs B will make a match of it one day. You must have noticed how close they've become.'

'I'd have to be blind not to have done so. What with you and Greg mooning over each other as well, Jack and I are feeling rather left out.'

She finished the final touches to the festive table and stepped away to admire her handiwork. The centrepiece was made from two fat red candles pushed into a cut glass bowl filled with glass baubles. The best linen had been used and the bone china dinner service would be in evidence too.

Satisfied the room looked as it should she stopped to ask if she was needed in the kitchen – she wasn't – so went to join the others. The room went silent as she entered. They were all looking serious and her dad was white as a sheet.

'What's wrong? Are you ill, Dad?'

'You'd better sit down, Ellie love, I've had a bit of a shock. I hadn't opened the last lot of cards that came yesterday. There was this letter from my solicitor amongst them.' He held out the expensive paper and she walked across to take it from him.

She scanned the contents with growing disbelief. 'I don't understand. I thought everything had been agreed before you signed the papers.'

'So did I. I reckon that nasty bugger is behind this. Charlotte, for all her faults, would never stoop so low.'

Twenty-four

'Can the lawyers make you sell the farm, Fred?' Jack asked.

'It's been in this family for over a century – I'd like to see them try,' Fred replied.

Greg wasn't sure if it was his business to comment, but as he was now engaged to Ellie he thought it would be in order to do so. 'Let me get this straight. Mrs Simpson's lawyers are saying she's entitled to half the value of your farm as compensation for the years of ill-treatment she suffered at your hands?'

'That's about the sum of it. I only agreed to allow her to divorce me on the understanding that I wouldn't have to pay maintenance or any other costs.'

'Did you sign a document stating this?'

'No, Greg, but I have it in a letter. Surely that's enough to prove my case?'

Ellie moved to stand beside him and he put his arm around her waist. 'Please don't let this spoil what might be the last Christmas we have together,' she said.

Jack laughed. 'Blimey, which of us do you think is going for a Burton then?'

'I didn't mean that; you know I didn't. But you could all be posted to different parts of the country, or even overseas, and wouldn't be able to come home.'

She handed the letter to her brother and he put it in a large manila envelope. 'Ellie's right, there's nothing we can do about this now and worrying about it won't change a thing.'

'I came to tell you that Mrs B wants everyone in the dining room. I'm famished, a couple of boiled eggs wasn't nearly enough to fill me up.'

*

The sideboard was laden with delicious treats. The capon, gammon joint and goose took pride of place. Dad carved each in turn and she acted as waitress. By the time they'd demolished second helpings they scarcely had room for the pudding.

Whilst Ellie and Mrs B got on with the washing-up Greg and the other men retreated to the safety of the sitting room. They had agreed Ellie wouldn't have to go out today, they would take care of the outside tasks between them.

Greg now appeared to enjoy the stench, cold and the less than friendly animals. He was happy to help but glad he'd never have to do this sort of manual labour to earn his living. The family estates had a dozen prosperous farms but these were run by tenants. His father would be horrified to think his son and heir was up to his ankles in pig muck – and on Christmas Day too.

The opening of individual presents had been delayed until no one had to go outside again. As he was rinsing the filth from his wellingtons he saw Ellie by the barn. She must be shutting up the chickens for Mrs B.

He'd bought her half a dozen novels and a bottle of a perfume called Joy. He'd been assured by the shop assistant in Harrods it was all the rage. He'd got the usual gloves, handkerchiefs, and scarves for the others.

'Drop your overalls in the boiler, Mr Dunlop, you won't be needing them again today,' the housekeeper told him as he came in.

'Thank you, but I'll want them for tomorrow morning. The men aren't coming in until the afternoon.'

'Bless you, we've plenty of spare. Nobody has to wear dirty clothes whilst I'm in charge.'

He nabbed the bathroom first and put his uniform back on. He supposed he could wear mufti but hadn't brought anything else with him.

Neil arrived as he left. 'I'll be down in ten minutes. Mrs B is bringing cake, mince pies and tea to the sitting room. Jack and Dad should be in shortly.'

Once all of them were assembled Ellie began to hand out the gifts. Greg and Neil received a similar rectangular box from her but Jack's gift was obviously a garment of some sort. She put her parcels to one side, as always putting other people before herself. Whatever she thought, he was certain she would make him the perfect wife and would adapt to being the lady of the manor without too many problems.

He opened his box and discovered a card with a picture of a bicycle. Neil had the same thing. She was bubbling with excitement. 'Both of you must go into the scullery – you'll find your gift there. I do hope you like them.'

Sure enough there were two shrouded shapes one on each side the scullery. His name was on the one on the left. He pulled back the dust sheet. 'Ellie, it's magnificent. It looks as good as new and I love the patriotic colour scheme. Nobody will be able to steal my bike.'

Neil did the same and was equally delighted. His was red and black, just as distinctive.

'I did most of the work myself but Jack and Dad helped with the chains. I'm so glad you like them.'

He picked her up and swung her around. 'The best Christmas present I've ever had, sweetheart. Every time I use it I'll think of you.'

'Thank you, little sister, exactly what I need to get around the base. If the snow stops, I think I might be able to peddle to Hornchurch when I go.

Ellie was thrilled with the books. He rather thought the expensive perfume was a dud as far as she was concerned. He should have known better; Ellie wasn't a girl who worried about her appearance and he doubted she'd ever use it.

*

By midday the house was ready for the invasion of partygoers. Ellie had reluctantly decided to put on a frock so she could use some of the expensive perfume Greg had given her. Somehow perfume and slacks didn't seem right together.

She'd allowed her hair to grow since she'd stopped flying and it was now long enough to put up. She spent a good half an hour fiddling around with hairpins and grips and was still dissatisfied with the result. The first guests would be arriving any minute. She ran her fingers through her curls, applied a smudge of red lipstick and was ready.

Jack was in charge of drinks but her brother and Greg were going to help as well.

'Ellie, you look lovely.' Greg kissed the top of her head and sniffed appreciatively. 'You're wearing my perfume. It smells quite delicious.'

'I thought maybe we could announce our engagement at the party, make it a bit of a celebration.'

'I'll speak to Fred, if he doesn't want to do it then I'll ask Neil.'

'I heard people arriving. I'm so glad it stopped snowing as several people will have walked.'

He brushed his fingers across her cheek and then went in search of her father. Jack had set out a temporary bar in the music room. He called out as she passed.

'You look a million dollars, Ellie, it's amazing what an expensive dress will do.'

'Thank you. Your uniform's very flattering – but I'm not sure it complements your red hair.'

They exchanged grins. 'What do you think?' He gestured at the impressive array of bottles, glasses, jugs and steaming punchbowl. 'Fred suggested I made this, he thinks people will need warming up. It's not very alcoholic – would you like a glass?'

'It smells wonderful, very Christmassy. Is the hot water to make squash for the children?'

'Mrs B's idea, but there'll be cold as well. I hope they won't be bored. I found some dominoes, a pack of cards, a chess set and a pile of paper and pencils. I've put them at the far end of the sitting room.'

'You've thought of everything. You mustn't spend the entire time in here, I want to introduce you to everybody. I've got to go; people are coming in.'

All the guests had arrived by one o'clock and as they all knew each other there were no need for formal introductions. The children, once they had a plate of food, settled happily in the designated place and were no bother to anyone.

She and Greg were congratulated on their engagement. However, by the end of the party she was heartily sick of being asked if they had set the day.

Gladys and Bert had come, as well as Sid and his wife. She hadn't seen them since the airfield closed and spent most of her time talking to them.

'I don't expect you're in a hurry to get hitched, Ellie,' Sid said after his third pint of beer. 'To tell you the truth I didn't think you were the marrying kind.'

'What you mean?' She spoke more sharply than she'd intended but he didn't take offence – after all, he'd known her since she was a schoolgirl.

'I thought you'd join the WAAFs, didn't see you as a girl to stay at home even if you are doing war work by being on the farm.'

'I was tempted, but when Dad had his stroke I decided I'd better stay to take care of him.'

'No need, my girl, your housekeeper will do that a lot better than you can.'

She obviously wasn't the only one to notice the closeness between Mrs B and her dad. 'I think I might join up, but it will be hard being so close to aircraft and not allowed to fly them.'

'Better than moping about here worrying whether your brothers, Jack or Greg are going to be shot down every time they fly.'

'You're right. Next time I go into town I'll ask at the library.'

'No need to do that, Ellie, you can go to the Drill Hall in London Road. It's been set up so girls can volunteer.'

'Then that's where I'll go – but I can't until the weather clears. Are you sure they actually want new recruits when nothing much is happening?'

'It will all start soon enough, and when it does, it makes sense to have people already trained and in place.'

The party ended as the sun set. Those who were walking home didn't want to do so in the dark. When the final person departed, she was relieved. She'd much rather spend time with her close friends and family.

'Is there any food left, Greg? I didn't get the chance to eat.'

'Neither did I, shall we go and investigate?'

Jack and Neil were in the dining room piling their plates. 'We're going to eat before we go out again. Mrs B is making tea and coffee and said she'll bring it through.'

'She and her friends did a splendid job. The washing-up's done and only what's left in here will need clearing later,' her brother said.

'I've not seen Dad for a while, is he all right?'

'He went upstairs for a lie down on Mrs B's insistence. I can't remember seeing him so relaxed in company before – I think he might have even enjoyed the party.'

'That would be a first,' she replied through a mouthful of cold chicken and chutney.

*

Whilst the men were outside taking care of the livestock she helped Mrs B wash-up the remaining crockery and put it away. 'You must thank your friends for their help, they worked so hard making sure everything went swimmingly.'

'They went home with a basket full of goodies – I hope you don't mind. None of them had done a lot of extra cooking as they were on their own. They all ate their Christmas dinner with family.'

'I'm glad you did. The boys have to catch the ten o'clock train tomorrow so I'm going to spend the evening with Greg – I don't know when we'll be able to meet again.'

If she did join the WAAFs it would be even more difficult to see him as she could be sent anywhere in the country.

'I just hope things can be sorted out with the solicitor, my Fred doesn't need the aggravation.'

Ellie was a bit startled that Dad had not only told Mrs B but that the housekeeper now considered him her property. Things would change if they got married and she wasn't sure she wanted to be here then.

*

Although she and Greg had spent a couple of hours alone together last night they'd only discussed how they were going to meet in the future, how they were going to

324

stop the lawyers forcing the sale of the farm, and what was likely to be Hitler's next move. She hadn't told him she'd decided to join the WAAFs, as he would probably object. Until they were married, as far as she was concerned, she was free to make her own decisions. Loving someone didn't mean they owned you.

Over breakfast Dad told her what he'd decided about the solicitor's letter. 'I'm going to put the farm in Neil's name, then they can't make me sell it. Not that I was going to. I'm taking Jack's car and going into the office this morning to get it sorted.'

She'd wondered why he was not in his usual overalls but in a smart tweed jacket and tie.

'That's an excellent idea, Dad, but I want Ellie's name down as well.'

She swallowed a lump in her throat knowing exactly why her brother had made this suggestion. Both he and George might be killed and they all thought she was going to be remaining here helping on the farm.

'Righto, son, I'll do that. If you don't get off, you're going to miss that train. Take care of yourselves, boys, and keep in touch.'

There wasn't room in the cab for all four of them so Jack volunteered to travel in the back with the two bicycles. Ellie was dreading having to drive to Romford when the roads were lethal but she wasn't going to ask one of the boys to drive as she would still have to do the return journey herself.

'I'll get the truck started, it can be a bit tricky when it's cold even though it's been standing in a barn with a blanket over it,' Ellie said as she pushed her chair back.

'The bikes are already in. We'll be out in a jiffy,' Jack said.

They arrived at the station without incident and she was rather proud of her driving skills. Neil got out to help Jack get the bicycles down, leaving her with Greg.

'I don't want you to ring at a set time anymore, Greg, just when you can. I'll write to you, but not every day, once a week seems sensible.'

'I agree, we are both too busy to keep up the daily correspondence. I don't suppose I'll see you for a few weeks – not until the weather improves anyway. I'm going to miss you, darling, but knowing you're safe here away from the action will keep me focused on what I have to do.'

Perhaps now was the time to tell him her decision – but she kept the information to herself not wishing to spoil their parting with an argument.

'I'll miss you too.' She swivelled on her seat and put her arms around his neck. His kiss was passionate and she responded willingly. Jack hammering on the window rudely interrupted them.

'Enough canoodling you two, the train will be here in a minute.'

She jerked away, her face scarlet, but Greg stroked her cheek and kissed her gently a second time. 'Ignore him, he's only jealous. Take care of yourself, sweetheart. Be careful on the drive back.'

'And you be careful cycling to the base,' she called after him.

Neil had already wheeled his cycle onto the platform but Jack was waiting for Greg. He winked and saluted and then they were both gone.

Her eyes prickled and she blinked back the unwanted tears. Hanging about at home would be unbearable. She would have far too much time to think about all three of them risking their lives every time they flew.

It wasn't too far to the recruitment office. She would leave the truck here and go and sign on right now. It might be only a couple of days after Christmas, but there was a war on and she was sure the office would be open.

Sure enough the dingy hall was ready and waiting to receive volunteers. She filled in the forms stating that she had a preference for becoming a radio or wireless operator. If she couldn't fly herself then the next best thing would be to talk to those in the air.

A wireless operator would be paid 2/8d a day, 2d more than if she was to be a radio operator. Whichever trade she was selected for, her food, clothing, accommodation and medical treatment would be provided free. By signing up she was agreeing to remain with them for the duration of the war and had to be prepared to serve anywhere in the United Kingdom or overseas.

She had handed over her log book, but they didn't seem particularly interested in her experience in the air. However, she walked out feeling proud to be doing her bit. Her papers would come through when the next draft was called, which could be anything from a couple of weeks to a couple of months. This would give her ample time to prepare her family for her imminent departure.

Twenty-five

The New Year came and went with little celebration on her part. She was now writing to both Jack and Greg and their replies were the highlight of the week. Mrs B now insisted that she called her Mabel but Ellie was uncomfortable with that. Although she was happy for her dad, she was beginning to feel she was in the way.

She had not told anyone she was joining the Women's Auxiliary Air Force. She kept the news to herself until a brown envelope arrived telling her to report to the WAAF depot the following week. The waiting was over and she would have to explain to her family and Greg that she would be leaving, possibly for years.

Greg was the first to be told. 'You've done what? What in God's name possessed you to do something so stupid? I thought we'd agreed you would stay where you are until we get married when this is over.'

'I didn't agree, you assumed. I'll be far more use as a WAAF than I will be here. I know it means we won't see each other, but...'

'There's a war on,' he finished for her. 'It's incredibly selfish of you. Now I've got to worry about what's happening to you as well as doing my job.'

'I'm sorry about that, but it can't be helped. I'd much rather be busy than waiting here for a phone call or telegram saying one of you has been killed. It's possible I'll get stationed at the same base as you, but if I don't we'll just have to get on with it like everybody else. There are several families in the village who haven't seen their husbands or sons since they were sent to France last September. At least we can talk on the telephone occasionally.'

There was a silence at the other end. This was the first disagreement since becoming engaged that they'd had and she hoped they could put matters right before he hung up.

'There's not much point in discussing it, Ellie, as it's a *fait accompli*. Do you know where you're going to do your training?'

'I was told I would be put in the next draft and it could be anywhere in the country. I haven't got my travel docket so don't actually know at the moment.'

'There aren't any WAAFs here, but the adjutant said they are thinking of putting up some Nissen huts to accommodate them. I'm sorry if I sound upset, it's just that I love you and the thought of you putting yourself in unnecessary danger is unbearable.'

'I love you too. I promise I'll be careful and not volunteer for anything I don't have to. At least the weather has improved as I don't fancy travelling in a blizzard.'

'I'm sure there will be a telephone box within walking distance of the camp. Ring me and give me your address. It's possible you'll get a weekend pass when you've finished your training. If you can get home, I'll meet you there somehow. By the way, my bicycle is the talk of the squadron. Much admired and will be bloody useful getting to and from the pub.'

'I'm glad you like it. I've got to go; I haven't told Dad yet. I wanted you to be the first to know.'

'Your entire family will be in uniform in a few weeks. No one can say the Simpsons aren't doing their bit for the war effort.'

After a few more pleasantries they cut the connection. She'd already written to Jack and Neil and promised to send them the address of the training depot. All that was left was to try and explain to Dad why she'd decided to leave Glebe Farm. One of the reasons was the growing closeness between Mabel and him – and she could hardly tell him that.

Both of them were in the sitting room – Mabel no longer used her own parlour. She poked her head around the door. 'I'm going to make myself a cocoa. Do you want one?'

'That would be lovely, and there's the last of the Christmas cake in the tin,' Mabel told her.

Ellie thought it would be easier to make her announcement when her father was happily munching cake and drinking cocoa. The reaction she got was quite unexpected.

'Well, love, you've always been a girl for adventure. To tell you the truth, I'd rather you were in the WAAFs than married. Don't get me wrong, I like your young man, but he'll take you away from me. He'll want you to become like him, like your mother, and I won't be good enough anymore.'

She put down her cup and dropped to her knees beside him. 'Dad, if I thought Greg was like that I wouldn't have got engaged to him. This is my home and I'll always come and see you as often as I can.'

To her astonishment Mabel was sniffing into her handkerchief. 'It won't be the same here with you gone, Ellie love. I never had children, but if I had I would have wanted a daughter just like you. You don't take any nonsense from anyone. I bet they have you made up to an officer in no time.'

*

The journey to the recruits' training centre was interminable, the train freezing, the sandwiches and flask of coffee Ellie had brought with her were like a distant memory when she eventually disembarked. She looked around the almost deserted station in the hope of seeing some other girls who were on their way to the same destination.

She was on her own, as she had been all day as the train had shunted in and out of sidings and stopped at innumerable anonymous stations. She was wearing her warmest slacks, long johns, plus a blouse and two jumpers. On top of all this was her thick leather flying jacket. At least she wasn't going to get cold, however far she had to walk.

The ticket collector shook his head when she asked him for directions. 'It's two miles to the barracks, miss, I don't think you should try and walk it, not in this weather. If you sit in the waiting room I reckon they'll send someone for you. Maybe there's a few more girls coming on the next train.'

'When is the next train?'

'That's anybody's guess, yours was over an hour late. Should be one before dark.'

Ellie thought for a moment. 'Thank you, but I'll walk. I'm a country girl and a couple of miles is nothing even in the snow.'

If she'd been wearing a skirt as most young ladies would be she would never have attempted it. But dressed as she was, she was sure she'd reach her destination without mishap. Her belongings weren't in a suitcase but in a knapsack. Dad had dug it out from the attic for her – it was the one he'd had in the last war.

She tied her scarf around her mouth, pulled the flaps of her flying helmet over her ears, settled the goggles on the end of her nose, and was ready to set off. There was no danger of her getting lost as all she had to do was follow the road she was on. Despite the swirling snow she made good progress and a little over half an hour later she spotted the gates.

She wasn't sure of the correct protocol – but decided she would announce herself to the huddled shape in the gatehouse. She stood outside for a few moments waiting to be acknowledged but she was ignored. The windows were so steamed up perhaps he couldn't see her.

Her second bang on the door elicited a response, but not the one she was expecting. The man's head jerked up and he stared back with open mouth. Then he was on his feet. The door was flung open and she almost wet herself when he pushed a rifle into her middle. She stumbled back and ended up on her bottom in the snow.

'Sod me! I beg yer pardon, miss, I thought we was being invaded by the Huns.' He reached down and hauled her to her feet with a sheepish grin.

'That's all right, I expect it's my goggles that did it. I'm Ellen Simpson, reporting for training.'

'Where did you spring from? We didn't expect the next lot until this evening.'

Ellie hoped this interrogation wouldn't take too long. The snow had seeped through her winceyette long johns as well as her slacks and they were both clinging unpleasantly to her rear end.

'I walked here from the station.'

'Good for you. Come in for a minute whilst I ring through. They'll send someone from admin to get you.'

Sure enough in less than ten minutes a female figure, muffled in a greatcoat, arrived at the door. 'Good heavens, Simpson, this isn't a good start.' The young woman stared at her and obviously didn't like what she saw.

Ellie realised she'd committed a major *faux pas* – in fact two – firstly by not wearing stockings and skirt and secondly by having the temerity to walk on her own and not wait for the designated transport. She was tempted to offer go back to the station, but that would be childish.

Despite the disapproving look she wasn't going to apologise. She had been instructed to report immediately to this place and she'd done exactly that.

'Don't stand there gawping, Simpson, follow me. I'll conduct you to your barracks, but I warn you it won't be very pleasant as the stove isn't lit until five o'clock.'

Ellie smiled pleasantly but didn't reply. The years she'd spent at school had taught her it was better not to provoke those in authority.

The inside of the two-storey building she was taken to was almost as cold as the outside. 'I've no idea which are your quarters. There are lists pinned to the wall. Find your name and wait in there.'

With a swirl of her coat the unpleasant woman left her to her own devices. Ellie shivered in her wet clothes but refused to be cowed. Being here was her choice, she was going to make the best of it and not allow anything to depress her.

She found her name on the third list. The dormitory, if that's what it was called here, was easy to find and was even colder than she'd feared. There were five beds either side, arranged head to foot against the wall, and a large black stove in the centre. The iron bedsteads were stacked with three flat brown squares which presumably made up the mattress. On top were four blankets and two rough cotton sheets held together by a fifth folded blanket. The pile was finished by a lumpy pillow – there didn't appear to be a pillowslip for this.

She was first in so could choose which bed she wanted and decided on the one nearest the door. It might be beneficial to be able to exit first in some circumstances. As she was on her own there was no need for modesty. She stripped to the skin, dried herself with the towel she'd brought with her, and then hastily dressed again. This time she put on the one skirt she'd brought with her and her lisle stockings. She wasn't sure what to do with her wet slacks and long johns, they certainly wouldn't dry in here at the moment.

She draped them over the end of the bedstead and put her knapsack on the floor beside it. There was a locker which doubled as a bedside table, a mat and a couple of hooks behind each bed – surely there was more storage space than that for each of them?

Her belongings went in the locker. She didn't want to get anything personal out until she was sure she wasn't going to upset anyone by having the place she'd selected. Her clothes looked untidy over the bed so she hung them on the hooks.

Her stomach rumbled loudly. She'd had nothing to eat today apart from the picnic Mabel had provided. She might as well explore the building as she was going to freeze to death if she remained in here much longer. Even with her flying jacket, scarf and gloves on she was perishing.

The floors were stone, a reminder of their Victorian past. The bathrooms were no more than functional and when she turned a shower on only cold water emerged. Hopefully there would be hot in the mornings and evenings when they wanted to wash.

To keep the blood flowing she marched briskly up and down the long corridor until she was tired and then retreated to her dormitory. There were no chairs; the floor was too cold to sit on and she didn't dare unpack the mattress or bedding so she could use the bedstead as a seat.

There was kindling, newspaper and two hods of anthracite. She wasn't going to remain in the cold for another minute. Perhaps she should light the stove despite the fact she'd been told it mustn't be done until five o'clock. There was ice forming on the inside of the windows, her breath steamed in clouds in front of her, and she couldn't feel her extremities. Then she noticed that the long johns and slacks were rigid – the wet patches had frozen solid.

She had to remove her gloves to get the stove going but it was worth it. Half an hour later the cast-iron was red hot and she was beginning to thaw out. When the other girls arrived, instead of finding a damp and dismal dormitory, they would walk into somewhere a little more cheerful.

Having broken one rule, she decided she might as well make her bed so she had somewhere comfortable to sit. If she was going to be put on a charge it might as well be for two things instead of one. She'd already blotted her copybook, according to the unpleasant corporal, by arriving on her own. So much for wishing to make a good impression in her new life.

If only she had something to eat and a hot drink everything would be tickety-boo. The strange three-piece mattress proved to be as uncomfortable as she'd feared, but at least there were plenty of blankets. She stretched out on her neatly made bed and dozed off.

She was woken by the sound of girlish voices approaching. Now she was for it – but she didn't care, she was warm and everyone else in the dormitory would be as well. She would be unpopular with those in charge but she was sure the other girls would be pleased.

Their voices echoed down the empty corridor. For a horrible moment she thought they were going into a different room but then someone tentatively pushed open the door.

'Golly, it's lovely and warm in here.' The speaker rushed in followed by the others. Ellie might as well have been invisible as they all ignored her. Her eyes filled. She slumped back on the lumpy pillow and put the blanket over her head.

Someone poked her none too gently. 'You shouldn't have lit the stove or made up your bed. You will have us all on a charge because of your selfishness.'

Ellie sprung out of bed expecting to be surrounded by a circle of accusatory faces. Instead there was just one girl, the rest were smiling at her. This gave her the courage to stand up to the bully.

'I arrived more than two hours ago and I was damned if I was going to freeze to death whilst I waited for the rest of you to turn up. Instead of moaning, you should be grateful the dormitory's warm.'

The girl, about her own age, but taller and thinner, raised her hand as if she was going to prod her again.

'I'm already in trouble so go ahead, I'll knock you on your backside with pleasure.'

The girl lowered her arm and moved a few steps away.

'Thank you for making this place bearable. Don't take any notice of Iris, she thinks she's in charge, but she's not.' The speaker walked across and held out her hand. 'I'm Mary Smith, pleased to meet you.'

'I'm Ellen Simpson, and I'm delighted to meet you.' Mary was a bit older than her, with fair hair and pale blue eyes.

Immediately Ellie was surrounded by the others and they seemed a pleasant bunch, apart from Iris, of course. Some of them had biscuits and they were happy to hand them over to her once they heard of her plight.

'Are we the only new recruits on this draft?' Ellie asked.

'The driver of our bus said the rest are arriving tomorrow. We are the odds and sods who travelled up individually. I believe the rest are coming *en masse* from a rendezvous point,' Daisy Jenkins said. Daisy was short and dark with a smile that made her plain face pretty.

Ellie hoped she would become chums with Daisy and Mary.

The other girls decided to make their beds up as well as they didn't want to sit on the floor any more than she had. The room looked less austere once this was done. There was one bed still stacked with the bedding.

'Where's bossy boots gone?' This question was posed by the girl who was next to the empty bedstead.

'I bet she's gone to fetch that nasty corporal,' Daisy said.

'I'm not going to be cowed by her, I'm sure there are plenty of decent aircraft women in admin – they can't all be like Fitzwilliam,' someone else said with a smile.

'I shall own up to lighting the stove. There's no need for anyone else to get the blame for that.'

'I think that woman should get the blame for putting you in here and not taking you somewhere warm to wait. You showed initiative and guts walking in the snow. I'm sure whoever's in charge will appreciate what you did.'

'Thank you, Mary, but I doubt it will ever reach the ears of the commanding officer. I'm quite prepared to be put on a charge – it was worth it to be warm.'

For all her bravado she jumped every time she heard a noise thinking she was about to get her comeuppance. When half an hour had passed and there was still no sign of Iris she became concerned.

'I'm going to put on my outdoor things and go and look for her. She should have been back by now.'

'Maybe there's a telephone extension somewhere in this barracks,' Daisy suggested.

They split into pairs and searched each icy dormitory with no success. This only left the sergeant's quarters. 'I'm going to look in here. The rest of you go back into

341

the dormitory. There is no point in all of us being involved in another breach of the rules.'

All the girls apart from Daisy and Mary vanished immediately. 'We're coming with you, Ellie, it's not fair for you to stick your head above the parapet every time,' Mary said firmly.

The door opened with a creak that echoed down the corridor. This room was no warmer than anywhere else. 'It's over there, on that table by the window.'

Ellie picked it up and waited for an operator to answer.

Twenty-six

Ellie was connected with a lowly being who promptly passed her on to the CO. She gave her name and then explained the circumstances.

'Let me get this straight, Simpson, you walked from the station and were then left in the barracks in subzero temperatures? I'm glad you had the gumption to disobey orders and light the stove. Duvall has since wandered off into the snow?'

'Yes, ma'am.'

'I'll organise a search party. You remain where you are until someone comes to take you to the canteen. Be at the door in half an hour.'

Daisy and Mary were waiting eagerly to hear what had been said. Ellie explained and they were delighted.

'Hopefully that horrible Fitzwilliam will get a strip torn off. I hope Iris is all right – I don't like her very much but wouldn't like to think of her freezing to death,' Mary said.

'I'm certain she went out to snitch on us so I've no sympathy for her,' Daisy replied.

'I'm sure the others will be pleased we're going to be fed soon. I wonder why our sergeant hasn't put in an appearance.' She led the way back into the wonderfully warm dormitory.

Someone had made up Iris's bed for her and put her suitcase in the locker which made the room look tidier.

'Does anyone know what's going to happen to us over the next two weeks? Do we get to choose what we do?' Ellie asked.

'The leaflet said we get a basic training here, medicals and inoculations, and then get sent for further training if necessary. I've put down for admin as I was working as a secretary.' The speaker was a short, plump girl with hair the same colour as Jack's. Being reminded of him brought a lump to her throat.

'I want to be a radio or wireless operator – but as they are both the same thing – I don't know what the difference is,' she told them.

Her flying jacket, helmet and goggles were much admircd, as was the news that she had made her living as a flying instructor.

'It seems a terrible waste of your skills not to be able to fly,' Daisy said.

'At least being in the WAAF will mean I'm close to the aircraft even if I can't fly them. I did train half a dozen RAF recruits before my airfield was shut down.'

The conversation became general and, by the time they were all muffled up in their outer garments, Ellie thought she was going to enjoy spending the next few weeks with them. Having spent a few years at boarding school it was going to be easier for her to adapt to the new environment than for those who were away from home for the first time.

They were escorted to the canteen and issued with a small canvas bag with a knife, fork and spoon inside. These were referred to as irons and had to be brought to all meals. The food was no worse than she'd expected and she wolfed it down. They were served a steaming mug of cocoa, at least she thought that was what it was, and then marched back to the barracks. There'd been no sign of Iris and nobody she spoke to knew anything about her whereabouts.

*

When they were woken the next morning by a jolly corporal, Ellie was so cold she thought she wouldn't be able to get dressed. The stove had burned out during the night and even if they were allowed to, there wasn't the wherewithal to get it going again.

Her teeth were chattering by the time she'd had a perfunctory wash – no hot water – and returned to the dormitory. The other girls were in no better shape and the cheerful mood of the previous night had vanished. No one chatted, they all did as instructed and gathered miserably at the main doors waiting to be escorted to the canteen for breakfast.

She was issued with a number and a uniform. They returned briefly to the icy barracks to change from their civilian clothes. Ellie, like her fellow recruits, became a second-class aircraft woman – or ACW2. They had been instructed to parcel up their clothes in the brown paper provided. They then had to address them and leave them on the table outside the barracks.

It was now clear why they only needed two hooks and a small locker for their belongings. She was relieved to be escorted to a recreation area where they were told to remain until sent for.

'I think we all look very smart in our uniforms, don't you?' Daisy asked.

'At least they're lovely and warm. I've never been so embarrassed in my life when I was asked if I wanted to wear my own knickers,' one of the girls said.

'I'm wearing both,' Ellie said with a laugh. 'I wish we could wear trousers like the RAF. I'm not used to wearing skirts all the time.'

'I wish I knew what's happened to Iris. Surely someone knows where she is and if she's all right?' Daisy said to a chorus of agreement.

'I'll go into the sergeant's room and ring when we return to the dormitory,' Ellie offered.

They discovered half a dozen board games, two boxes of dominoes, a chess set and several packs of cards in a cupboard. The remainder of the morning was spent in these pursuits and despite her concern for the missing recruit, Ellie was feeling more positive by lunchtime.

They had been told to report to the canteen at twelve o'clock precisely. They no longer needed an escort as they were becoming more familiar with the depot. She walked with Daisy and Mary. As she pushed open the doors of the canteen the noise almost overwhelmed her.

The long room was heaving with an assortment of girls still in their civilian clothes. Automatically she straightened her shoulders and marched briskly to join the line.

*

Ellie didn't discover what had happened to Iris until several days later. The girl's belongings had disappeared and she had thought nothing of it. However, Iris Duvall had been given the option to change her mind about joining up and she'd taken it.

The next few days were spent in learning how to drill, listening to lectures on 'Kings regulations' and several visits to the medical centre for a variety of inspections. One girl was mortified to discover she had nits – but they rallied round and cheered her up.

Two weeks later she went before the selection board whose job it was to decide if any of the candidates had special qualifications. She did – but she didn't think they would be of any use to her in the WAAF.

They were seen in alphabetical order so she had to wait all day for her turn. Thankfully the waiting area was heated. Eventually she knocked politely on the door and stepped in, her log book and flying licences tucked under her arm.

The room was vast. In the far distance was a table behind which two grim-faced WAAFs and three male officers sat. They watched unsmilingly as she did her best to march smartly. She halted in front of them – and saluted.

'You may sit down,' said one of the WAAF officers, gesturing towards the chair placed centrally in front of the table.

Ellie was relieved to sit as her legs were about to give way beneath her.

'It says here that you are a qualified pilot,' the other female officer said.

'Yes, ma'am. I have my licence and log book here if you would care to see them.'

The woman snapped her fingers impatiently and Ellie pushed them across.

'There are no flying posts for women in the WAAF,' one of the male officers said.

Did he think she was a complete idiot? 'Yes, sir, I do know that. If I can't fly, then at least I can be close to those that do.'

This response failed to impress the men but the women exchanged glances that were slightly less frosty. She was asked about her education and work experience – which was nil apart from farming and flying– neither of which would be much use now.

They ignored her for a few moments whilst they talked in hushed voices together. 'I see that you expressed a preference for being a wireless or radio operator. We are in need of some girls for a classified operation. Are you prepared to volunteer without knowing the details?'

Ellie hesitated, remembering that she promised her family she wouldn't volunteer for anything but keep her head below the parapet. They were all looking at her, waiting for her answer.

'Yes, ma'am, I should like to volunteer.'

Finally, all the board looked relatively pleased with her. 'Good show. You will receive details of your posting in the next few days. Are you aware what the Official Secrets Act means?'

'Yes, ma'am, I am.'

'Then that's all. You may go. Good morning.'

Ellie jumped to her feet, her heart thudding, and hastily smoothed down her skirt which had ridden up her thighs. This time her salute was perfect. She about-turned and marched out. The drill sergeant would have been proud of her.

The next day postings were on the board. She desperately wanted to tell her friends that she'd volunteered for something important but remembered the warning about official secrets.

'Ellie, I'm so pleased you're being posted with us,' Mary said. 'There's only a few of us on this list. Isn't it exciting?'

The following morning the select group were ferried to the station and told to get on the next train. They were accompanied by a less than friendly male sergeant. They steamed and rattled for the remainder of the day, stopping and starting, reversing and shunting until eventually they were told to disembark. She had no idea whereabouts they were. They could have been travelling in a circle for all she knew.

There was no transport waiting for them. They were expected to march through the countryside, down winding lanes with high hedges over which they couldn't see. These new escorts were equally taciturn, and also male.

'I can smell the sea, Ellie,' Daisy whispered.

'You're right, I can too.'

After an hour's brisk marching they arrived at a wooden jetty which stuck out into a silent estuary. Not the sea – but close. This was deserted apart from three rowing boats.

If anyone dared to speak they were immediately told to be quiet. In silence, they stowed their bags and scrambled in to the boats. Fortunately, they weren't expected to do the rowing themselves, this was the job for their escorts.

A further thirty minutes was spent on the water. Night had fallen, but from the light of the full moon she could see they were travelling inland. The boat bumped against another wooden jetty, but this one was more dilapidated and much smaller.

It moved and swayed under their feet and she was glad to be on terra firma. They marched in the darkness until wrought iron gates appeared. They continued and there was the crunch of gravel under her feet. This was the drive to a large, stately home of some sort. It was impossible to see clearly exactly where they'd arrived.

There was no supper offered before they were directed to their accommodation. She fell asleep hungry and still not sure exactly what she'd volunteered for.

*

Jack had only to complete the navigational sections of the initial training as his log book made the basic training unnecessary. He found himself billeted with half a dozen blokes with similar experience and they were all destined to be fighter pilots.

They seemed a reasonable bunch although none of them had the flying hours that he did. He passed the exam with no difficulty and was shunted off to an

Operational Training Unit – known as OTU – where he would learn how to fly a Spitfire or a Hurricane.

He'd become close pals with a fellow recruit. Ian was the same age as him, but there the resemblance ended. Whereas he was an inch under six foot, Ian was several inches shorter. He was best described as wiry, with thick black hair. His father was Chinese, which you could see in his slightly oriental features.

They were lounging about in the local pub when another member of the group burst in. 'What's up with Rollo? Never seen him so animated,' Ian said as he slurped his warm beer.

Jack beckoned him over. 'Bad news, mate? Has the missus run-off with the milkman?'

Rollo shook his head. 'Worse than that. I've just heard there aren't going to be any Spitfires to train on – we'll have to make do with Hurricanes.'

'Is that all? I thought Hitler had invaded. They can't build them fast enough to let us loose on them in case we go for a Burton. I'm sure you'll get to fly one eventually,' Jack said unsympathetically.

'I suppose you're right, as usual. I need a couple of pints to cheer me up. Are you buying?'

'Bugger off! It's about time you stood us a round.'

The banter continued and became noisier when the remainder of their group arrived and joined in. He left them to it after three drinks and made his way through the inky streets with only the pinpoint of light from his pocket torch to stop him breaking his neck.

*

The instructor was a veteran from the previous war, but he'd flown Hurricanes and Spitfires often enough to be able to fulfil his job efficiently. Rollo had been right and they were to complete their training on Hurricanes.

The next few weeks were spent on night flying, navigation, cross country and all-weather practice. The final two weeks of the six-week course was devoted to flying mock battles. They were divided into two groups and took turns chasing each other around the sky. At the end of each day Jack's neck was raw where the stiff collar of his shirt bit into him every time he turned his head.

Staying alive in a fighter plane was dependent on the pilot being able to see an enemy plane approaching. Firing blanks at each other wasn't the same as using live ammo, but obviously a lot safer.

At the end of the training four of the blokes were commissioned and only he and Ian became flight sergeants. It hadn't been suggested that he became an officer and he thought that was because of his association with Joe who was now languishing at His Majesty's Pleasure in Wandsworth.

He was being sent to Croydon to join 17 Squadron and would be flying a Hurry as expected. He was pleased his friend Ian was coming with him. He began to regret that he hadn't been commissioned when he discovered that the Officers' Mess was where most of the pilots congregated. The Sergeants' Mess might have better beer but it wasn't where you got all the gen about what was going to happen.

He was a bit cheesed off about being treated like an inferior specimen by the toffee-nosed lot. No doubt when it all kicked off, and he proved his worth, things would be different. The RAF only took volunteers which meant that even the lowliest ACM2 had chosen to be there.

It rankled that he had ten times the flying hours than anyone else in his squadron but he was still spoken to as if he was in need of advice. Until the weather improved, there wasn't even the pleasure of taking his kite up for a spin. He played cards, but as he wasn't a gambler he didn't join the games of pontoon and poker.

He and Ian, now nicknamed Bob, played darts and dominoes together most of the time.

'Hey, Ginger, there's a letter for you,' an orderly yelled across the room.

'Chuck it over then, I'm too bloody idle to come and get it.' His response was received with a rude gesture but the envelope spun across the room and landed in his lap.

'That from Ellie?' Bob asked as he stared morosely at his hand of dominoes.

'Nobody else writes to me, so it must be.'

He looked forward to his weekly letters from Ellie. The dogs were earning their keep as there had been no further visits from the fox. Fred and Mrs B were happy and there'd been no further aggravation from the ex-Mrs Simpson.

He'd been surprised when she'd written to tell him she was joining the WAAF but didn't blame her. She was the sort of girl who needed excitement in her life and planting spuds wasn't going to suit her. The last letter he'd had she'd told him she'd just finished her training and was about to be posted. He'd heard nothing since and it was more than three weeks.

He examined the envelope and the writing was unfamiliar. He tore it open and pulled out a single sheet of paper.

Dear Jack,

I'm sorry to tell you that your Uncle Joe passed away last week. The doctors said it was his heart. I got your present address from Mr Simpson. There will be a letter coming from the solicitors about his will.

The funeral will have taken place by the time you receive this. I hope you're keeping well,

best wishes

Joe dead – terrible for the poor old bugger to end his life in prison, even if he did deserve to be there. There was no forwarding address on the letter so he couldn't reply.

'What's up, mate? Bad news?'

'My uncle died last week. I told you about him. I don't think he was more than fifty, but I expect the strain of being inside did for him.' He tore the letter up and tossed the bits into the nearest waste-bin. 'It should have been from Ellie. I'm going to give Fred a ring just to make sure everything's all right.'

There was no queue for the one phone. He dialled the operator, gave Fred's number, put sufficient pennies into the slot and waited with his finger poised. As soon as he heard Mrs B he pushed the button and heard the money drop.

'Mrs B, it's Jack. I've not heard from Ellie and just wanted to know that she's okay.'

'My Fred's that worried about it, Jack. He told her not to volunteer and heaven knows where she's been sent or what she's doing. We have to send our letters to an office and then they forward them for us. I can give you that address if you like.'

He wrote it down. 'Thank you, just what I wanted. I expect she's too busy being trained in whatever it is and hasn't got a moment to write.'

'She could always give her dad a call.'

'If it's a secret establishment I doubt that they have access to a telephone.'

He spent the remainder of the time before the pips went enquiring after Fred and the farm and then said goodbye. Whatever hush-hush job she was being trained for, she couldn't be kept incommunicado indefinitely.

Twenty-seven

Ellie was none the wiser as to what she might actually be doing at the end of the course even though she'd spent the day sitting with Mary inside a blacked-out cubicle. Half a dozen of these little boxes had been constructed in the main hall of this stately home. An RAF man stood behind them giving them instructions.

The girls emerged blinking from their confinement, none of them speaking, all of them looking as bewildered as she was. They had half an hour's free time before they had to go to the canteen for their evening meal.

She was sharing with Daisy and Mary and as soon as the doors closed she said what she'd been holding back until that moment. 'What on earth have we been doing? I can't see how staring at that screen and twiddling the knobs to find a green blob is of any use to anyone.'

'I've got a splitting headache,' Mary said, 'do either of you have any aspirin?'

Daisy gave her a couple from the bottle she kept in her wash bag. 'Half the time we didn't see anything apart from flashes and lines on the screen.'

'I wish I hadn't volunteered, I really don't want to spend the rest of my time in the WAAF shut away like we have been today,' Ellie said.

'There's not time to have a lie down or proper wash before we go to eat, I'm not particularly hungry, but if the food is as good as it was at lunchtime I expect I'll force it down.' Daisy rubbed her eyes and went to collect her irons from the bedside table.

'The work might be peculiar, but it's a very comfortable billet we've got here. A real mattress and proper sheets is a luxury I've learned to live without,' Ellie said with a smile.

'There's no telephone we can use and it doesn't seem as if we're going to get any opportunity to go outside and get fresh air or exercise.' Mary swallowed her aspirins with a glass of water and ran a comb through her hair.

When they were all sitting at the large dining table one of the male officers repeated even more forcefully that they were not to discuss anything they did or saw under any circumstances.

As they weren't allowed to make telephone calls or write letters or even walk in the grounds there was no chance that any of them could break the rules.

*

The days became weeks and Ellie became more adept at the task of locating the little blobs of light. She now knew they were called 'echoes'. She was puzzled by the compass scale on the locating control but used it as instructed.

Already three of the girls had left but fortunately her roommates were still there. As the course came to an end they were told to assemble in the lecture hall where what they had been doing would become clear.

The Commanding Officer stood up and smiled at them. 'Thank you for your hard work and for putting up with the monotony and lack of exercise. What you have been doing is learning to use radar interception.'

Ellie had vaguely heard about this new invention. It was something that could detect enemy aircraft approaching and would give the RAF a huge advantage over the enemy. To have been involved in something so worthwhile made the three weeks of boredom and incarceration acceptable.

'Imagine that,' Daisy said as they left the lecture room. 'We'll be doing really valuable work – much better than anything else that was on offer when we signed up.'

'If I can't fly then this is the next best thing. Being able to keep our boys safe in the air is a great job. Do you think we'll get any leave before we're sent to our postings?' Ellie said.

'I doubt it. Someone said there's going to be a leaving party tonight. There will be music, alcohol and men,'

Mary said gleefully.

'I think that a couple of the girls have already got to know their instructors quite well. The chap we had suffered from bad breath so we had to keep facing front and I don't really know what he looks like.'

The others laughed. 'Any port in a storm, Ellie. I'm not averse to a bit of how's your father as long as they smell a bit sweeter than the one we had teaching us,' Mary said.

'I think we were unlucky because somebody told me they'd had a nice bit of slap and tickle with their bloke.'

'I only intend to canoodle with a Brylcreem boy, officers only for me.'

'Daisy, I'm shocked. I'm glad that I'm engaged to Greg and don't have to worry about being chased by officers or other ranks.'

'I'm not surprised you said yes, he's a bit of all right,' Mary said as she led the way into their accommodation.

*

The following day Ellie was posted with her friends to a radar station at Rye on the south coast. They were received enthusiastically by the male operatives as these poor chaps had been working every day without respite.

The nearest town was miles away and none of the men had been allowed leave because of the shortage of trained personnel. There was no suitable accommodation at the camp so they were billeted with a local doctor and his wife. This meant a two-mile walk morning and evening, but it did mean she was getting plenty of fresh air and exercise now.

Another girl was added to their group as they had to work in teams of four. Vanessa was an ex-deb and talked as if she had a plum in her mouth. Despite her initial reservations Ellie thought she was a good egg.

The first morning they were escorted to the hut where they were to work. Although it was a mile or two from the coast the bitter wind from the channel battered its wooden sides relentlessly.

'Right, ladies, this is how things work,' they were told by a depressed looking male officer. 'You will work eight hours on and sixteen hours off on your watch. One of you will operate the screen, one fix the position of the echo and inform central control. The third is to record everything in a log and the fourth to act as telephonist and tea maker. Is that clear?'

'Yes, sir. How do we decide which duty we have?'

'Simpson, isn't it?' Ellie nodded wondering how he knew her name. 'You change your duty every two hours. It doesn't matter where you start – you'll do each task in a shift.'

No one minded who did what first. Her first duty was as a telephonist. The hut was totally blacked out, rocked in the wind from the sea, and even with greatcoats, scarves and balaclavas on they were still cold. Only constant mugs of hot, sweet tea kept them from freezing to death.

Occasionally Ellie had the energy to go into town when her time off coincided with daylight – but usually she was too tired to do anything but catch up on her sleep. So the months drifted past with only her weekly letters from Greg and Jack to break the monotony. Nothing much was happening to either of them and they were both bored and eager for the war to start in earnest. The only telephone available was in town so calls were now a thing of the past.

'It's not so bad being in this beastly hut now the weather's improved,' Vanessa said as she and Ellie sipped their tea and Daisy and Mary got on with the real work. Answering the telephone and scribbling down anything that was spotted on the screen were less stressful than the other two.

They were conversing in whispers although the other two couldn't hear them as they were wearing headsets.

'It might as well be winter the amount of sunlight we get to sit in. It's May, a heatwave out there, and we're all as pale as ghosts.' She finished her tea before continuing whilst Vanessa jotted down a few things in the log book. 'The news isn't good, is it? Hitler has stormed across Holland and Belgium and the Prime Minister has resigned.'

'We'll be better off with Winston Churchill – he's a man who knows what he's doing. My brother is in

France and Mummy has heard nothing from him. General Gort is in charge of the army, you know, and Clive thinks the world of him, so I expect he's fine.'

Unfortunately, accommodation had now been built for them at the base and they had to leave their cushy billet with the doctor. Ellie wasn't looking forward to being there next winter as it was basic to say the least, and they didn't have a wireless. If they wanted to hear the news they had to remain in the recreation room with everyone else.

As a non-smoker she found the blue haze created by the smoke unpleasant so spent as little time as possible in there. This meant she often got news second hand.

Weekends no longer existed – they didn't get days off. On Sunday, 26th May, her watch had been from midnight to eight o'clock in the morning. When she and the other members of the team headed for the canteen later that day, everyone off duty was congregated in the recreation room listening to the wireless.

Hitler was driving the British and French armies back to the coast and they were being fired at and bombed. The RAF fighters were protecting the soldiers as they retreated and British warships were trying to evacuate as many as they could before they were killed or captured.

*

Greg decided to ask for a transfer to a fighter squadron. That was where the main action was going to be and he didn't want to be a bus driver any longer. He wanted to take a more active role in shooting down enemy aircraft. Dropping bombs on civilians wasn't supposed to happen, but he knew, like everyone else in the squadron, it was inevitable. He wasn't comfortable with the idea of killing innocent people; by becoming a Spitfire or Hurricane pilot he wouldn't have to do that.

When he handed in his request the adjutant looked less than pleased. 'I see from your log book, Flight Lieutenant Dunlop, that you have some experience flying a single engine plane. We are desperately short of pilots of any sort and I don't expect you'll get a transfer as this would mean losing an experienced flyer from here who I doubt we would be able to replace.'

Greg was about to reply but the adjutant continued.

'Nevertheless, I'll put this through, but don't get your hopes up, old chap.' He waved his hand and Greg was dismissed.

There was nothing to do apart from the occasional night flight to keep their skills honed when weather permitted. He'd got a forty-eight-hour pass but as Ellie was away somewhere training there was no point in him leaving the base.

He was cycling around the apron just as a Tiger Moth landed. He pedalled furiously towards it and arrived just as pilot jumped out.

'Can you give me a lift? I don't care where you're going – I just want to get away for a bit?'

'I'm delivering spare parts – if you care to give me a hand unloading them, I'd be happy to.'

Greg discovered the middle-aged airman was returning to Hornchurch where he was based. Neil was there; it would be grand to catch up with his friend as he hadn't seen him since Christmas, almost four months ago.

He grabbed his overnight bag, made sure his whereabouts for the next twenty-four hours had been logged, and was ready to scramble into the front seat of the little plane.

Even with his flying jacket and helmet on it was cold in the open cockpit. At least he had a heated flying suit when he went up in the Blenheim.

The short hop to Hornchurch was over too quickly. The pilot landed smoothly, they shook hands, and Greg went in search of his friend. He found him in the Officers' Mess.

'Good God! How the hell did you get here?'

'I cadged a lift. I've got two days' leave and this seemed as good a place as any to come.'

Over a beer he told Neil about his wish to become a fighter pilot. 'I doubt I'll get a transfer, but I had to ask. I just hope my CO doesn't think I'm lacking in moral fibre and has me demoted and sent to scrub latrines for the duration.'

Two chaps overheard his remark. One of them, Greg realised, was wearing the insignia of a Wing Commander. He was about to leap to his feet and salute but the man waved him back.

'Ever been up in a Spit?'

'No, sir. But I've logged twenty hours in single engine kites.'

'Bus driver, are you? What's your squadron?'

Greg told him and the man pulled a face. 'Bloody Blenheims are absolutely useless. Not fast enough and vulnerable to enemy attack. Simpson, let him have a spin in your crate. See how he goes. Do three bumps and circuits.'

His friend didn't look too pleased about this but could hardly refuse a senior officer. Once they were outside he gripped Greg's elbow. 'If you prang my Spit I'll kill you. There aren't any spares – not enough coming from the factories at the moment.'

Neil stood on the wing and ran through the basics. 'Pre-op flight check is the same. Good luck – take care of her.' He jumped down and a couple of ground engineers took over. Moments later the Merlin engine roared into life – the propeller turned and it was chocks away.

Greg taxied from the apron onto the runway. Waited for the green light and then took off. The Spitfire was a joy to fly, a bit claustrophobic inside the closed cockpit after the space in the Blenheim, but this was more than made up for by its responsiveness.

He did a circuit and came in to land. He repeated this manoeuvre three times and each one was perfect. He felt as if he'd been born to fly this fighter and it made him even more determined somehow to win himself a place in one of the squadrons.

'That was capital. Thanks so much for allowing me to take her up. She's everything I've heard, and more.' He clapped his friend on the back and Neil laughed.

'You handled her as well as anyone in the squadron. If the Wing Co agrees I'll see if you can borrow Digger's kite when we go for a mock sortie later today. Digger's wife has just produced their first sprog and he's got compassionate leave.'

Greg couldn't believe his luck. If he proved himself then it would make his application more attractive as he wouldn't need to receive any further training. He and Neil spent the next couple of hours together. By the end of it he was sure he understood what he'd have to do.

'You must keep your eyes peeled, constantly look from side to side for enemy planes. Be able to manoeuvre, spin and loop in order to evade the enemy gunners,' Neil told him. 'You only have a couple of minutes of ammunition so you have to make it count. Our job is to shoot down the bombers before they can drop their load.'

Neil drained his glass before continuing. 'Talking about acrobatics reminds me of Jack Reynolds, I think he'll make an ideal fighter. He's had years of experience.

Ellie said in her last letter he's now stationed at Croydon and flying a Hurricane.'

For some reason hearing about Reynolds gave him an uneasy feeling. Why was his fiancée writing to another man?

He enjoyed every minute of the exercise and believed he slotted in as if already an experienced fighter pilot. The Wing Co sought him out just after they landed and said he would do his best to facilitate a transfer as Greg was exactly the sort of chap he was looking for.

That night there was a social at a nearby village hall and he had no option but to attend along with everyone else. He was also to spend the night in the bed of the absent Digger.

The hall was full of eager partygoers. There was dancing for those who wished to do so, card tables at the far end and silly party games for the children. Only tea and buns were served, but there was a convenient hostelry a few doors down and, like everyone else, he nipped down there for a quick pint every now and again.

As the event got going a group of land girls walked in – to his astonishment he recognised one of them. It was Elizabeth Hamilton, a deb he'd had a brief relationship with before he'd joined the RAF.

'Gregory Dunlop, I can't believe it's you. Or should I say Flight Lieutenant Dunlop?' Elizabeth hesitated for a second and then stepped in as if expecting him to kiss her. Instead he offered his hand and she shook it vigorously.

'Elizabeth, I never imagined you would join something so mundane as the land army. But I must say you look very well on it.'

They stepped to one side so they could continue their conversation in private. He told her he was engaged and that his fiancée was doing something hush-hush in East Sussex. She said she'd joined up to escape a persistent suitor.

He was introduced to the other three girls and in turn he introduced them to Neil. A very pleasant evening was spent dancing and chatting. Although he'd left his old life behind he was still pleased to hear how his erstwhile friends were coping with the war.

He returned to his temporary billet three sheets to the wind and humming the hokey-cokey. Elizabeth had the day off tomorrow and they'd agreed to meet up for a picnic. He felt the same way about her as Ellie did about Jack. When he explained to Neil, his future brother-in-law told him life was too short to miss out on a bit of light relief. If his friend didn't see any harm in seeing an ex-girlfriend then there was no need for him to feel guilty.

Twenty-eight

Ellie and her friends walked to the cliff edge to watch the appalling inferno of bombs and shells that were dropping on the BEF trapped on the beaches at Dunkirk. The fact that all three of them had been promoted to ACW1 no longer seemed important.

Wave after wave of fighters roared overhead in a desperate attempt to protect the men from the Luftwaffe.

'I don't see how they can survive for much longer,' Ellie said to Daisy.

'I know we can't actually see what's happening, but the flashes and explosions on the other side of the channel are quite clear.'

Mary wiped her eyes. 'My brother's an officer over there. My parents are beside themselves with worry. The warships won't be able to get close enough to the beach so the men must swim. Nigel can't swim very well.'

Ellie pointed to the sea. 'Look at that – people have responded to the call on the wireless last night. There are hundreds of little boats heading for France. They are

371

going to fetch the soldiers too. Maybe their help will be enough to save them.'

They remained, sitting on the grass, until it was time to return for their watch. The sky was still noisy with Spitfires and Hurricanes and she wondered if one of them was piloted by Jack or Neil.

There were now more trained radar operators so they no longer worked continuous watches. The news was more encouraging and by Tuesday, 4th of June, the newspapers were reporting that hundreds of thousands of British and French troops had been saved. Churchill was calling it a victory but Ellie didn't think the families of those who had died would agree. She was aware just how many fighters had failed to return.

She was returning bleary eyed from the night watch two days later when she was waylaid. 'ACW1 Simpson, you are to report immediately to the CO.'

Her heart sunk. She could think of only one reason why she'd been summoned. With both her brothers, her fiancé and Jack in the RAF she'd been dreading getting this call. Mary had been on edge since the evacuation started and still didn't know if her brother was safe.

As soon as she stepped into the office she knew the news was going to be the worst possible. Someone she loved had died. She saluted and remained at attention ignoring the suggestion that she be seated.

'My dear, I have the sad task of informing you that your brother Flight Lieutenant Neil Simpson died yesterday. His aircraft was so badly damaged that he couldn't land it safely. He was unable to bail out for some reason.'

Ellie heard the words but they didn't make sense. Her beloved older brother couldn't be dead. She stared at her CO unable to respond coherently.

'You have been given a week's compassionate leave, Simpson. You may collect your travel docket from my secretary. I have arranged for you to get a lift to the station.'

Ellie nodded, dry eyed, saluted a second time and marched out having not spoken a word. She ran to her quarters relieved the hut was empty as the girls would be getting their breakfast. After tossing all her belongings into her kit bag she raced off, praying she wouldn't meet anyone and need to explain where she was going.

If she didn't say the words, then maybe it wouldn't be true. The thought that she would never hear Neil call her his little sister again was too awful to accept. A staff car was waiting and she scrambled into the back, not wishing to sit beside the driver and be obliged to talk.

The journey to Glebe Farm passed in a blur. She remained sunk in her misery, unable to cry in public, torn apart by guilt that she was glad it wasn't Greg who had died. When she emerged on the station at Romford she realised she should have let her dad know she was coming. She wouldn't be able to get a taxi so late – none of them liked to work in the blackout.

She slung her bag over her shoulder and decided to walk. There was sufficient moonlight to be able to find her way safely and it shouldn't take more than a couple of hours. Despite having spent so much of her time huddled in front of a screen these past few months she was still fit and strong.

It was two o'clock when she trudged down the drive. Only then did she think about the problems of getting into the house. She would have to wake Mabel and get her to open the back door.

She was still half a mile away when the dogs arrived at her feet whining and barking with excitement. She'd forgotten the animals were left out overnight to protect the birds.

'Good boys, I'm glad to see you too. Stop jumping, you'll have me over. How did you know I was coming?' Somehow it made things a little easier talking to the dogs as though they understood.

She was a hundred yards away from the dark bulk of the farmhouse when a tall figure appeared from the darkness. He didn't have to speak, she recognised Greg's outline immediately.

Dropping her bag, she ran towards him and threw herself sobbing into his arms.

'Sweetheart, I thought it would be you coming when the dogs shot off. I'm so sorry. Neil was a good chap.' He held her close and his strength was enough to comfort her.

She gulped and snuffled, wiped her eyes and nose and was finally able to speak. 'How's Dad? He must be devastated.'

'He's taking it as well as can be expected in the circumstances. The funeral is the day after tomorrow. George and Jack have got leave to attend.'

'I hadn't seen him since Christmas – but we wrote to each other most weeks.'

'Actually, I saw him a couple of weeks ago.'

Greg explained how this happened and told her that he'd got a transfer and was joining Neil's squadron after the funeral.

'The next few weeks are going to be difficult for all of you. I think almost two hundred planes were lost and God knows how many soldiers were killed on the beaches. We won't be the only family mourning the loss of a loved one this week.'

'I hope you didn't wake anyone when you came out. Did the dogs bark?'

'I haven't been to bed yet. I've been wandering about out here. Which reminds me, darling, why didn't you ring? Nobody would have minded being woken up and I could have come and got you.' He still had his arm around her waist and turned to guide her towards the house.

'Hang on, I dropped my bag. I better collect it; in case it rains.'

'No, I'll get it.' She stood, numb, whilst he raced off and fetched it. 'I'll chuck it on the porch and then we can sit in the garden for a bit and talk.' He kept his arm firmly around her waist and guided her towards the house. The kitbag thumped nosily on the porch and the dogs barked in excitement.

'Shut up, you two, you'll wake everyone up,' Greg said and they slunk off.

She was so tired she could hardly see straight and would be better off in bed but didn't want to be alone, not tonight. Greg guided her towards the rose arbor. She stumbled and he swore. Next thing she knew she was in his arms being carried and she felt safe and comforted by his love and strength.

He didn't continue to the garden but returned to the house and shouldered his way in and took her to the sitting room. He sat on the sofa with her in his arms and then let her cry. She woke later in the morning still in his arms but now they were in her bed and she was in her underwear.

She shot up in bed. 'Greg, you shouldn't be in here...'

'I wasn't leaving you alone, not when you were so devastated. Are you feeling any better, darling?'

'Not really, but I'll be able to cope with you beside me.' His hair was tousled and he needed a shave but she had never loved him more. 'At least you are fully clothed, unlike myself.'

'I'm not an idiot. If you're okay I'd better get washed and shaved.' He leaned closer and kissed her gently before rolling off and striding to the door. Only then did she see he had left it wide open.

'See you downstairs in half an hour. I love you, sweetheart, and I'm so sorry.'

His parting smile was sad and belatedly she remembered Neil had been his best friend. He was grieving too but had put her first as he always did. She dragged herself to the wash-stand and quickly sluiced herself down with the cold water from the jug. She put on a clean shirt and stepped back into her uniform skirt and jacket. She was glad she didn't have to wear black.

The house didn't seem the same. It wasn't just that her beloved brother was dead – she thought it was her. She'd changed, she wasn't the naïve girl who had left home all those months ago.

Dad had already gone out to work. Farming wasn't something you could take a break from unless you'd got someone else in to do your job. Even the death of a son didn't mean you got compassionate leave.

Greg joined her outside on the terrace – it was too hot to eat in the kitchen. She moved willingly into his arms and they kissed. If anything happened to him she didn't think she would ever really recover. He was the most important person in her life now. He tucked a strand of her hair behind her ear. 'Your father has had a letter from Mrs Simpson in response to his telling her about

Neil. It seems she will be coming to the funeral. Will you be alright seeing her again?'

'It's almost a year since she left. She and Dad are no longer married, but Neil was still her first-born. It wouldn't be right to stop her coming but I hope Sir Reginald doesn't accompany her. Which reminds me, why hasn't he been arrested? Isn't it treason to support Hitler?'

'I'm sure he wouldn't be so crass as to come here after what happened the last time. And you're right, people like him should be behind bars.'

She'd lost her appetite and put down her cutlery, feeling guilty she was leaving a perfectly good plate of egg and bacon when there was a war on and rationing in place. 'If you're not going to eat that, Ellie, do you mind if I polish it off? Pity to waste it.'

She drank her tea in silence trying not to think about the reason she was home. 'By the way, I don't even know how old you are or when your birthday is. In fact, how have we got engaged when we know so little about each other?'

'I'll be twenty-four on 28th June. I have two sisters, one ten, the other eight years older than me. My parents don't live together and I've not spoken to my father either for over a year.'

'I think you told me that before. My birthday's not until October and I'll be twenty then.'

The telephone rang and she jumped to her feet and went to answer it. The caller was another neighbour ringing to give their condolences and ask when the funeral was. She replaced the receiver and scrubbed her cheeks dry with her sleeve.

Mabel spoke from behind her. 'I've just heard that three families in the village have lost someone too. I don't suppose it's going to get any easier. Them blooming Germans will be over here dropping bombs on us soon.'

'I keep telling myself that Neil died fighting for us – but it doesn't make it any less horrible.' She swallowed the lump in her throat and pushed herself away from the table she'd been slumped against. 'Do you need any help getting the rooms ready?'

'Bless you, Ellie, but that's not your job. My friends are helping out with the wake. We'll give your brother a good send off, don't you worry.'

*

Having Greg there helped to ease her grief. He understood how she was feeling and was there for her to cry on whenever she needed him. The mantelpiece and windowsills in the sitting room were crowded with condolence cards. Greg made himself useful on the farm while she took the dogs for a walk, answered the telephone, and replied to the cards.

Somehow, she staggered through the two days, but couldn't have endured it without Greg being there. Dad turned to Mabel for comfort and this was how it should be. This was no longer her home. She had grown up, was a responsible member of the WAAF doing essential war work, and she knew that in future she would be a visitor to Glebe Farm not a member of the household.

George and Jack shared a taxi and arrived on the morning of the funeral. Because of petrol rationing there would be no procession, the coffin would be taken directly to the church by the undertakers.

Her brother hugged her, not something he usually did, and he seemed genuinely distressed. 'I thought it would be me that would go first, I can't believe he's gone. Bloody war – bloody Germans.'

'Mum's coming – did you know that?'

He looked uncomfortable. 'Actually, Ellie, I took Fiona to meet her and Grandpa. Don't look so horrified, Sir Reginald has learnt his lesson and cut all ties to the fascists. He had nothing to do with that unpleasantness, it was someone else on the list.'

She stepped away from him, shocked by his admission. Jack was waiting his turn to embrace her. 'You look good in your uniform, Ellie. I'm pleased to see you, but wish it was in better circumstances. We lost fifteen from our base – some of them good friends of mine.'

'George just told me he's been visiting my mother and that horrible man. How could he betray the family like that?'

'You told me that he's always been your mother's favourite. Stands to reason he'd want to keep in touch. You don't have to see any of them again after this if you don't want.' He dumped his kitbag by the door and put his arm through hers. 'Let's go for a walk in the garden. There's something I want to tell you that might cheer you up a bit.'

She couldn't think that anything he had to say would make her feel any better.

'Did you know that they are taking on female pilots in the ATA? A girl turned up at the base the other day. She was delivering some spare parts and left with a bloke who needed a lift. She was flying a Tiger Moth like the one we had. Why don't you apply?' He handed her a form he'd been keeping in his inside pocket. 'I picked this up for you in case you want to have a go at getting in.'

She took it and quickly scanned the page. It appeared she had exactly the qualifications they were looking for. 'I wondered what ATA stood for, now I know – Air Transport Auxiliary.'

'It seems they only had male pilots, but we've lost so many blokes they've decided they're going to take on suitably qualified women. This means the men can leave and join an active squadron. It's a civilian operation so I'm not sure exactly how it works.'

'I'm going to apply. The WAAF would never have let me leave a few months ago, but they've got plenty of radar operatives now so they might well agree. I'd be better off doing something very few girls can do.'

This information had definitely cheered her up. She threw her arms around his neck and kissed him on the cheek. He hugged her back then gently removed her hands.

'Don't encourage me, Ellie, I never could resist a pretty girl even when she's spoken for.'

'Thank you so much. Now I've got something to look forward to. I'll fill this in right away – would you post this for me when you leave this evening?'

The leaflet that accompanied the form explained they were only looking for female pilots with more than two hundred hours in the log book and she had over two thousand. There were stamps in the drawer downstairs and she thought she'd get one and bring it up, rather than take the envelope down. This was the second time she'd applied for something without telling anyone – she wasn't sure why she hadn't told Greg. Being a civilian would be better as far as he was concerned as she could leave whenever she wanted to.

*

Dad was driving his truck. She and Mabel were sitting in the front and George, Jack and Greg had to make do with the back. George obviously wasn't pleased but got in without comment. They arrived only minutes before the hearse.

There were no wreaths on the coffin, just a large bunch of garden flowers. Sombre music could be heard in the church. Greg, George and Jack took one side of the coffin and three other RAF officers took the other side. The vicar moved in front and led the procession into the church whilst solemnly intoning the words from the funeral service.

Ellie put her arm through Dad's and dropped in behind. Mabel had already taken her place in the congregation. Mum should have been there with them.

She bit her lip and marched as she'd been taught by the drill sergeant. As long as she concentrated on her steps she wouldn't break down. The church was packed. Even with her eyes firmly to the front she was aware there were a dozen or more grey-blue uniforms.

A pew had been reserved for them at the front. Mum and Sir Reginald were already occupying two of the seats but there was plenty of room for Dad, George and her, but Jack and Greg would have to sit elsewhere.

The service followed the usual pattern, too many hymns and too many prayers before they got to the eulogy. She'd expected George to do this but it was left to the vicar, who'd scarcely known Neil, to tell everybody what an exceptional young man her brother had been, and how much he was going to be missed. He ended by saying he died for King and Country and to keep his family safe.

Her handkerchief was sodden and she wished Greg was beside her and not George. Eventually the service was over and the entire congregation traipsed outside for the burial. Neil wouldn't be lonely here, with more than two dozen Simpsons in adjacent plots. Their family had bought this corner of the churchyard one hundred and fifty years ago and she hoped, when her turn came, she could rest with them as well.

Greg was beside her and she turned her face against his shoulder needing his comfort. As one by one people moved to the grave to pay their respects he led her to a quieter spot. 'Come on, let's get it over with, darling.'

'I don't want to speak to her or him…'

'I know, but you must. They're waiting for you.'

Without his arm moving her forward she would have run away. She had expected her mother to look more elegant. happier, but the reverse was true. The woman standing nervously beside Sir Reginald couldn't meet her eyes. Ellie's animosity evaporated. Suddenly she was sorry for her. Dad was happy with his new life but her mother obviously wasn't.

'Mother, thank you for coming…'

Sir Reginald interrupted her. 'It's not your place to thank your mother, miss. Of course my daughter would attend her son's funeral.'

Ellie ignored him. 'I'm glad you came. I hope we can stay in touch.'

Again, the bully spoke for her. 'My daughter is no longer part of your life, young lady. She is back where she belongs. Come along, Charlotte, the car's waiting.'

He grabbed her mother's arm and marched her away. 'That was quite horrible. Mum wasn't allowed to even speak...'

'Sweetheart, don't feel sorry for her. It was her choice to leave Fred and go back to him. Forget about her.'

'I'm going to try and get her on her own at the wake. I can't bear to think of her being unhappy.' She looked around at the crowd of RAF personnel milling about the graveyard. 'Who are all these men?'

'His entire squadron is here to pay their last respects. I'm so sorry, darling, you know I was intending to stay the night but I've got a lift in the truck. I've told them they can come back to Glebe Farm. I think his squadron leader wants to have a word with you and Fred.'

'That's a shame, but duty comes first.'

George didn't travel back in the truck with Jack and Greg – he must have been in the car with the others.

'Don't you worry about anything, Ellie love, my friends and I have got everything in hand. You spend as much time as you can with your young man before he leaves.'

'Thank you, Mabel, I'll do that.'

The wake was being held outside and if it wasn't for the fact that those not in uniform were in black, it could have been a garden party. Nobody stayed very long and her mother, George and Sir Reginald failed to attend at all. It was as if she'd lost two brothers today.

Jack had hugged her and she'd shed a few more tears as he too was going back in the RAF transport. There was something she needed to say to Greg before he left and she took him to the rose garden where they could be alone.

'The Germans will be invading Britain soon. You could be killed next. I don't want to wait – I want to get married as soon as we can. We just don't know how much time we've got left.'

His arms tightened. 'If you're sure, sweetheart, then I'm all for it. If you talk to the vicar he can call the banns immediately, then we can get married as soon as we both get leave at the same time.'

He kissed her and wiped away her tears with his thumbs. 'Having a wedding to plan will give Mabel and Fred something to think about. It needs to be a low-key affair, just immediate family and friends. We won't be able to live together until the war's over, but knowing I have a wife to come back to will keep me safe.'

Someone called his name and it was time for him to leave. She stood in the centre of the drive waving until the lorry was out of sight then returned to the house to give Mabel and her father the good news.

To be continued...

Acknowledgement

My thanks and love to my brother Tony and sister-in-law Susan. Without their support I couldn't do what I do.

I am immensely grateful for the work of the brilliant authors of the books listed below. I had all the information I needed from them in order to write this book. The more I learned about the ATA girls, who ferried aircraft for the RAF, the more fascinated I became.

I couldn't find any novels about a ferry pilot that included aircraft and flying. I'm hoping my books will fill this gap in the market. This is a story that needs to be more widely known and by fixed normalising it I believe the brave young woman in the ATA will get the recognition they deserve. No one I spoke to had heard of them and the remarkable job they did in World War II.

The second book in this series will be published in 2019 and the final book later in the same year. I hope you enjoyed reading this book as much as I did writing it.

Fenella J Miller

Spitfire Women Giles Whitehall

Spitfire Jonathan Glancey

Debs at War Ann de Courcy

Spreading My Wings Diana Barnard Walker

Fly & Deliver Hugh Bergel

Contact! Britain! Nancy Miller Livingston Stratford

Bomber Girls MJ Foreman

The Female Few Jackie Hyams

Spitfire Girl Jackie Moggridge

Lettice Curtis Her Autobiography

Spitfire Pilot Flight Lieutenant David Cook DFC

Wartime Britain Juliet Gardiner

RAF Airfields Jonathan Falconer

Dictionary of RAF Slang Eric Partridge

Opie's The Wartime Scrapbook

Oxford Dictionary of Slang

Britain at War Unseen Archives Maureen Hill

Bomber Boys Patrick Bishop

The Home Front Marion Yass

Looking into Hell Neil Rolfe

Christmas on the Home Front Mike Brown

HELLO FROM ARIA

We hope you enjoyed this book! Let us know, we'd love to hear from you.

We are Aria, a dynamic digital-first fiction imprint from award-winning independent publishers Head of Zeus. At heart, we're avid readers committed to publishing exactly the kind of books we love to read — from romance and sagas to crime, thrillers and historical adventures. Visit us online and discover a community of like-minded fiction fans!

We're also on the look out for tomorrow's superstar authors. So, if you're a budding writer looking for a publisher, we'd love to hear from you. You can submit your book online at ariafiction.com/we-want-read-your-book

You can find us at:
Email: aria@headofzeus.com
Website: www.ariafiction.com
Submissions: www.ariafiction.com/we-want-read-your-book
Facebook: @ariafiction
Twitter: @Aria_Fiction
Instagram: @ariafiction

37647330R00217

Printed in Great Britain
by Amazon